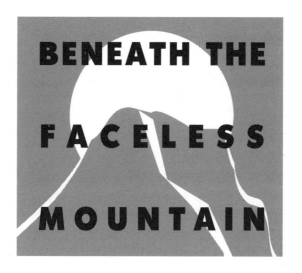

BENEATH THE FACELESS MOUNTAIN

A NOVEL

ROBERTA REES

*To Audrey,
For the
magic in
mountains*

Roberta

RED DEER COLLEGE PRESS

The Publishers
Red Deer College Press
56 Avenue & 32 Street Box 5005
Red Deer Alberta Canada T4N 5H5

Credits
Cover design by Dennis Johnson
Text design by Dennis Johnson
Printed and bound in Canada for Red Deer College Press

Acknowledgements
Financial support provided by the Alberta Foundation for the Arts, a beneficiary
of the Lottery Fund of the Government of Alberta, and by the Canada Council,
the Department of Communications and Red Deer College.

COMMITTED TO THE DEVELOPMENT OF CULTURE AND THE ARTS

Canadian Cataloguing in Publication Data
Rees, Roberta.
Beneath the faceless mountain
ISBN 0-88995-106-3
I. Title.
PS8585.E434B46   1994   C813'.54   C94-910307-1
PR9199.3.R43B46   1994

Portions of this novel have previously appeared in the *Calgary Herald Sunday Magazine*,
the *New Quarterly* and the *University of Windsor Review*.

NOTE: While some of the names in this novel are of historical persons, this is a
work of fiction and the characterizations and some of the events are fictional.

AUTHOR'S ACKNOWLEDGEMENTS

Thanks to Aritha van Herk for advice, support and encouragement in the early drafts; Hiromi Goto, Elizabeth Haynes and Sarah Murphy for sensitive and challenging edits; Anne Spatuk, Laura Johnston and the Crowsnest Historical Society for the wonderful book *Crowsnest and its People*; Albert Goodwin and Orestes Serra for the talks about coal mining; members of the Bellevue Seniors' Drop-In Centre for cake and stories; Matt Elliot and Basil Whalley for sharing war stories with me; Bud and Jo Henning for the latenight use of the printer; Mrs. Pierzscala, Grant, Dambois, Maxwell, Fortunaso, Mr. Gray, Norma Jean McKay and Andy Stojak for nurturing me and my writing; Jane Corkish for reminding me about women and horses; Betty Hersberger for a catalogue story; Barb Pielecki for advice on Polish words; Lynne Podgurny for a reader response; my friends and family for love and support. Thanks also to Alberta Community Development, Arts and Cultural Industries, for the award. Special thanks to Michael Whalley for space and encouragement, and Jane Warren for the wise, enthusiastic, generous edits all along.

In memory of my father, Robert Rees (1935–1985)

There's two things you've got to be careful of. You gotta watch out for the black-damp. It will explode and kill you. And if you're not careful the after-damp will come and kill you again.

—LYNNE BOWEN, *Boss Whistle*

There is no text without context.

—CHARLES STEELE

ROLL DOWN your car window, taste the wind. Pine, poplar, sweet wolf willow. And river mixed in. Run the fingers of your right hand over the cover of the book lying against your thigh, frayed cloth you have touched and opened again and again. Run the tips of your fingers into embedded letters. Trace the words, *History of the Crowsnest Pass*. Trace mountains pressed into cloth.

Flip back the cover, glance down quickly, this book you bought at a garage sale, carried home in your backpack, opened to a black-and-white photo of a dead baby in a wicker buggy and the white eyes of miners staring out at you from darkness.

Across the inside cover and title page, a panorama of mountains. Rocky Mountains. Turtle, Crowsnest, Seven Sisters. Jagged and bare. In the foreground, a coal town at night, houses and horses and hotels and shops, softened by the dark. Pricks of light from windows, from the coal tipple standing sentinel at the edge of town.

Look for the green handwriting wedged into margins, scrawled over photos, in spaces between paragraphs, lines. Someone's hand, woman's or man's, you don't know, speaking to the miners and hotel keepers, the widow running the maternity home on the edge of Blairmore, the family on ponies in front of a mine washhouse, the men, women and children marching through the boulders of the Frank Slide to the drums and pipes of the marching band, singing "Unionize, unionize, we must unionize."

There, over the tipple blowing smoke down the valleys, the grey cloud raining soot on the widow's sheets flapping on her line, all the living and dead asleep or digging under the earth—a patch of green.

The history of this place tunnels under my skin. Whose tunnel? Whose light? Whose dark?

Ahead of you, Turtle Mountain rises out of boulders, humped and deep green, shock of grey slice down the middle. Flip to the picture of Turtle the morning after it fell. April 23, 1903. Dust hangs in the air over the slide. Miles of boulders. Huddled in the foreground, broken clapboard houses, smoke. Men, women, children duck around jagged boulders, rummage through rubble, stand still in the dust and smoke and silence, and listen. Across Turtle's missing face, grey in the morning light, grey in a black-and-white photo, a patch of green.

90 million tons. 90 million tons of rock in 100 seconds. What did they see, the people awake or asleep beneath the mountain, three or four in the morning? An enormous black shadow? A winged shade in the corner of the eye? An angel perhaps, a mote or moment of angel?

Shift down to fourth. Turtle just ahead in the sun. Crowsnest Mountain, dizzy crags way up the valley, the Seven Sisters' jagged spires. On your right a sign, WELCOME TO THE CROWSNEST PASS, and a carved tree, giant crow with two babies in an enormous nest. Flip back to the first page, glance down to the black-and-white photo, the green writing woven into the nest.

Some night I'm going to climb up here and sleep with crows. There's too much tragedy on the ground.

Down the hill into the river valley, your car slides past the cement mouth of the Bellevue Mine on the right. You don't have time before the turnoff to flip to the section on Bellevue, the two photos of the mine on facing pages. A close-up of the opening, 1905, dark hole boring into rock. Three men in suit jackets and dress hats, seven in dusty shirts and miner caps, sit or stand, stare out at you. Only one smiles, sits on a piece of machinery, looks off somewhere else. His hands hang relaxed between his thighs. On the opposite page, a long shot down the tracks to the tipple and washhouse. Snow covers the ground. The tracks pull you through blowing snow, coal dust, to the tipple, black and skeletal. Above the tipple, through plumes of smoke and fog, houses perch on the edge of the cliff. On the photo of the mine and men, inscribed into a wedge of rock, green handwriting.

Do me a favour, please go on the mine tour. Then you'll know what I mean about coal swallowing light, about vertigo underground, about coal breathing when the lights go out.

On the opposite page, faint green among the houses perched in smoke and snow.

For women, another kind of vertigo.

At the sign that says HILLCREST, turn off the highway, cross the railway tracks, make a sharp right before the bridge. You don't have time before the sun slips behind Turtle to visit the Hillcrest graveyard on the other side of the river. But you know what it looks like, under the shoulder of Turtle. You know the words written into the shade of a pine tree at the edge of the mass grave, people in black huddled on both sides of the long trench, words from a stranger to you.

And the graveyard, you must spend a few hours at the Hillcrest graveyard. Do you know they found many of the men still standing or crouching, the ones who weren't blown up? Afterdamp, that's what got them, after they survived the explosion. Air without oxygen. Look at them all in one plot, all with the same date. June 19, 1914. June 19, 1914. Two months before W.W.I exploded. What the earth knows or holds. The shock waves through the soles of your feet. Close your eyes, think of the women waiting at the mouth of the mine, the last words they spoke or wished they'd spoken before their men or boys went on shift, aching in the backs of their throats. Close your eyes, listen for whispering or moaning or praying or singing.

Drive along the dirt road, Turtle Mountain's green-black shoulder on your left. Past four horses grazing, tales flicking, past three ruined stone towers, around a corner.

Turtle Mountain. Grey gash two thousand feet straight up. Ahead of you, miles of boulders. Before the first boulder, pull off onto a small side road, into poplar shade. Turn off the engine. Stand beside your car, listen to the wind in the leaves, taste the air. Poplar, pine. River, just there through a stand of cottonwoods. Shade your eyes, gaze up Turtle's missing face, up to the sun balanced on one of Turtle's humps. Think of the writing scrawled across the picture of rocks filling the valley.

Hillcrest Mine Disaster. Frank Slide. Bellevue Fire. They run together under the earth here.

Slip through the trees down to the river. Green and clear and fast. Kneel in the shade of a poplar, rocks and mud under your knees, lower your face. Shock of cold. Lean back into sunlight, river drops prickling your cheeks. Close your eyes to the glare off the water. Close your eyes, but you still see them, the pictures you look at every night before you go to sleep. The words you look for, thrill of finding. A photo of the Crowsnest River, 1910. A girl in stockings, boots, dress, hat. A boy in short pants, jacket, hat like the girl's, round with a turned-up brim. Between them, a string of fish. Rainbow trout. The children, very small, squint in the sun. And written on the silver sides of the trout—

I want more than I can read about this place. I want the flutter of heart, heat up the neck, between the words. I want to breathe this place in.

Pitch your tent on a flat spot among willow bushes. Roll into your sleeping bag as the sun dips behind Turtle. Lie on your back, grey dancing in front of your eyes, your book solid against your side. Listen to Crowsnest River, the wind in the poplars. Darkness presses into your eyes.

A groan outside your tent, deep and long. Turn your head toward Turtle looming through the thin skin of your tent.

A sharp bang. Hold your breath.

Silence.

Let your breath out. Roll onto your side, away from Turtle. Your arm brushes the book. The wind shakes your tent. Sigh. Lift and drop your shoulders. Run your fingertips over the letters embedded in the cover. *History. History.* Press hard. Try to feel the green writing inside each embedded letter.

History. Herstory. My story. Your story. Their story. Who's telling? Who's listening?

Behind you, closer, a deep moan.

Sit up, unzip your bag, throw it over your shoulders, hoist your book under your arm, slip out into the cool night. Breathe deeply the sweet air—cottonwood, willow, undertaste of limestone, dank and sour. Let your eyes adjust to the dark. Above you Turtle Mountain looms.

Your bare feet find the path down to the river. Branches comb your hair. Deeply, breathe deeply.

Beside the river, sit wrapped in your bag. In the dark, in the damp, listen to the river's deep running, the wind in the trees, rocks rumbling down Turtle.

Lay the book down beside you. Wrap your bag tighter. Ease yourself down onto your side. Your thigh, your ribs, your shoulder, your cheek press into the cool dirt. Your ear cups the ground.

Soft tickle. You shiver. River damp in the soft whorls of your ear. River gurgle deep inside. Sift and shift of bones under the earth, through your blanket, into the skin along your arms, thighs, temples.

Concentrate on the wind buffeting your bag, fingering your scalp, blowing words in your ear. Words mixed up with the green writing in the book close enough for you to smell.

Rescuers brought bodies and pieces of bodies out at night, carried them to the washhouse, stripped and washed and pressed gas out of them, then sewed them together. Stitched arms and legs onto torsos. Tried to make them fit. Make them whole. Did anyone laugh while marching down the hill out of town behind the wagons to the tune of Saul's Death March? Mothers, sisters, daughters, wives, lovers, friends? When one team bolted into the ditch, the wagon lurching, coffins lifting, white bundles bouncing and rolling? Did anyone laugh, laughter being all that was left?

Behind you in the trees, a sob, deep belly sob. Close your eyes. Try not to flinch.

In the wind, voices. Coming from Turtle, from the river, from the bones under the earth.

Listen. Listen with your whole body.

FISH

THROUGH THE CROWSNEST PASS, before Bellevue, Hillcrest, Blairmore, Lille, Frank, Coleman, before black holes in the earth, before ninety million tons of rock fell off a mountain in the night, before thirty-five nationalities and all their tongues, after the Blood of the Blackfoot nation camped beside the river and the green, green lake, he ran cattle on golden hooves. Some say twenty-five thousand acres. Some say two thousand head.

One summer morning, his wife walked down to the lake, watched clouds roll across the water, fish swim through trees and hills. She knelt over her reflection, pushed her finger into water, her reflection pushing up until their fingers touched. Fish darted through her eyes, around her ears.

"You must go fishing," she said to Samuel S. Reed. "You and Henry. But not here. You can't fish a still lake. Go to the river and fish upstream."

AFTER BANNOCK and slices of seared beef and thick coffee, Samuel Reed and Henry set off on foot.

"Catch bait as you go," his wife says, "worms by the river and devilscratchers under rocks." She wraps bannock in paper, hands it to Henry.

They walk along the lake, three of them, the sun rising over their right shoulders. Samuel and Henry carry packs. Samuel looks over his left shoulder up the mountain pass where his bulls graze. His wife watches their reflections in the lake.

At the end of the lake, a creek runs out into the field. "Don't look back," she says, "and keep fishing upriver." She points along a line of lush cottonwoods, into the mountain pass, then turns and walks back along the shore. Her reflection walks upside down in the lake. Fish dart through her legs, around her swollen belly.

HENRY AND HER FATHER FOLLOW the creek across blowing grass, toward poplar and cottonwood leaves. Henry sniffs. "I smell water and roots, but my legs miss the feel of a horse."

Her father nods. "Good for your legs to miss what they're used to. Good for a man to walk on his own two legs."

Henry watches her feet swish through the yellow grass. "But a man's two legs aren't fast enough for cattle."

"Your mother's people hunted buffalo on foot. You have to know what you're after, Henry, and how to go after it."

Ahead, the creek disappears into grass. The tops of poplar and cottonwood, there ahead.

Henry's feet swish the grass. The back of her nose sings. "This creek must run underground. How can a creek run under the ground?"

Henry's father looks down, his eyes fixed on the top of her cowboy hat. "Same as above ground. Water finds a way, Henry—openings between rocks, in the earth—and runs through. If it doesn't find a way, it makes one. Keeps trickling or flowing or rushing until it carves its own way."

Across the field, long yellow grass blows against their ankles. Samuel hums. "I walk across a field, my field, with my child." He watches Henry, her arms swinging. "But what if this new baby is a boy? What if I get a son?"

Henry listens and thinks, This field has a spring in it and a river beside it. A spring in it, a river beside it, and I can, I can carve my own way.

Above the river valley, Samuel and Henry stand still for a moment, gaze up at the mountains.

Samuel points at cottonwood and poplar snaking ahead. "A twisted river, Henry. A man must know how to follow a river."

Beyond his fingers, poplar and cottonwood leaves turn their bellies silver and pale green to the sun. Henry looks from her father's fingers, dark as her own, to the dancing leaves and back to her father's fingers.

She laughs until the long grass asks her to sit.

ON ROCKS DRY above the river's running, they squat. Samuel squats downriver.

He rolls up his sleeves, sinks one hand into the fast water. "Keep your hand close to the bottom." He flips a rock over. "Grab the bugger before he crawls away." He pulls his hand out, smooth, holds a dripping black bug. Impales it, legs flailing, onto his hook. "Devilscratcher," he smiles. "Who else could live under rocks at the bottom of a river?"

Henry rolls back her sleeves. Concentrates on the rocks at the river's bottom. Sinks her hand in quickly, cold across her wrist. The current tugs her fingers. She runs them up against rocks, holds them against a blue-grey rock, leans over the water to hold her hand still. Slides her fingers around, grit under her nails. Ah, she flips the rock over.

The rock rolls, bumps downstream. Tiny rocks jig up from the hole. Henry watches her fingers glide over stones, wrap around the edges of a long low rock, buried deep. Squeezes so she can feel.

Squeeze, jiggle. The river sucks on its stone. Henry pulls. A low sucking. She leans back, pulls straight up. One great sucking sound, and the rock flies into the air.

Henry's arm flies up over her head. She tips back, back. Sees the world roll by—pine, cottonwood, river grass. But she won't, won't let herself fall. She arches her body forward, arcs slowly toward the river, arms out stiff. One hand slides in, jams into gravel. The other aims. Plunges.

Her first devilscratcher. Between her thumb and finger. She squats back on her haunches, opens her other hand, holds the crawler while it scratches her palm.

The river brought my father to Canada, thinks Henry, and now I am beside the river beside my father. Eight years ago my mother had me inside her. Now she is beside the lake with someone else inside her, and I am beside my father by the river.

AFTER LUNCH, Samuel packs up the flour, pots, fat, and arranges them in his canvas pack so they won't rattle or spill. He picks up Henry's blanket, waves it at her standing beside a cottonwood, staring up into the top branches.

"Do you need this?"

Henry shakes her head, stares up into the cottonwood. My mother is a Blood. The men are fierce warriors. While the women stay in camp, the men go steal horses. "Thou shalt not steal," my father's Bible says. But the men on the ranches steal from each other all the time. The women steal my mother's name. Frown or laugh when she tells them Coyote Woman. Another biscuit, Mrs. Reed? Another cup of tea? Mrs. Reed. Mrs. Reed.

"Keep him fishing," her mother had said. "Keep him moving upriver."

Henry turns toward Samuel, takes the blanket, stuffs it in her own pack. "I was watching a grey squirrel eat its cousin."

THROUGH THE AFTERNOON, while the sun moves upriver, Samuel and Henry look for deep green pools below rapids, swing their rods back, flick their wrists and, *zing*, their lines sail out over the river. With each cast they hook a piece of sun, arc it down into deep green.

Samuel holds his rod low over the water, quickly reels his hook back. For this one, his wife has sent him fishing. But he was there for Henry, when Coyote Woman's waters slid down her inner thighs and she kneeled on all fours, rocking back and forth, grunting. Between her buttocks, Henry crowned shiny black, stretched Coyote Woman's skin purple. Samuel touched the top of Henry's head, hot and wet. My son. Coyote Woman looked over her shoulder at him. Her belly heaved. She bunched forward, groaned. Thighs trembling, she eased back on her haunches. Henry's head and shoulders slid onto the blanket. Oh, my son. Samuel slid his fingers down Henry's tiny shoulder. Coyote Woman's buttocks bunched, quivered. Wrapped from the waist down in afterbirth, Henry slid breathless between Coyote Woman's legs.

Coyote Woman put the baby to her breast, cradled the baby pulling on her nipple. "Tomorrow Woman," she whispered.

Samuel leaned close to Coyote Woman and the baby girl. He shook his head. "You should be my son. My son." He looked up at Coyote Woman. "We'll call her Henry." He stroked Henry snuffling at Coyote Woman's breast. "I will raise her as my son."

For this one, she has sent him fishing.

Samuel watches Henry reel in her hook. My son. Yet, if this baby is a boy. A boy. What if this one is a boy?

HENRY WATCHES the green water for her hook, sees it just before it rises dripping into the air.

Around oxbow after oxbow, jutting out from the river, so that if they look back an hour, they are closer to themselves than they were five minutes ago. She drops her hook into a pool on the other side of the river, reels in as it floats downstream.

Henry's line jerks. She reels in. Not too fast. Her line slackens and she reels faster. *Bang*. It jerks again, tremors up her arms. She holds her rod low over the water, tremors up her shoulders. The rod jerks, slackens, jerks. She walks upstream, pulls on her line. Green and rock shadow. Her arms shake. Her line trembles, and she sees the fish, silver and thrashing. Henry pulls the fish through green and rocks. Its whole body thrashes. She pulls the fish into the shallows. It heaves its body against rock. Henry kneels, plunges in both hands, an explosion of muscle. Smooth under her fingers, flinging its body against her wrists. She squeezes. Hooks a thumb through its gill, sharp against her skin, the hook through its jaw. The fish arcs its body, slaps against her arm.

Henry brings the rock down against its skull. Under her hand, the
fish pants. She lifts it into the air, slams it onto the rocks. It jiggles as
she presses her knife point into the flesh under its tail. Sliding her
knife forward through its belly, she slits a clean line, runs her thumb
inside, hooks out soft masses of organs and roe, flicks them into the
middle of the river.

Henry closes one eye, leans her other into the fish's.

WEST AND SLIGHTLY NORTH, they fish all afternoon. Sandstone
bluffs, limestone, into the mountains. The river narrows, deepens. If
they cast too hard, their hooks drop onto rocks on the other side.

Samuel watches Henry through the dark trees aim her rod, flick
carefully to avoid tree snags, watches her reel in, feet squarely apart,
pelvis forward. Listens to the river sing deep-throated, "A girl's a girl,
a boy's a boy, but when is a daughter a son?"

TREES GROW taller, darker. Pine, cottonwood, willow. Henry
sniffs.

The shore Henry and Samuel stand on shrinks. A bank of bush
against their backs, round licked rocks underfoot. They ease themselves around tree trunks, brush through thick willow. Hold their
rods straight up or straight ahead or low to the ground, but still they
snag and bend. Branches scratch the backs of their hands, cheeks and
necks. They cast without pulling their rods back, a sharp flick straight
up or sideways or backhand.

Upstream from her father, Henry straddles a cottonwood growing
sideways from the vertical bank, lays her rod flat against its trunk,
slides one leg over. Bark scratches her leg through her jeans. She balances, cannot see through the leaves below her boots. She presses her
palms into the rough bark, leans forward, picks up her rod with both
hands. Through the leaves in front, the river slips deep green. Old
Man River, her father calls it. Napi, her mother says.

Napi-Napi-och-a-tay-cots
Place where Napi plays

A tremor runs out of the river along Henry's line, along her rod, up her arms. She reels in. Her rod bends low over the pool she has cast into. Henry grips the handle hard with one hand, cranks the reel with the other. Her rod bends, its tip touching water.

She looks downstream at her father, his face shaded under his hat, the sound of running water between her and him, whispers to herself, "The river has my hook stuck in it, and the river must have me in it to get my hook."

Her father's face blank under his hat, his line loose in the water, hands loose around his rod. Henry slides from the tree, takes a few steps downstream toward him, yanks her rod sideways, gently, harder. The river holds her hook tight.

Henry glances at her father. He has not moved. Yanking her rod straight up, straight back, sideways, she hoists herself over the tree trunk, walks upstream around a sandbar, around a clump of wolf willow, as far as her line will let her.

She looks back. Between her and her father, the clump of wolf willow, the cottonwood hanging over the water, roar of the river. She examines the wolf willow's silvery green leaves, murmurs under her breath. "The river must have me in it to get my hook." Henry breathes deeply, too-sweet willow and river.

She props her rod between two stones. Undresses quickly. Boots, pants, shirt, underwear. Hangs them on the wolf willow. The leaves tickle her bare skin.

She reaches up, pulls off her hat. The sun overhead blinds her. She runs her finger around the sweatband, puts her hat back on.

Henry stands for a moment in the soft mud and grass, warm in the shallow water. Takes a step deeper, puts all her weight on the slippery stones. Cold grips her ankles. The river rocks dig into her instep.

She sucks in her breath. Not long, not long. Reaches out a foot. The river pulls it downstream. She pulls back, curls her foot around a stone. Pain shoots up the inside of her leg.

She reaches downstream for her line, taut between river and bank. Lifts her other foot. The river pulls. She teeters, clutches the fishing line. Shoves her foot down hard between two large slippery rocks. Finds balance, water over her knees, legs numb and aching. Looks down the line, where it enters the river. How far? Three steps, four steps?

Up to her thighs in freezing water, Henry looks downstream for her father. Only a clump of thick willow curving out into the river. She opens her mouth, the river roars. She runs her hands down the line, plunges them in.

Cold. Ice cold. Pulling her feet, her hands. Henry hunches forward, bends her knees.

Her feet lift. Her body slowly tilts. One shoulder slides into the river. Her neck, ear. She reaches out, sinking into cold, cold water. Her cheek, eye, nose. Water over her head. The river rolls her onto her back. Water cold in her open eyes. Above her clouds and mountains and trees wash apart, flow together. A tree with a mountain top, a mountain with leaves, a crow with butterfly wings, a frog with the legs of a deer.

A black shape floats over Henry's face, blots out mountains and clouds and trees.

Her hat floats by.

A fish in the sun's eye. And the river with her in it, not roaring, but quiet. She listens. Pebbles, fish, devilscratchers.

Henry laughs. Water in her mouth, her throat. She hiccups, cannot breathe. Water.

The river tosses her into the air. She coughs, water and bile down her bare chest. Gasps, and the river sucks her to the bottom. Green, green all around. A trout nibbles her ear, and a yellow water snake snakes past her eyes.

On the bottom of the river, Henry sucks water into her lungs, coughs, sucks, retches. Her chest jerks violently in out, in out. Against her face, arms, eyes, ears, the river whispers.

>*Napi Napi*
>*Napi-och-a-tay-cots*
>*Napi Napi*
>*see how Napi plays*

Ah, through the water, layers and layers above her. Henry stops trying to breathe. Sun's rays scatter down to her, eyes open against water flowing over them. She lays her head back, looks through the sun. An eagle with a horse's tail. A butterfly with moose antlers.

Without moving her head, Henry looks for shore. Her eyes slide through water. Along the shore runs a bear, shoulder muscles flowing back and forth. Cinnamon tip. It looks down through the water at her. Her mother's face.

It does not smile. Her mother runs beside the river in a bear's body. Henry opens her mouth, but her mother cannot hear her. Henry looks up through water, sun, into her mother's eyes, her mother loping alongside the river, lips shut tight. Between her front legs, her swollen breasts swing. Through shimmering water, Henry watches them splash white drops on the water above, but she cannot reach them. She opens her mouth like a fish. Her mother the bear lopes past the willow bush, brushes leaves silver-green with her humped shoulder.

Beside the willow, her mother rises upright, lifts her great head high into the air, swings her head from side to side. Between her hind legs, a dark slit opens wide. Rips her belly up to her throat. Her skin flaps back in the breeze. Underneath, jeans, a checked shirt. Her eyes change shape, colour.

HENRY LOOKS up through shimmering water at her father's wild blue eyes. He lifts a giant paw into the sky, giant shadow on the water over her. Falling toward her. Claws and blackness.

On her stomach, cheek ground into gravel, Henry's eyes flicker open. A blue knee, blue calf, brown boots, on the ground beside her. Uuuhhhhhh. *Thump* between her shoulders, her chest pushed into the ground. Up from her stomach, into her throat. She chokes. Closes her eyes.

Thump. Water and bile stream out her mouth, her nose. She gags, coughs, laughs. Tears run down her face onto smooth river rocks. She has stolen time.

TUCKED DEEP BESIDE the earth's river, Henry huddles under a Hudson's Bay blanket. No matter how hard she clenches her muscles, she cannot stop shivering.

Everything around her appears bright and shivering. The cliffs across the river, above them the limestone peaks thrust into a blue shivering sky, the leaves, the trees, Samuel gathering twigs, piling them into a fragile teepee.

Henry does not look at the river, makes her eyes jump from the shivering cliffs on the other bank to the trees on this one. Makes them follow her father's hands, picking up a twig, snapping and laying it on the small teepee in a circle of stones at Henry's feet. Her father's hands shake.

He slides them into his jean pocket, pulls out a flint. A flick, and the twigs crackle and smoke. Flames curl up around their stems.

Henry breathes in sweet smoke, holds her breath. Listens for the steady thu-thump, thu-thump inside until she is inside, thu-thump, thu-thump, and her trembling shoulders, legs and head are outside with the crackling fire and the snapping twigs and banging pots. And the river, slipping, roaring, gurgling, is inside and out.

She closes her eyes. The ground beneath her lifts, swells.

She opens her eyes, focuses on the fire. The logs sizzle and blacken. Heat waves dance overtop. Her skin prickles.

"I've been to the bottom of the river." Henry speaks to the side of Samuel's face, shaded under his cowboy hat. He does not answer, does not look at her. He dumps flour into a pot, walks to the river, dips the pot. His shirt strains over his back as he bends.

"I saw new things from the bottom of the river." Henry speaks to Samuel's face bent in the shade of his hat. He carries the pot back to the fire, mixes the flour and water with a stick. Henry watches the stick stir the flour and water into a sticky mass. Samuel's hands squeeze the dough, roll it over, squeeze again.

"I saw how things come apart and how they come together." Her father drops a chunk of beef tallow into a frying pan, holds the pan over the fire, swirls it around as the fat melts and sizzles. He dumps the dough into the pan, covers it with the pot, slides it into the coals.

"I've been a fish after my own hook." Henry watches her father's back move away, the muscles under his shirt bunch and dance as he saws at poplar seedlings, shaves the ends with his knife.

"Barely alive when you fished me out." His back muscles flatten.

He strides toward her, face in shadow, kneels, awkward, pulls her slowly into his chest.

Henry presses her face into Samuel's neck. Salt and fear. "I won't swim again, except on horseback." She presses her ear to his chest. Thu-thump, thu-thump. Inside her father. And inside her mother, oh, her mother.

OLD MAN. NAPI. Crowsnest. This river rushing past you in the dark. This river that Henry and Samuel fished and camped beside. Now you beside this river, more than a hundred and twenty years later.

And Henry. Lift your ear from the ground, listen for Henry's voice. Henry as a girl of eight. Fishing.

Flip the pages of your book. Somewhere around the middle. Here. Yes, here. Tip the book toward the river, try to catch a bit of moonlight rising through the trees.

A black-and-white photo. An old man on horseback. Checked shirt, suspenders, cowboy hat. But the wind and river and trees and rocks tell you about Henry Reed, the girl.

Tilt your book left and right, try to read the history given with the picture:

> Samuel Reed moved to the area in 1872. In 1873 he married a native girl from a tribe east of here. Whenever anyone from ranches nearby needed help, Samuel was there. Henry Reed was Samuel's oldest son, a quiet and reserved boy. After he sold the family ranch, he worked for awhile for West Canadian Collieries, before moving onto his place in the Upper Old Man, where he raised horses. He died in the spring of 1969. The Reeds were pioneers in the truest sense of the word.

And there, in the margins, the green handwriting.

Always the problem of projecting. Native as Innocent, Wise, Exotic, Primitive, Savage, Environmental Protector, Drain on the Government, Inarticulate, Trouble (won't farm their land, what's wrong with them), Good (White like me), Mysterious, Sneaky, Untrustworthy, Absolutely Trustworthy, Hopeless, Healer of the World. We can't pre-

tend that Henry didn't exist. But did anybody know Henry? Who are we, and how many Henry's are there? Question, question, remember to question what you read or hear or write or say or think or do.

Push yourself up on your side. Listen to the river rush over boulders. Question, question, question.

Quest. Sit holding your book to your ribs. Girl or boy? Who is Henry? Who are these voices speaking to you from the river, the mountains, the wind, the bones under the earth? Who are you?

As the moon rises above the trees, slip through poplars to your tent. Step into your shoes, cool and damp where you left them outside your tent flap. Your book under your arm, sleeping bag around your shoulders, step out onto the road. To your left, Turtle Mountain's missing face changes shape in the moonlight. To your right, the road disappears around a corner.

Turn right. Follow the road past trees and a few houses and horses appearing and disappearing in the moonlight. All around you, whispering. Who are you? Where do you come from? Why are you here?

It's a long walk along the road, across the river, up the hill, but you want to sit there with your book, in the dark, among the gravestones.

BELLY UP

"GOLD," PEOPLE SAID, "in the mountains. We know it's there. We only have to find it."

Prospectors from France, Britain, America, Ontario, tied tin plates onto pack horses, cinched pick handles tight to their horses' ribs, headed for the Crowsnest Pass.

Coal is what they found. Heaving, pitching seams of coal. They ate off their tin plates, swung their picks at the black seams, dug and blasted. Underground, hardly able to see the noses between their eyes, they mined blackness for all it was worth and more.

"BELLY UP to the bar, boys. Belly up to the bar."

"You bet," I say and clink my money on the counter. "And a pint for my dirty friends here."

We laugh in our beer. No sense crying when the coal seam's thick. Might as well come up singing so you don't notice the sun hurts your eyes. Might as well come up singing, start way down deep. Swing your pick, last swing for this shift. Up and back, weight of metal pulling your arms out, down. Whiz past your ears into solid black. Your body stops dead. Tremors run up your arms, along your skull. "Last swing, boys." Then crunch, crunch up the tunnel, lights on our caps, buckets under our arms, our feet lost in the dark below. In the flicker of the lamps on our heads, a face floats by. Blackness all around us coughs, wheezes, then hums sweet and low.

Sleep my child and peace attend thee,
All through the night.
Guardian angels God will send thee,
All through the night.

Long miles through the tunnels, our tired bones ache. Eyelids heavy with coal, throats dry, we swallow dust, chew, spit. We sing. Solid blackness swallows our voices, sings back to us, cold and breathy.

Soft and drowsy hours are creeping,
Hill and vale in slumber sleeping;
I my loving vigil keeping,
All through the night.

Cut off by the sudden dark beyond your lamp, sloshing inside your boots, your feet can't tell you in the dark, but your knees bend, and you know you're walking uphill. Sweat trickles through the roots of your hair. Singing, your throat vibrates.

While the moon her watch is keeping,
All through the night.
While the weary world is sleeping
All through the night.

So tired your bowels gurgle deep inside, and you clench your ass cheeks tight. A shiver runs up your spine, fingers your scalp. Lost in the dark that your light merely probes, measuring the depth of blackness in coal, the tiny bones in your feet send sharp pains along the nerves of your legs into the dilated nerves behind your eyes. Quick slices with each step. You can almost see. You stand still at the cage. Blood drains from your fingers and toes. You stamp your feet, finger the leather strap on your bucket. From the miles of blackness at your back, a horse snorts, water drips, a smell like that from the outhouse hole on a dark winter morning rises around you. Into the cage, you rattle for surface. Your mates warm against you in darkness. Singing.

O'er thy spirit gently stealing,

Visions of delight revealing,
Breathes a pure and holy feeling.
All through the night.

"Might as well come up singing," I used to say. Hands, arms, feet cut off from each other underground, come together in the light you ride up into. You look down at the puzzle of your own body fitting itself together. "Stand you a pint."

"BELLY UP to the bar, boys. Belly up to the bar."

"A pint for my dirty friends," I said.

I was new in the Crowsnest Pass. Two weeks on the train from Nova Scotia, backside numb against a wooden bench all day. A black pot-bellied stove in a corner. Greasy smoke. A few women with hair covered by babushkas heated pots of coffee, fed their children green-smelling meat, bits of bread. Mostly men. Thin, dark shiny pants. Eyes on the women bent over the greasy stove. Harvesters' Excursion, August, 1912, and the sun long over lake and granite and prairie. Endless sun I was not used to. Endless sun after endless dark. My hands, feet, legs, head, lost in the dark. Dissolving in sunlight. My hands cold, gripping the rough wooden bench, growing away from me. My head expanding—so much light, so much space. Ache of thin skin stretched tight, tighter. Pounding in my temples. Wrench of bone at the base of my neck. Head lifting from my body. Running my icy fingers through my hair, digging them into my scalp, holding. Holding on.

Lakes and rocks and grass and sky, and a young woman with three half-pints and a Scottish accent.

"How far you going?" Her eyes dark grey on my face.

"Crowsnest Pass. To the new mine in Hillcrest."

"Where you coming from?"

"Sidney Mines, Nova Scotia. Come from the valleys a year back. Time to move on. I have an old friend come out two years ago. He wrote and said coal's thick and the valleys are like home."

She laughs, lifts her baby to her shoulder, pats it on the back. "I could tell you're a miner just by looking at you. Don't know what to do with your hands and feet in all this light, do you? By the way, my name's Susan. Susan McRae. We're on our way to join their father. He came out a year ago, hasn't seen the baby yet."

She holds out her hand, small and rough and firm.

My hand in hers. My hand connected to my arm by her warm hand. "The name's Evan Thomas. Where did you say your husband works?"

"Hillcrest Mines."

"BONNIE WANTS to know if she can curl up with you."

Susan McRae in the clickety-clack train across from me, wrapping coats around her half-pints. In the dusk, her hands white, solid.

I pat the bench beside me. "I'm sure there's room on this bench for a little Welshman and a littler Scottish lass. As long as you don't snore now."

Susan's hands around her child's waist, floating out to me in midair. I lie on my side, tuck the girl, all elbows and knees, into my coat. My nose brushes the top of her head, her hair smelling of stale milk. Across from me, Susan on her side, a child curled on the floor, a baby tucked under her breast.

"I'm grateful, Evan Thomas. It's been a long journey on the boat, now this train. Who knows, maybe we'll wake up back in Scotland in the middle of a strike, no money, no babies, no flour. We can go dancing, Evan Thomas, on the platform down by the lake. I hear tell you Welshmen like to dance and sing. Grant loves football, but he won't dance. I'll grant you, I tell him, two babies is enough to make any man serious. He can't sing a note either. Doesn't mind listening as long as it doesn't sound like church but can't sing a note."

The back of my head tightens. I shiver, focus on Susan's hand stroking her baby's hair. Ache up the back of my head. My scalp ice cold. Sharp pain in my temple. All the darkness. All the light. This child curled inside my coat, my heart pounding, breath stuck in my throat, sick flutter of stomach, my head growing, tingling, buzzing, and I imagine Susan's hand on my head. Warm and rough and solid.

"Tell me about yourself, Susan, before you married."

She sighs. Strokes her baby's hair. "Oh, I worked, Evan Thomas. Went into the factory when I was fourteen. A winder, I was, thirty cops of jute to look after. Didn't know my mom and dad. Sent me away when I was four to my auntie's in the next village. Have nine brothers and sisters but don't know none of them either. Who's got time? But I love to dance, Evan Thomas, and I love a good voice."

Susan's fingers on her baby's face, softly stroking. "How about you, Evan, do you dance?"

I breathe out slowly, my chin tucked into her daughter's hair. "I was born dancing, Susan. Danced in my nappies, danced with my aunties and uncles, danced into the mine after my da."

She laughs in the dark, her child rolled inside my coat. Elbows and knees and feet pressed against my chest, my stomach, my legs. Her daughter's skin soft and warm.

> Sleep my child and peace attend thee,
> All through the night.
> Guardian angels God will send thee,
> All through the night.

I sing into Bonnie's hair. Susan on the bench, hands around her child, sighs. "You have a dark voice, Evan Thomas. That's how I think of death. A dark voice sets every nerve in your body vibrating until you can hardly stand it, and the only thing you can do is strain toward the singing. You fall into it, fall and fall into blackness, every nerve singing. Then you're gone, just like that."

"BELLY UP to the bar, boys. Belly up to the bar." I'm new here, and they're standing me a pint, telling stories. About me. The new taff. Beer in my belly. Hanging onto their voices, here and alive and whole, and the pit just up the hill. The pit black and yawning, waiting. My hands in the light over the bar. Connected to my arms. Pulse in my wrists up to my chest. Their voices. My hands. Hang on, hang on.

"Sing us a song, Evan Thomas, you little Welsh bugger."

"Cautious little bugger, too. Never blasts from the solid, no siree. Holds his pick like this, slices down the face neat as a surgeon. Slides a stick in, boom, singing the whole time. Before you know it, coal's sliding down his chute. Have a drink on me, you crafty bastard."

"Come on, Thomas, sing us a song, recite us a poem. That's what you do over there isn't it. Listen, about this Thomas here, first day down No. 2 cold as hell, rest of us hung over, can't see, thank God, in the dark. Thomas gets to his room, climbs straight up the coal, hardly needs to bend his neck. I follow him up. 'Ever worked a pitch so steep,' I says. 'You'll need them tools. Too steep for power equipment. Bastards give us three dynamite or one can of black powder. Don't want us blasting. Say it shatters the coal too small. Insist we break our backs with a shovel so they get the big bloody chunks, then turn around and sell the fine stuff for coke. And we don't see a cent of it. Not one Christly cent, by God. Careful with your can there now. Bastards who own this friggin' mine are sabotaging it. Fireboss in Frank held his lamp over a box of caps, blew his hands off.' While I'm talking, Thomas here's chunking away in the dark. At least he speaks English, but he's not saying nothing, humming away like he thought he was in the goddamned opera house in Blairmore. 'My room's down 6,' I says. 'If you need me ask.' His auger hums in the black, and I can't see his face, just one arm. 'Thanks Grant,' he says, formallike. 'Thanks.' Keeps on Christly humming. 'By the way,' says I, 'slow down.'"

"You'd best slow down on the ale there, Evan Thomas." Grant's hand slaps my shoulder. Black cracks, red knuckles. Knocks the sound out my mouth, ale all over.

"Slow down?" I shout, laying my head back, the lights over the bar spinning. Hum from my balls up to my throat. "Slow down, Moses." I sing low. "Slow down, Moses." Louder. "Slow down, Moses." Fill the whole room. "Slow down, Moses." My arm brings a pint to my lips.

> Hush me child and peace attend thee
> Blew his hands off
> Now can't mend thee
> Guardian angels God will send me
> All through the night

The lights, two bright augers boring through my eyes, the room spinning faster and faster. "Have a drink on me," my voice shouts, and my arm tips a pint over my face. Can't blink, beer in my eyes. "Don't bore me," I shout, fixed to the floor, head back, room spinning.

"Put him in the snake room. He can sleep it off until the whistle blows."

"What shift is he on?"

"Days."

Black spinning all round. A face leans into mine. "You're okay, you crazy bastard. I'll have Susan make you a bucket. Come down when the whistle blows."

On my back alone in the dark, the only one left. They have gone home, gone down, gone by. Can't tell if my eyes are open or closed. Back, arms, legs, hands, feet, stomach, toes, muscles, flesh, meat. Bones. "Come up singing," I used to say. The sun bleaches bones.

"Jesus H. Christ," says a voice in the dark in the next room, "a pack rat traded me a leg bone for a cheap spoon." His voice gravel. Maybe my leg, maybe not.

SUSAN ON THE TRAIN, clickety-click clickety-click, swallowed by dusk. "Your voice is dark, Evan Thomas, dark and clear. Makes the back of my neck tingle."

Granite, trees, grass, sky. Clickety-click clickety-click.

"Goodness me," she says, "what do we want with so much sky. A little bit would do after Scotland, but all this blue pushing down on the land. No wonder it's so flat. You want to watch you don't dissolve in it, Evan Thomas. Keep a little of the black stuff on you. Grant never scrubs his hands clean on a day off. He's always checking them out on the football field as if the sun will dissolve them right under his nose. He checks them when he eats, hardly says a word to the rest of us. At night, he tucks them under the blankets, looks for them first thing in the morning. And in the pub, he laughs and tells jokes, but he's always watching his hands each time he picks up his glass. Here, can you hold Duncan for me?"

Her hands small, fast, freckled in the daylight. Her hands knitting her children, holding them together.

I look down at my forearms. Lost underground in the dark. My fingers, thighs, feet. Unravelling in the light. And my mind. My hands cannot, no cannot.

Susan's hands around Duncan's waist, reaching across.

Clickety-click clickety-click. Susan's fingers white and freckled under strands of wool. "I'll knit you some socks, Evan Thomas. Thick wool. The only colour I have left is blue, but who'll know inside your boots down there in the dark?"

Clickety-click clickety-click. Blue rolls off her needles. Daylight blue, sky blue. Susan's fingers knitting prairie towns. Lydiatt, Hazelridge, Winnipeg. Carberry, Brandon, Moose Jaw. Then dusk.

"Your voice slides between a man's and a woman's, Evan Thomas."

Regina, Swift Current, Medicine Hat.

"Like the night, Evan Thomas. Makes the hair prickle on the back of my neck. Can you hold?"

Her hands quick against her child's cheek. My socks forming blue light. Her hands in the light. Her children, whole.

CLICKETY-CLICK clickety-click.

Pincher Creek. Ahead, blue hills, mountains, valleys.

Burmis. A river valley beside us and a glint of water. The mountains ahead, one mountain face gone, grey in the sun, grey boulders across the valley. Tipples black against the sky, blowing smoke. Mountains. Valleys. Smell of coal, black and oily. Tipples, yards, shacks, ovens, hoists, stacks, engines, cars, cables, wheels. Black, black, black.

Clickety-click clickety-click. HILLCREST painted on the station roof. A group of men on the platform, hands behind their backs.

We step out into the air, crisp and sulfur, me first, hands up for Bonnie and Duncan and Alex as Susan hands me her children. Her eyes on the tall man, red hair, coming down the platform. He swoops her into the air, swings her around, presses her against his chest. "How's me lass?" Her eyes over his shoulder, dark grey. Then Bonnie, Duncan and the baby, Alex, swinging above his head and pressed against his sweater, dirty brown in the sun.

I pick up my trunk, head for the station, clapboard, not stone. Dizzy beneath a faceless mountain.

"The name's Grant." Pressure on my shoulder to turn around. "No doubt Susan's told you. Loves to talk, that one. Can cook like the devil."

His hand around mine, black around his nails, across his knuckles. His eyes pale blue, friendly. "Ride with us why don't you. I've hired a wagon. Town's only a mile or so, but all up hill. We can drop you at the hotel. Not much of a hotel, mind. Full of us filthy moles. Couple of Chinamen do your cooking. Can make soup out of a fish head."

I WAIT for Grant McRae in the six o'clock dawn, my breath steaming. Across the valley, the sun reddens the sky above Bellevue. Over my left shoulder, Turtle Mountain hunches black against grey, its face gouged and strewn.

I pull my Dai cap over my forehead, hear them before I see them, faces black off the night shift.

"Mornin'."

"Mornin'."

"Mornin'."

A face pale and clean hovers behind them. I hoist my lunch box under my arm.

"Ready, Evan Thomas?"

I clear my throat. "Ready as I'll ever be, Grant McRae." I turn and start walking, say over my shoulder, "How would you like to climb Turtle on Sunday, take a route beside the slide?"

In the grey light, Grant laughs, flips the back of my cap. Cool air fingers my scalp. I pull my cap down hard, fist my hands into my pockets. Beside me Grant chuckles, takes big steps. "By Christ, you taffs are a strange bunch, Thomas. Next thing you know, you'll be suggesting church or the library. Can hardly understand a word you say, but don't matter here. Surrounded by Russians, Slavs, Italians."

He stops walking, glares at me. "Look, you're a friend as long as you're not Blackleg. Or Whiteshirt." His eyes fierce and blue. I hold my breath, focus on his mouth, thin and tight. Tight as my scalp beginning to stretch, tingle. I imagine Susan's fingers warm and rough smoothing his lips, my forehead. He smiles, tips his head back, laughs, his teeth white. "Come on, Thomas, we've a way to go yet."

Through town beside the creek, past sleeping houses. My hands and ears growing warm. Grant points. "See that big son-of-a-bitch? Belongs to Whippet. Mine manager. Went to Coleman and hand-picked the boards, by Christ. I can see him out there in the yards running his fat fingers up each one, peering one eye down the length. 'Won't do, not straight enough.' Bastard wouldn't know straight if it upped his arse. Married to Hill's sister, a Yank who owns everything—tipple, spur line, houses, all the shops except the union store. Your opinions, too, Evan Thomas, so keep them to yourself."

He frowns down at me, chews the corner of his lip. "They laid off a bunch last year, one at a time. Said they had too much rock. Too much rock, my ass. Too much English and too many guts. Hired on a bunch who don't have enough English to say, 'I need more money.' Don't even know when they're blacklegging, the poor bastards. Fire-boss has to draw a big X where there's gas, or the poor bastards would blow us all to hell. See that church there? Brand new. St. Francis. Preacher's a Welshman, Reverend J. Watkins-Jones. Sings his sermons. Starts with talking but ends up bloody singing. Makes my hair stand up. Played against a team in Cardiff once. Soon as we ran out onto the field, every mother's son stood up and sang at us. Sang at us, for God's sake. In harmony, as if they were the whole bloody sky and all its angels. My knees shook so hard I could hardly kick the bloody ball."

Up the hill behind town, our feet follow a dirt track. A bead of sweat rolls down my spine. My spine. My head. My hands. This moment.

We hear the swish of their jackets, thud of their feet before we see them. Grant's hand on my shoulder. "Stop a minute there, Thomas. What's the use in racing yourself?" Grimed faces, bright eyes, drift down through the dark. We step aside, and they drift by.

"Mornin'."

"Mornin'."

Up the hill, smell of sulfur on my tongue. Cold stings my eyes. Behind my shoulder, Grant takes a deep breath, stops walking. "Smell the trees, Thomas? Haven't killed all of them yet, by God. Like putting your face in a jar of gin after a shift of smelling your own sweat and sweat of the guy next to you. Used to have a spike team hauling the stuff out. Horse sweat, horse shit. Cleaner than human though, by God. Still have horses down deep. Too steep for the engine. Dinky they call it here."

Behind me, he sighs, his voice soft. "When did you start down, Thomas?"

My feet attached to my legs here in the dawn. Susan knitting me socks, wool wrapped around her fingers, around my calves, carrying me up this hill to the mouth of the mine, into darkness. I turn and face him standing still, hands at his sides.

"Born into it, man, born into it. Slipped kicking and screaming down one tunnel straight into another. Only difference is my mother's kept squeezing me out, the other closing me in. 'Job for you down under,' my da says one night. 'Need a boy small like you to mind the fire door, said I'd bring you down.' First day, I stepped in freezing water up to my groin. All shift I lay shivering, pressed into a hole above the fire doors, coal against my spine. Lights bobbed in the dark below me. 'Swing 'er open, boy.' The fireboss' voice. 'Swing 'er open, boy.' My hands, which I couldn't see, felt for the chain, pulled, both arms pulling. I leaned back all my weight, coal pressing my chin into my chest. At last the door groaned open. Lights crossed below me, disappeared into blackness. My hands fed the chain out slow, couldn't risk falling. The door shivered shut, cold wind on my face. Been down ever since."

Grant's voice soft in the dawn. Far enough away that I can't see his eyes. "Must be fifteen years or so, eh, Thomas?"

Cold creeps under my collar. I shake my head, turn up the hill, a mountain of coal slag looming above us. I swing my arms, walk quickly. "More like twenty. You're not so Scottish as to cheat me out of a few years are you, Grant-the-Haggis?"

My bucket solid against my ribs. His feet running behind me. His breath fast. "Go on. Twenty years. You must thrive on the single life then. Keeps you young. No mouths to feed, no one waiting up top for whistles. You can't get hurt when you have kids, can't afford to. Can't afford not to go down either. But it's worth it, Thomas, if you can stand the loneliness when they're not around."

His fingers around my arm. "But good Christ you're a dangerous man. Got me talking daft. Here, up this way now."

In morning grey, my lunch box cold under my arm. Climbing straight up the dawn, grey as dusk. Smoke, thick and sulfur, burns my throat.

Beside me walks a man with a grey-eyed wife. Come down when the whistle blows. When the whistle blows.

IN THE CHURCH on the edge of town, Susan kneels next to me, bows her head. For the first time, I see her without children, Grant at home. She kneels with her back straight up, does not lean back against the pew, her hands white and freckled across her round stomach. She kneels and I smell warm bread, cotton, lily of the valley.

Reverend Watkins-Jones bows his head. "Let us pray." His voice echoes from the wooden roof, pews, floor. The silence after echoes louder, and we wait for his praying voice. Outside, the sun catches on limestone boulders strewn across the valley, their cracks and fissures like ancient writing, gravestones to the men and women and children bedded beneath ninety million tons of rock. The sun catches on faces of stone. Susan beside me, warm bread, cotton and lily of the valley, and her white freckled hands across her round stomach. She will lean forward when the minister sings, toward his voice. I am here beside her, she will lean forward, and I cannot, I cannot. I grip the pew in front of me, close my eyes, wait for his voice. The first word he sings echoes in the wood around us.

"Grant. Grant, grant, grant . . . "

I am here beside her, and I cannot.

"Grant, O Lord, that as we are baptized into the death of thy blessed Son, our Saviour Jesus Christ, so by continual mortifying our corrupt affections we may be buried with him; and that, through the grave and gate of death, we may pass to our joyful resurrection; for his merits, who died and was buried, and rose again for us, thy Son, Jesus Christ our Lord. Amen."

Susan beside me, freckles on her wrists, leans into the clear dark voice of Reverend Watkins-Jones, then whispers in my ear. "He sounds like you, Evan Thomas."

My knuckles white on the pew in front of me.

"Amen." I sing it an octave higher than Watkins-Jones. Our voices echo together from the ceiling, walls, pews, floor. "A-a-a-a-men."

THE WHISTLE BLOWS and blows, but they keep running and kicking, skirts blowing between their legs. The men, women, children lined along the playing field cheer and laugh.

"No regard for rules, women, no regard at all."

"Spent her whole life kicking, that one. Might as well give her a leather one to boot."

"Remember what I told you, Nettie. Use your head. And your elbows."

The whistle blows. The wind blows their blouses out from their bodies, back against their breasts. The tipple here in Michel blows soot. Grey shacks up the valley. Grey sheets, pants, bloomers, vests on the clotheslines.

"Dirty play. We'd never get away with that one."

"Did you talk her into this, Evan Thomas?" Grant's hand on my shoulder. He watches Susan, small and round. She bends over, running, scoops up the ball, drops it down her blouse. Runs the field, soot in the air, runs, the ball bouncing inside her blouse.

Grant's hand on my shoulder.

Susan runs up to the goalie and hugs her, the ball between them, the two of them dancing in a circle.

"Everybody to the hotel."

"Bloody women."

We move together, Susan between Grant and me, for the hotel beside the tipple. Susan, Susan my heart is ready. I will sing and praise thee.

"Belly up to the bar, boys. Belly up. And you, too, ladies, if we can still call you by that term. Rougher than men on the football field, slower, but rougher. What time are you heading back to Hillcrest?"

"Dunno. Hey, Grant. What time does the Fernie Flyer pull out?"

"Not for a long time boys, not for a long time. Fill your gullets while you can."

His hand black and creased on Susan's neck. Pale freckles beneath her hair, close enough for me to smell. Wind and soot and skin. Down the bar, men in striped shirts, short pants from the playing field. Women, skirts and blouses, and Susan's neck. White. Sweaty. Grant's fingers curled against her skin.

My loins are filled with burning, and there is no sound part in my body.

"What are you reciting now, Evan Thomas?" Susan's face level with mine. Beer on her breath. She lowers her voice. "Listen, I'm going to smuggle a bottle back and I need your help. He'll have to know later when I give it to him, but you mustn't let on now. When the train pulls up, I'm going to run back in here for my coat. That's where Shorty behind the bar will put the bottle, in my coat. You keep him on the train. I'll only be a second."

Her eyes dark grey, nose crooked.

The fig tree putteth forth her green figs, and the vines with the tender grape give a good smell.

"I'll need you again in Hillcrest, as a decoy. The police will be there nosing because we're coming from B.C. As soon as the train stops, I want you to grab the club bag and run. By the time they figure out it's full of sweaty towels and footballs, we'll be home safe and you can join us for a drink. What do you say, Evan Thomas?"

THE WHISTLE BLOWS and blows. Ash. Smoke. The train shudders. I grab the bag, sweaty leather in my palm, race for the door.

"Hey, Thomas."

"What the hell?"

"Thinks he's on the field."

"Gone mad."

"Crazy Welsh bugger."

I clang down the step, the train moving past Turtle Mountain. Across the platform, hollow thud under my feet, head down, the bag thumping my hip. Light behind me. I crash into the bush.

"I'm warning you, buddy. Stop in the name of the law. Stop." Through poplar. Uphill. Knees bent, pumping. Head down, panting. Uphill, the tipple smoking.

Every man hath his sword upon his thigh because of fear in the night.

Come and drink with me. I run, I run, I run.

Thy word is a lantern for my feet. Until the daybreak and the shadows flee away, I will get me to the mountain of myrrh and to the hill of frankincense.

THE WHISTLE BLOWS and blows and blows and blows. Down here in the pit in the black. Blows and blows. The nations are sunk down in the pit that they made—no hands, no feet, no one. Water drips—no eyes, no hands. In the same net that they hid is their foot taken. I am black but comely. Look not upon me because I am black. The earth trembled and quaked. There went up a smoke out of his nostrils and a consuming fire out of his mouth. I love you, Evan Thomas. Grant loves you, too.

HAVE MERCY upon me, O Lord, for my bones are vexed.

Bone-tired, bone-chilled, we slosh toward the prick of light so bright the back of my eyes ache. Mud around our calves, in our boots. Blackness around us, breathing. No singing here. I hum low. Behind us water drips. The light grows bigger, fills my eyes, a great pressure. Hands and knees visible, we speed up but do not look at each other. At last, the wind blowing in the entrance needles the back of my throat. One of us coughs, spits, and we find our voices. Dave, Tony, Albert, Guido, Vlad, Sesto, Orestes, Grant, Evan.

"What do you think, this Jesus Christ mud will give us more money, eh?"

"Can't wait to crawl between the sheets."

"Sheets aren't all I'd like to crawl between."

"Maybe what we need is to order more women from the catalogue, no? That hotel is cold like Siberia."

"Just be glad you're not a horse down there weeks at a time."

We are in the light, low sun, snow bright. I pull my muffler tight around my neck and blink. Below, Hillcrest, spirals of smoke, coal in every stove, every fireplace. Susan kneads bread dough on a floured board. Punches, rolls, digs with her knuckles. Slides the dough risen in pans into the oven. Rubs her hands down her apron. "I'm feeding the world now, Evan Thomas. First couple times, you couldn't eat the stuff, hard as rocks. Threw the loaves out against a tree. Birds couldn't eat it. Next day a man from down the street knocks on the door. 'Can I use these bricks to prop up my wagon?'"

We stand black in the sun. Blink at the boiler house exhaling steam. Grant's hand claps my shoulder. "Race you to the washhouse, Thomas. Last one there is a filthy miner going to hell."

Black pants and shirts, pale underwear, man shaped, hang in the steam rising from the boilers below. "What took you so long, Thomas? Dreaming of those Welsh lasses again I'll bet. Good thing my Susan's plain and homely, though maybe you'll be looking at her soon enough."

His underwear floats through the steam, drapes my shoulder. "Hurry up, my friend. I'll wash your back."

BETWEEN WAKE AND SLEEP in the night, in the dark. My fingers, toes, legs swollen numb. Roll over, cold sucks my skin.

Down the main entry, mud sucks rubber, sucks my flesh. My toes, dead lumps. Roll over half asleep, can't move my arm, lift it with my other hand.

Grant's voice speaks to me out of the dark, lost between wake and sleep, he in their bed among rows of miners' cottages, Susan asleep beside him. "This is a mild winter, Thomas. Not like last. Balls clenched up tight in November, didn't loosen until May."

I roll over, my breath a grey fog, cold wind down my neck, lost underground between waking and sleeping. Grant's voice. "Here, let's take this cross-cut." This cross-cut, this cross-cut.

Pull the blanket up, can't move my leg

    black

turn right black

            my toe bangs iron rail black
                 rings ahead
      rings behind rings above
            black all around
                       rings up the back of my neck.

"Like a pick in the skull, eh, Thomas." Eh, Thomas, eh, Thomas. Grant's face floats above me, beside me, underground, under sleep. My fist curls around blanket, pick, auger, shovel, can, stick. Here in the dark, walls breathe. Wooden planks, ice in the cracks. In the hotel, in the mine. In blackness. Walk black, dig black, eat black, breathe black. Uphill, can't see my feet lost in black. Up. Drip, drip, drip onto the back of my neck.

I pull closer my blanket, my muffler. Up the counter tunnel, between black rooms, between pillars of coal. Thud of metal on coal all around. My feet heavy into coal, into the mattress, into . . .

Sleep, I dig into sleep. My lamp shines on blackness.

Wheezing in the dark. Grant's hand on my shoulder. "Into your room, you little Welsh bugger. Not called stalls here, like a horse buried kicking." Buried kicking, buried kicking. "Rooms, they call them rooms in Canada." Canada . . .

He disappears into blackness, his voice ringing behind. "Stand you a pint, Thomas." A pint, Thomas, a pint, Thomas.

I swing my legs, lost in double dark, here in my hotel room, here in my room at the coal face. My sock sticks to floor nails, my boots bend around ladder. Straight up blackness. One hand clutches my blanket, pick, shovel, auger, the other scrapes glass, coal. My legs and arms shake. Ice and grit under my fingernails, raking darkness, window glass, coal, ice and grit—my fingers tingle.

I grab brattice cloth hanging between me and window, between me and coal. Susan's face on the other side, her voice seeps through.

"I was a winder, Evan Thomas, jute. Held the strands between my fingers like this, dug into my skin fearsome but you need brattice down there, need to keep the gases out of your face."

In my room, in my dream, I drop my blanket, shovel, auger, pick, two fists around the curtain, the brattice, pulling down, down.

And behold, the veil of the temple was rent in twain from the top to the bottom, and the earth did quake, and the rocks rent, and the graves were opened, and many bodies of saints which slept arose, and came out of the graves.

Cold gas on my face. Below my room, a horse coughs down the tunnel through blackness. Horses starving outside in the dusk press ribs, cheeks against the glass.

"I have to go feed them, Evan Thomas." Susan's hands, white in the dark, pull the white sheet over my face. "It's better this way, Evan Thomas."

POOR BRATTICE CLOTH SPELLS DANGER
Buy only Genuine Jute
Cloth of Recognized Quality

There are mine operators who buy inferior grades of brattice cloth because the first price is attractively low. But the last price they pay for it is the loss of property and life occasioned by explosions caused by air leakage. Nothing of this kind ever happens when Colonial Brattice Cloth is used. It is absolutely non-inflammable and is practically air and water tight. The Standard for Years. Satisfactory Service always and the Cheapest in the end.

Special prices now—ask for quotations.

Colonial Supply Company

I WAIT for him outside the hotel, snow falling. The door swings open, shut. Men trudge up the street, stamp into the pub, snow on their caps and shoulders. Men push out into the street, blink at the grey flakes falling through the air like brattice. Snow muffles their footsteps, their voices. Two men coming out nod at me.

"Evenin', Thomas."

"Evenin'."

"Goin' to the meetin', my man?"

"Wouldn't miss it."

They trudge off into the falling snow toward the Miners' Hall. Bits of their talk drift back to me.

"And then the bastard said . . . "

"Bent over, nearly burnt his ass off . . . "

"Why should we pay for our own goddamn powder? . . ."

Beside me, the door swings open, shut. Warm ale, smoke, sweat blow across my cheek. Three pints in my gut, fish head soup warm to my toes. Loosen my muffler, breathe deeply. Soot and snow. Hum, wave to the full moon.

Grant's hand on my back. "Good God, Thomas, mooning again? Maybe tonight we should wave aside trivial matters of safety and wages and talk about sending you across for one of your dark Welsh lasses. Put you up in a room for a few days, and see if you don't come running back to the pit looking at your boots."

Warm and whole and solid. I hoist my arm around his waist. "You've got it wrong there, Grant-the-Haggis. I wasn't mooning. I was standing here digesting my latest bowl of fish head soup when that shiny face there poked through the clouds. You want to watch you're not undone by her, you Scots, used to the fog. Did you ever see the moon, Grant-the-Haggis, before you came here?"

He laughs, his back big and thick under my arm. "Good Christ, Thomas. If you're not mooning, you're moonstruck. Susan says come for Christmas dinner, roasting a fat goose. I'd stand you a pint, but we want seats don't we, close to Hill and Whippet. God himself and his anointed son. Remember, Thomas, you taffs have a reputation for agitating. Hill or Whippet would send you sacking before you could load a blast. Silence is the word."

Grant's voice snow muffled. His voice, my voice, our footsteps, through snow and grey air. Down Main, past miners' cottages. Wooden verandahs, wooden scrolls and swirls carved above lighted windows. His voice excited.

"LISTEN, THOMAS, I don't know how he survives underground, that Petrovik. What a partner, but a softhearted bugger. Lunch box full everyday, sausage and cheese, stinks like the inside of my gum boots in July. 'You want eat some cheese,' he says, 'you want eat some Kielbasa, you want eat real food, eh, eat, eat.' Works hard, too—finished chute 116, onto 117. Grunts when he hoists the timber onto his shoulder. About your height, Thomas. Broader in the back. Grunts, his sweat like garlic. 'Jesus Christ, you little bohunk,' I say, 'you don't have to kill yourself timbering at five bloody cents a foot. Let the timbermen lug them to the cross-cuts. You'll be digging seven little bohunk graves and a fat one for your wife working for starvation pay.'

"He laughs, Thomas. The bugger grunts and laughs. 'Don't be mistake me for Jesus Christ, you big one Scots,' Petrovik says. 'You gettink your own timber, eh.' He swings away at the face. Falling coal knocks him on the side of his head. The bugger laughs. 'Looks like glory hole, eh, you big boogair Scots. No diggink, no blastink, just you pushink down the chute. She slide easy, boom, out bottom.' All in that bohunk talk, Thomas. Gets me talking bohunk by the end of the shift.

"I'm still planking the middle wall for Christ's sake, thinking about lagging the ceiling, laying brattice. But a little bohunk magic as the bugger rattles and bangs, and the chute's ready to roll. 'You remember Petrovik,' I say, 'you're no bucker. No climbing on the chute if she gets stuck. I won't be carrying you home in bits and pieces in your lunch box like an old Kielbasa.' Can't see his face in the dark, but I hear him slap his leg, laugh. Room smells like garlic, old cheese. 'No worry,' he says, 'no worry. You come my house. My wife, she give you dandelion wine, vodka, halubcha. Is good for you, good for your wife, good for little Scotches pale like you. You too much worry, eh, too much worry.' I saw his wife one day, Thomas, making bloody dandelion wine in the same damn tub Petrovik washes in.

"Then I turn my back on Petrovik's light, Thomas, start stretching brattice. Digs into my bloody fingers. Can't wear gloves and lay brattice. I look up, and he's at the face again. Swings his pick. Coal falls, can't see, but that smell, Thomas, cold and wet. Christ, I can taste it. That Petrovik swings down hard, then back. His pick and arm disappear in the dark beyond his lamp. Then he brings her down hard again. Sweat rolls down my back. 'Slow down you Jesus Christly bohunk,' I say, 'you're making me sweat laying bloody brattice.' He laughs, swings over his head, brings her down harder into a solid rock. Knocked the bloody wind out of himself. He gets madder than hell. 'Piss on the king,' he grunts, trying to catch his breath. 'Shit on English King George.'

"He can't even pronounce it right, the bohunk, but he chuckles, horks. His back to me, his light aimed on a bit of the face. I can't see what he's doing. I hear everything though—water dripping, tapping from other rooms. You know what it's like, Thomas, how you can hear your partner breathe. Petrovik breathes through his mouth, scrapes away at the face. His auger hums around and around. I'm still laying brattice, pitch so steep I lean back. Can't tell if my Christly head is up or down. Then in the dark, that crinkle of the Eaton's catalogue as Petrovik makes his funnel, pours powder in, tamps in the dark, his breath and the powder sliding. Christ, Thomas, you know how it sounds, like a mountain of slag sliding down on you, can't stop it. 'Okay,' he says, 'now we're be blowink' and disappears around the pillar. His light flickers on and off down the tunnel, twisted as your guts, by God, gas trapped inside seeping and swelling. I swipe my hand, grit across my forehead before the sweat runs in my eyes, but I'm cold, Thomas, cold with damp seeping off the bloody coal.

"He's back soon enough with Ironmonger lugging his box. Don't know it's Ironmonger until he speaks.

"'What did the Scot say when he woke up with a blue ribbon under his kilt?'"

"I hold my lamp up to Ironmonger's face. 'Same thing any self-respecting Tartan would reply, Ironmonger, but you tell it since you seem to have personal experience with this matter.'

"'I do, I do,' he says and looks down. 'Don't know where you've been, but you've won first prize.'

"'Go on,' I say, 'take your first prize and fire us a shot.'

"I trust Ironmonger, Thomas, Christly good fireboss. Deserves to lug that big bloody box blowing holes in the face. Knows his powder, knows its smell, its feel, like I know my Susan. Never an accident on his crew, not one. Don't know how with all those bohunks, wops, taffs.

"C'mon then. Up this way, Thomas. Don't think I'm telling you this for anything but a good laugh.

"So Ironmonger lifts his lamp, one of those tarted up safety lamps, less light than a fart in the dark, all that glass and steel. Says, 'This is the whore that leads us to hell. Walked Kroli into water over his head, bloody near drowned. Don't you laugh there Petrovik,' he says, 'could've been the belt or between cars.'

"Ironmonger walks over to the face, puts his lamp down in the pitch black, rubs powder between his fingers, that dry rubbing. Brattice still in my hand, sweat runs down my neck. He breathes slow, Ironmonger, deep and slow, Petrovik through his mouth. My own breath seeps back at me. She shifts, moans, breathes out, and I trust Ironmonger, Thomas. You know that black powder lust you can taste. Pour in all ten pounds, twenty, forty. Blow her wide open, just once.

"'Good Christ, Ironmonger, you're not paid to play in your powder,' I say. My voice bounces back at me.

"Then Petrovik speaks up. 'Slow down, you big one Scots. They not payink you for worry. We be diggink big Barley grave, too much you worryink.'

"And I can't stop laughing, Thomas, there in the dark. 'By Christ, Petrovik,' I say, 'if you aren't learning English, and the king's at that. If I could see it, I'd shake your bloody hand.'

"I swear the mine laughs at me, Thomas, the black bitch laughs back at me in my own voice.

"Up this way, Thomas, look at that Miller and Hawkins at their larders feeding their fat chops. Never come to meetings. You ever heard them? Don't believe in unions. Pork on their English breath, where in black bloody hell do they think the bacon comes from? Next time we're doling out, we'll hand their hundred pounds to someone needing it. Bunch of Judas priests. Could do with a stick in the maw they could.

"But that's not the end of the story, Thomas. There's a better end, by God. Petrovik and I stand in the dark, listening to Ironmonger flick the last bit of powder off his fingers, slow and careful.

"'Christ,' I say, 'you're not preparing to drag a bairn kicking and screaming from out between his mother's legs there, Ironmonger. No need to disinfect your palms.'

"Keeps rubbing his hands together like he never heard, and Petrovik in the dark breathing out his mouth.

"'Or maybe a christening,' I say louder. 'Rub a bit of the powder between the wee bairn's eyes. Holy Father bless this child.'

"And she groans overhead, Thomas, and I want him to hurry, want the blast. I'm not telling you this in fear, Thomas. Never been afraid. But my arms shake from holding up the brattice, and I want her blown wide open.

"'Good Christ,' I say, 'have you gone to sleep man?'

"'Right,' he says at last, 'ready to fire this bastard.'

"But he takes his Christly time unwinding the cord wrapped around his leg.

"'Is that your line to God there, Ironmonger, or are you still tied to your mother?'

"'You know as well as I, McRae,' he says, 'no miner has a line to the Almighty. Now you're holding us up here with your fine religious talk when all I want is a damn pint, so if you don't mind Reverend McRae, would you lead this holy procession behind the nearest holy pillar.'

"And there we are—Ironmonger, yours truly, and Petrovik noses to the coal, already tasting in the dark the dust of her shudder. Any minute, any minute. Ironmonger slides the handle down slow, sighs.

"The silence, Thomas, the silence."

NOTICE
Mine Rescue Bulletins, April 28, 1913

Bulletin No. 1—Qualifications for Mine Rescue Team:

1. You must be a mining man between the ages of 22 to 50 years old.

2. You must pass a thorough medical examination by the mine doctor, especially regarding the heart, lungs, nose and throat.

3. You must be temperate in your habits and of calm and deliberate disposition.

Bulletin No. 2—Signing Up:

1. By signing up with the mine's rescue superintendent, Mr. Henry James, you could attend classes in Mine Rescue No. 1, a remodelled passenger coach obtained from the Canadian Pacific Railway Company.

2. You could make use of lecture room, office, kitchen, bathroom, and one of six standard berths.

3. You could stand beside Mine Rescue Car No. 1, roll a cigarette, lick the paper sweet under your tongue, squint at her clean in the sun against tipple blowing smoke, black slag rising in the sun, and there, held open by wooden beams, the black mouth into Coleman, Blairmore, Frank, Bellevue, Hillcrest, Burmis, and when you crawl bone weary into bed, you could sleep easier, dreaming her there on the siding, cool steel in the mine's cold exhalations, just in case.

Waiting.

LISTEN
LISTEN
LISTEN

A HEAD, THE RIVER VALLEY OPENS WIDE. Samuel's feet slip, rocks tumble, he jumps, lands beside Henry sitting on grass, dumping rocks and black dirt from her boots. He sits beside her, pulls off his boots.

"How does a rock turn black?" Henry turns a flat rock over and over on her palm. "Why does it shine like the sun but isn't bright?" She takes both hands, twists. It separates. "How come it looks like wood?"

Samuel watches her face, high cheekbones, dark eyes. Where do you come from? he wonders. Watches her hands, square and brown. "Coal," he says, "comes from plants crushed under the earth for millions of years."

Henry sits absolutely still, stares at the coal in her hands. Samuel points across at the other bank. "Sometimes coal gets pushed to the surface, but mostly men go underground, dig it out. They take ponies down, too, to pull out the coal carts. If the ponies are down long enough, they go blind."

Henry stares at her hands. Samuel lifts a chunk from her palm, turns it over and over. "In Europe, people burn coal. To heat their houses, run their trains, build their cities bigger and bigger, closer and closer, until you can't get away from people, Henry, can't get away from grime and poverty." He closes his eyes. "Someday they'll want to come here, too, and start the whole thing all over again."

IN 1849 ON HIS BACK, in a room under the eaves, over the garden, Samuel Reed dreams of gold in America.

English roses and begonias and hydrangea creep up the wall, push their heavy scents up into moist air, into his open window, his open mouth.

He dreams of gold, hard dry nuggets. Gold in his teeth, gold marking time in his fob, gold around his mother's middle finger.

Down by the parlour fire his mother runs her finger around the garden on her cup. Around and around, there is no way out.

The heavy scents of roses and hydrangea and begonias and asters and lilies and lilacs rise in the moist air, through floors and walls and up the stairway, into his open mouth. Send roots down his throat, along his spine, out his back, down through bed, floor, parlour, cellar, into English soil.

He dreams of deer along the Ohio River, pulling him north.

His mother shouts up the stairs, "Samuel, will you be having bacon with your tea? I've cut flowers for the table."

After he sails, she tells people, "Except for a bit of dirt and a few fine hairs, you'd hardly know he grew here."

HE STEPS off the ship in New York, one foot in front of the other, west to California.

In California, tongue scorched to the roof of his mouth, he climbs over hills of sand and mountains of clay. Inside his new leather boots, his feet swell and swell. When the sun falls, Samuel, careful of cactus, lays his bedroll in the sand. After dried beef, bread and thick coffee, he sits on his bedroll and pulls at the heels of his boots. His swollen feet push into leather, defy his hands. He sighs, rolls into his gritty blankets.

In the middle of the night, he is awakened by his own teeth chattering. He opens his eyes, and the stars shiver. Inside his boots, his feet shrink from cold leather. Without sitting up, he toes his boots off, burrows deeper into sand.

Dizzy in the midday sun, Samuel Reed watches his brown leather boots, coated and scuffed, plant themselves one in front of the other, one in front of the other, in white dirt. When they seem to walk toward him, he knows he is going uphill.

His boot toe hangs in midair. He watches it hesitate, swing back and plant itself safely beside his other foot. He looks straight down into a swarm of dust and clapboard shacks and wooden walks and hitching posts spilled together in the gulch. His tongue slides out between his teeth, sticks to his top lip. His feet turn north. Carry him relentlessly greenward.

ALONG THE OHIO RIVER, among giant cottonwoods and long green grass, Samuel Reed sights along the barrel of his Winchester.

A mule deer doe turns her head almost right around to face him. If she holds her body still, a predator can't see her.

A coyote slinks through brush, head down, lifts each paw almost before it contacts earth. She turns eyes yellow on Samuel Reed sighting along his barrel.

Up on her hind legs, a grizzly sow swings her head slowly side to side. Swings cottonwood and sweet willow until her tiny eyes make him out, yes, there sighting along his rifle.

His finger against trigger, his cheek against wooden butt. "Give me grace, give me cunning, give me courage," he prays who has never before prayed.

His finger squeezes.

Brown and yellow and piggy eyes.

He steps lightly to his kill, his Winchester warm against his side. Cuts a clean line down her belly. Warm entrails under his fingers.

Brown eyes and yellow eyes and little round eyes.

His fingers strip hide from flesh in one piece. "Give me courage, give me grace, give me cunning."

Over his fire, venison spits and sizzles.

In his fire, a grizzled claw sends up singed hair, begins to bubble.

Beside his fire, the coyote dances with her carcass.

NO ONE STOPS HIM at the border. He snakes along beside the river, fighting willow snags and boot-sucking mud and round rocks. In the wind, he sniffs sweet, sweet grass.

"Watch for the Indians," said the man at the post. "Just as soon scalp you as look at you."

"Noble savages," said the woman, "poor noble savages."

"Horseshit," said the dancer at the saloon. "Whether they mean to or not, people speak a lot of horseshit about people they know nothing about."

"They know the land," said the trapper, "they sure as hell know the land."

Samuel watches. Listens. Scans above cottonwood, willow and pine, and across field, bluff and meadow for thin spirals of smoke. Hides his rifle against riverbank or tree and sets out, one holed boot in front of the other, toward the smoke.

"Grant me grace, grant me cunning, grant me courage." When he can just see the cluster of teepees, he sets his canvas and leather pack on the ground, rummages inside. His fingers grasp the liver of the doe, tail of coyote, claw of bear. He walks toward the teepees, cradling his offerings in the crook of his arm.

"Bless me that I may have your grace. Bless me that I may have your cunning. Bless me that I may have your courage."

The children see him first, run to the edge of the meadow.

Samuel S. Reed holds out the liver. "For you," he says, "grace." He holds up coyote's tail, dancing beyond his fingertips. "For you, cunning." He holds bear's paw on his palm, long yellow claws curled down between his fingers. "For you, courage."

He stands still, hands out before him. Sweat trickles down his neck. His legs shake in the wind. Liver and tail and claw warm on his hands, he drops his eyes. A child's moccasins swish through the grass, away, into the ring of teepees.

A horse's whinny echoes through the trees, the song of the cicada sings up his spine, poplar leaves whisper in his ears, listen, listen.

The grass hums, and he sees walking toward him a pair of moccasins, swirls of beads, bright red and blue and purple.

They stop a few feet from his boots, cracked and curled.

Samuel S. Reed looks into her eyes. "For the mighty Bloods on their swift horses," he says, stretching out his palms.

VOICES FROM TOWN

ABOVE LUNDBRECK FALLS, the Crowsnest River narrows to an oxbow between steep rocky banks. If you could be in two canoes at once, there are spots on each side of the horseshoe shape where you would meet yourself going in opposite directions, even though you're following the same current.

Lundbreck Falls is a true waterfall, not just a steep rapid. Some people say it resembles a small Niagara. Many people say that it is far more beautiful. Keen, sharp, focussed. A pure slice of freezing water.

A little above the falls, the CPR built a black bridge back in 1897, the year Samuel S. Reed died of pneumonia. Floating downstream, you must get your canoe out of the river as soon as you sight this bridge. You don't have much time. Nobody survives the fall.

You can stand on the edge of the falls behind wire mesh. You only have to stand there to see how water rushing below makes you want to fall forward, plunge in. The falling part must be wonderful for instinct to work that way.

A few years ago, a woman from Brocket went over. Some campers at the campground below saw her silhouette at the top of the falls against a full moon. They don't know how she got over the fence, but they saw her fall, black against the water lit up white by the moon.

Some said she had a man with her, and he pushed her. Some say she was drunk. Some say pregnant. None of them knew her name or where on the reserve she lived or anything about her. None of them said that maybe what they were thinking about her, had thought or done since their grandparents came here, helped push her. But they talked just the same, even those who had friends from Brocket and should have known better.

In the early 1880s, when Samuel Reed and Henry Reed went fishing, there was no train bridge, no mesh fence, no campground, no road even.

Behind the falls, foothills run back into mountains. Henry Reed used to winter his and later other peoples' horses back there. They'd come out crazy in the spring, lean and tough from fighting snow and each other. You could go on spring roundup with Henry, chasing through trees after wild horses.

He rode on into his nineties, Henry. Straight as a poplar sapling, legs shaped by horseback riding. Didn't speak much, real gentle. People from town here said it was the Indian in him made him gentle. Then it was the Indian in him made him ride so wild. And the English, or was it the Indian, that made him so reclusive. Always taking it upon themselves to decide once and for all what someone else is. You know how small towns are. Henry once looked a woman right in the eye in front of the hotel on Main and said he was Dutch.

SUN

A FEW MILES ABOVE LUNDBRECK FALLS, in a deep bend in the river, Samuel casts his line. It arcs over the water, for a moment hangs there silver in the sun, then plops into a deep pool.

"When you feel the river grab your hook," he says, "reel your line in slowly, evenly." The handle of his rod against his belt buckle. His hand rolling round and round, brown, from the wrist. And the river singing by.

Samuel's hook rises, dripping, from the river. "If you feel a jerk on your line," he says, "don't jerk back. You'll either lose a fish or hook a snag." His arm swings back, snaps forward at his wrist. The line arcs over the water, green singing.

Henry swings her line back, flings it out over the river. Her line sings.

"The river still has more fish in it . . . "

A silver arc.

" . . . and the land has a lake in it with fish in it and those fish have my mother in them who has another inside her . . . "

In the river, Henry's line trembles. The tip of her rod bends, straightens, bends.

"That's no snag there, Henry. Roll her in steady now." Samuel watches Henry watching the tip of her rod bend, straighten, bend. Henry winds back slowly. The river plays with her line. Tugs, releases, tugs.

"River, lake, fish, father, mother, me . . ." Henry turns the words around and around.

Her mother said the river is Napi, Old Trickster. Henry's rod jigs. Faster, she winds faster, around and around. A steady beat on the end of her line. And her father said the river is the Old Man.

"Him or her, boy or girl, I will carve my own way."

Flash out of the water in front of her. The fish bounces on her line, thrashes its tail. Henry holds her rod straight up, stares at the fish white and dark against blue sky.

Before she flicks the fish off her hook, slippery thrashing, before she takes it pinched in both hands to a tree, bangs its head, thwack, against the trunk, before her father says, "See those two lines on its throat like it's been cut," before they roast it over a fire, pick at its pink flesh with their fingers, tasting river and fire and fish, before they throw its bones back into the river, Henry turns from the Cutthroat thrashing the air and says, "Now even the sky has a fish in it." Smiles at her father.

TREADLE ME AN ANGEL, LORD

IN THE GRASS at the edge of the mass grave, watching. The moon overhead makes the gravestones shimmer. Smell of grass and horses somewhere in the field next to the graveyard fence. Always the wind in the trees, the boulders along the valley, the bones under the earth. Henry and Samuel. Evan Thomas and Susan and Grant McRae.

Here in the Hillcrest graveyard, curled in your sleeping bag, ear to the ground. "Fire," you hear on the wind. "Fire," from under the ground.

Sit up quickly, sniff the air. "Fire," says a voice from Turtle Mountain. But you do not smell smoke. "Fire, fire, fire," whisper the leaves of the poplar.

Unzip your bag, stand and look around. Surely there would be fire trucks, sirens. Surely you would smell smoke. "Fire," says a voice on the wind. "Fire in Bellevue. Whole of Main. Quick."

Bellevue. A mile away. Down the hill, across the river, and up the long, steep hill behind the Catholic Church. Half-run, half-walk, your book wrapped in your bag, slung over your shoulder. Words on the wind, from the river. Words in green from the book bouncing against your back.

What about the stories behind the stories behind the story? What about another way to write the tragic?

"Hurry," from the wind in your face.

TUESDAY, AUGUST 28, 1917. 7:30 a.m. Bellevue, Alberta, Canada.

It is believed the fire started in a small barn back of the Southern Hotel where the proprietor's son, a mute child, spent hours squatting with a magnifying glass aimed at dry hay, his eyes a kaleidoscope of bright slivers going around and around down into his pupils. When magnified smoke rose in wisps toward him, the boy laughed a deep slow laugh, rather like a cow's moo. But nobody was there to hear him.

It is believed the fire started when a horse suffering from a hangover induced by his owner feeding him fermented mash kicked over a lantern left lighted in his stall. There were three charred horse corpses in the ruins, all on their sides, their legs poised as if in full gallop, their lips grinning over their teeth.

It is believed the fire was set deliberately. The hotel's only out of town guest, a Mr. Excoffin, in town for the express purpose of measuring grief in coal-mining communities, had stored his calipers and flasks and weights and scales under a pile of straw. At 9:30 a.m., the sky thick and black, he stood over the pile of smouldering rubble. Beneath the horses' galloping hooves, his calipers and weights and scales bubbled in one molten mass. Out of the corner of his eye, he watched men, women and children wander up and down the street, stopping where yesterday they had passed or entered the bakery, theatre or meat shop. Such dark circles under their eyes, such bereft silence. Tears rolled down Mr. Excoffin's cheeks. Despair filled his stomach. If only he had his apparatus now.

It is believed the fire started spontaneously, no explanation needed, thank you very much. Except that it would have stopped spontaneously, too, if the brisk north wind hadn't tossed flames into the air, where the west wind picked them up and threw them east. Only later did residents south of Main marvel that the flames blew from north to east, and not south, where they had already moved grandfather clocks, treadle sewing machines, Sunday waistcoats, bone corsets and children out into their gardens.

WHILE MOST OF THE MEN, women and older children, including her husband and five oldest daughters, dashed uptown where flames licked the bottoms of the clouds black, Mrs. Toleco sat at her treadle machine between a row of string beans and a row of pea vines, pumping her treadle back and forth. Sweat ran down the tendrils of hair on her forehead, into her eyes, extinguished cinders that blew in when she blinked. Her fingers guided white cotton under the pulsing needle. Her daughter's wedding dress, this Saturday, no time to lose. Angela marrying a Canadian boy. Maybe now she won't be called wop, deepee, bohunk. Mrs. Toleco did not look up at her three youngest, three girls, always girls, crawling among plants, eating warm peas and carrots and rutabaga. All morning she rocked the treadle back and forth, back and forth. The clouds grew darker.

The bottom of the clouds burned completely black, Mrs. Toleco used firelight to sew by. The whole uptown blazed. The smell of burnt wood, metal and cooked sausages filled the air. Pumping her treadle back and forth, back and forth, Mrs. Toleco glanced up. Across the black sky flickered a cowboy on a white horse. "Tom Mix, Tom Mix," the children shouted, mouths stuffed with cooked zucchini, spaghetti squash, kohlrabi. Mrs. Toleco shook her head, pumped faster, thinking, Ah, now the Lyric Theatre burns, no good, no good, and the Lord God says, no idols but me. In her belly, her baby, maybe this time a boy, kicked in time with the sewing machine. Next door, Mrs. Oakley carried a pan of rising dough covered with a tea towel down to the end of her garden, planted it among potato leaves. No sense wasting the heat.

FIREMEN AND APPARATUS ARRIVED from Coleman, Hillcrest, Blairmore, Frank. Men jumped from their fire wagons, coupled lengths of hose, screwed nozzles onto one end, the other onto hydrants, took aim, in mere minutes. "Okay, crank her open." They waited beside their hoses for the burst of water strong enough to lift the nozzle holder off the ground. "Crank her open, crank her wide open." One nozzle aimed at the roof of the Lyric Theatre, one at T.M. Burnett's store and post office, another at the Italian Pool Room and

Barber Shop. "Good God, man, open her full out." The hoses undulated, snakelike, water burped from nozzles, then the hoses went limp, burped.

C.W. JOHNSTON WATCHED flames leap onto the wooden roof of his theatre, watched the thin stream of water splash the hand-painted LYRIC over his theatre door, watched the water evaporate in a puff of steam as soon as it hit, watched the letters evaporate one by one, LYRIC LYRI LYR LY. He raised his hand to the crown of his hat, partial insurance, son-of-a-bitch, raised his hat to the fire that razed. His fingers groped for his hat, but the crown connected with his own burning hair. C.W. Johnston banged the top of his head. "Mummy look at Mr. Johnston with a burning bush on top." Laughed so hard he could hardly see through his tears as his theatre dropped off the wooden sidewalk, like a Sarah Bernhardt falling offstage.

T.M. BURNETT TURNED his head as the whole Eagle Block crashed in a sheet of flames. He brought his fist down hard on his thigh—Christ who would think to fully insure a goddamned warehouse. Carloads of flour, hundred-pound sacks of sugar, barrels of currants, what a goddamned cake. Burnt to a crisp. Serve them right, grubbing wops and bohunks and limeys and yankees and, yeah, even his own kind. All mouths and stomachs set up in a Christly company town. He turned, marched down the street, flames on one side, wooden fronts on the other lit up, a bloody bonfire—bring your fat wives and big-eyed babies, Burnett will give you credit. Can't say no, the stupid bastard. He banged his heels into the ground. The fire roared in his ears. He raised his fist at the blackening sky, shouted. But not Pat Burns, no credit there. Pat Burns can undercut Burnett when it comes to meat, sure as hell, has the whole damned cattle world drinking from his trough. T.M. Burnett shook his fist, the fire roared, the sky grew blacker. Around him, wooden buildings flared into the night, spit, crackled, roared, collapsed. Around him, men with soot-smeared faces heaved buckets of water onto the flames. Firemen stood with water trickling from hoses. Burnett shook both fists. Not even enough water in the goddamned reservoir. Suddenly, across the sky flickered the image of a cowboy bent low on his horse's neck. The cowboy leaned out from his saddle, grabbed a woman around her waist, hoisted her up behind him. Turned in his saddle, flashed the woman a Tom Mix smile. She smiled back, her eyes moist, but they began to flicker up and down, melt into the burnt clouds. Burnett stood before the windowed front of his store and post office. Inside, letters on tins and boxes and books turned brown, lifted in swirls of smoke into the air. *EDGEWORTH, Extra High Grade Sliced Pipe Tobacco. Club House Brand Pure Spices Whole Nutmegs. Farmers' Needle Book.* First the words, then the haystack and ducks and the needle stuck through the haystack and the woman running toward it turned brown, lifted in a swirl of smoke. T.M. Burnett closed his eyes, rocked back and forth. Inside the mail bin at the back of his store, *August 25, 26, 27, 1917, Dear Mother, We Regret to Inform You, Love Elizabeth, Sincerely Yours,* lifted from the pages of letters, disappeared in the hot closed air. He opened his eyes as the wind tossed a ball of flames onto his wooden roof. Over the door, his sign turned brown, lifted letter by letter, T.M. BURNETT M. BURNET BURNE.

ON THE EAST END OF TOWN, Frank Toleco stood with four of his daughters between the Italian Pool Room and Barber Shop, and P. Burns & Co. Store and Stables. Flames leapt down both sides of Main Street toward them. Sweat trickled from his daughters' ringlets, down their cheeks and foreheads. All daughters, but such girls. Look at that thick hair and those dark eyes, and good, they are all good girls. But please, God, just one son, this one, then no more mouths to feed. I will name him Primo or Consolato, maybe Ezio Primo Consolato Toleco. Such a name, he could be a saint.

Ines Toleco blinked through the sweat beading her eyelashes at her father. Flames and heat waves engulfed the town behind him. He could be in hell. Ines crossed herself, mumbled, "Forgive me father," then couldn't help it, snorted out loud. Imagine God right here in Bellevue, his jacket sleeves smoking in the heat, mumbling just one son, just one, from those lips, how could your own father have such thick dark lips? Primo, Primo, Primo. If Jesus would only kiss her, once, just once, she wouldn't have to see him. Ines crossed herself again. "Forgive me mother." Better to think of the Virgin. Did she sew Jesus' clothes? She must have had some Italian in her—in all the pictures, same big eyes and pointed chin as Momma. Pumping her treadle in the garden, yet, another one planted in her belly, and how did it get there? She looked at her father's lips, soft full lips, moving up and down. Consolato, Consolato. Oh, God, forgive me. "The Father, the Son and the Holy Ghost." Crossed herself quickly. Safest to think of the Holy Ghost. She patted the smoke rising from Frank's sleeves. "Poppa, you watch the fire too long, you're gonna burn up."

Without moving her head, Dozalina watched her older sister cross herself three times. Always crossing herself. So much movement, such waste. Easier not to think sin. Through the flames and heat waves, men ran back and forth with buckets and sacks of dirt. The flames drank the water, ate the sand, grew bigger. Dozalina smiled slowly, arched her head back slowly. Ah, the fire made her drowsy. She closed her eyes, watched the flames on the insides of her lids. Like sleeping, you can watch and watch, float on your back. Ah, the heat on her cheek, inside her closed lids, her sister Ines brushing at Poppa's sleeves. Such movement, such waste. Dozalina breathed in deeply, smoke and cinders, metal and, and what was that . . . that odour? Dozalina waited, her head back, eyes shut, and let it come to her. Mmmmmm, in her mouth, around her taste buds, such a smell— pepper and anise and garlic and warm soft fat. Yes, sausage, roasting sausage—Mortadella, Pepperoni, Capicola. Her mouth watered.

Vera and Elsa watched the balls of flame leap from roof to roof, watched flames shoot out of windows, watched as one after another, the Bellevue Café, Boston Café, Lyric Theatre, Southern Hotel trembled, burst into brilliant flame, shuddered and collapsed.

"Why can't they put the fire out?"

"Why is Ines crossing herself?"

Beads of sweat ran down their backs, under their petticoats, into their bloomers. Elsa and Vera wriggled. The flames grew closer and closer, leapt into the sky where a cowboy lifted two little girls onto the back of his flying white horse. Then the horse and man and two little girls began to flicker up and down, flickered out. Vera and Elsa looked at each other, giggled, turned back to the fire.

"What's a LYRIC?"

"What's a LYR?"

Sausage. Pepperoni, Salami, Mortadella, Chorizo. They looked at Dozalina's nostrils flare gently in and out.

"Do you smell sausage?"

"Do you smell cheese?"

The flames leapt, roared. Ines patted her father's sleeves, crossed herself. Dozalina drowsed. Vera and Elsa sniffed. Ah, there from the Italian Pool Room. Holding hands, they crept to the wooden board-walk, one foot up, then the other, crept across, into the arched vestibule, pushed open the door where only men had gone before.

A wall of heat and cooking vapours stopped them on the thresh-old. They closed their eyes, breathed in steam. Capicola, Mortadella, Pepperoni, Chorizo. And melting cheese—Provolone, Reggiano, Romano, Sardo. Steam so thick and hot their ringlets swelled, pulled out of the tight coils that Angela made this morning and cascaded down their backs.

"Are your eyes closed?"

"Is your mouth running?"

Steam beaded on their lashes, weighted down their lids. By drop-ping their faces forward, they forced the fatty drops down their cheeks, opened their eyes a crack. Around their boots, the wooden floor planks heaved and warped, sent waves of sizzling fat and white melted cheese washing over their toes. They pried their lids higher. All around them, dark floorboards creaked and heaved, waves of fat cresting with foaming cheese splashed the legs of wooden chairs, wrought iron chairs, huge wooden tables with balls on top, all rolling and cracking into each other. A stuffed chair with one leg spun around and around.

"This is where men play?"

"Do we have time?"

Vera lifted the hem of her pinafore to her left eye, Elsa lifted the hem of her pinafore to her right eye. They flicked the last beads off their lashes, their eyes opened wide. There, hanging from the rafters, immense sausages dripping through net coverings and split skins, coils of Garlic sausage sizzling inside sheep casings, sausage-shaped cheeses growing longer and longer. Elsa shook her head, her hair straight now to her bum, pulling back on her neck. Vera nodded, her hair also straight to her bum.

"Do you smell burning wine?"

"Can you chew with your head back?"

Outside, the roar of the fire grew louder and louder. Inside, the air grew hotter and hotter. The cheeses and sausages stretched lower, hung inches above Vera and Elsa's heads. Drops of fat and white cheese rained past their noses. Outside, the air thundered, and a great light leapt past the window. In an instant, the sausages and cheeses multiplied in the light, glowed orange. In the next, the roof above them crackled, roared. Elsa and Vera looked at each other, their heads almost too heavy to move.

"Is your nose twitching?"

"Is your belly rumbling?"

Their heads balancing their sliding feet, Vera and Elsa stepped from wave to wave into the raining forest, pulled down coils of Salami and Garlic sausage, wrapped them around their necks and shoulders, pulled down Mortadella and Capicola and Chorizo, hoisted them hot under their arms. Above them, the roof roared, shook the hanging sausages. Under the roar, a strange silence. The balls on the green table melted into each other. The chair on one leg whirled faster and faster. The cheeses too soft to carry, Vera and Elsa let their heavy hair pull back their heads, opened their mouths. Such cheese, Provolone, Reggiano, Sardo. They sucked, swallowed, licked their lips, swallowed.

"Who said fishes and loaves?"

"Why not sausages and cheese?"

Above them the roof quivered. Their mouths caught soft bits of cheese, one more drop, one more. Romano, Sapsago. Above them, beyond their sight, a bellow. Then silence. In their mouths, soft plop of cheese on tongue, on throat, on teeth. Around their necks and down their sides, thick warm sausage.

Above them a deep inhalation. The roof lifted, sucked up air and sausage and cheese. And Vera and Elsa. Dresses full of oil, heads back. Flying up into the burning air.

"What is that sucking sound?"

"Are your feet leaving the floor?"

Flames leapt through the gap between ceiling and walls. Hot wind blew their pinafores against their legs. Higher, they floated toward the ceiling.

Whoof, the roof crashed onto the crackling walls, burst into flame. Beams and sausage and cheese and boards crashing in flame around them, the coils around their necks buoying them, Elsa and Vera drifted slowly back to the floor.

Dozalina let her feet carry her toward the smell. Every morning they carried her, no hurry, across the room she shared with Angela and Ines and Vera and Elsa, their beds empty, down the stairs, toward big bowls of strong coffee and slices of thick warm bread. She smiled, eyes half closed, trusted her feet. Ah, Provolone and Pepperoni, Romano and Mortadella. On both sides of the street, fire roared. Her mouth watered. Behind her, Ines brushed flames from her father's jacket, crossed herself. Frank muttered in Italian. Such movement, such sound, such waste. Dozalina's feet followed her nose, her nose followed the smells of cooking on the wind.

Dozalina stood outside the Italian Pool Room and Barber Shop, breathing slowly and deeply. Ah, such smells, such drowsy heat. Through her half-closed lids, she watched her little sisters, coils of sausage around their necks, sausage under their arms, mouths open to melting cheese, lift inches off the floor. Such dreams, where you can watch others move without moving yourself. Through her half-closed lids, she watched without moving her head the flames suspended in the sky. She breathed in deeply, held in her lungs hot cinders and sausage and cheese. As she breathed out, balls of flame fell in slow motion around her sisters.

Flames snapping the air across the street, Frank Toleco muttered

under his breath. "I don't say I don't want to go down. I just say
sometimes I love the mine, sometimes I hate her. You never know
when she loves you, when she hates you. She keeps you excited all
the time. You never know. You take a good lunch, eat a good breakfast,
kiss each one before you go, even lazy Dozalina still in bed. You never
know. But give me one son, just one boy, and I'll stop. Find work,
who knows, maybe the railway, maybe the coke ovens. Who knows.
Eight already, all girls, such girls, but a boy."

Ines patted the sparks on her father's collar. Her fingers brushed
the back of his neck, flicked his damp black curls. Jesus must have
been dark. Such skin. If only she could touch him on the back of the
neck, she wouldn't have to see him. "The Father, the Son and the
Holy Ghost." She crossed herself with the same hand. "If your hand
offend thee . . . "

"A boy would carry my name, a boy would look like me, a boy I
could understand." Across the street, the roof of the Italian Pool
Room and Barber Shop shot up into flames. Eight girls already.
Angela, Ines, Dozalina. Frank looked into the flames, into the flames
in Ines' eyes. "Where are Vera and Elsa?"

". . . cut it off." Ines shook her hand, so hot. When did this start,
this wanting to touch Jesus, kiss him? She just wanted to hold baby
Jesus, rock him, sing him lullabies. When she was their age—Vera
and Elsa. Maybe this burning started a year, two years ago, when she
was Dozalina's age. Dozalina who smiles in her sleep, smiles with
food in her mouth. Across the street, the roof of the Italian Pool
Room and Barber Shop lifted in flame, her father shouting, "Where
are Vera and Elsa?"

Dozalina breathed evenly, slowly. Through her half-closed lids, she
watched her small sisters step across the waving wooden floor,
through falling flames, weighed down by sausage, their dresses plastered against their bodies. Through her half-closed lids, she watched
her father and sister cross themselves, begin to run and shout, "Elsa!
Vera!" Such movement, such noise, such waste. Better not to think of
death. Dozalina yawned, waited.

Frank Toleco reached the long vestibule of the Italian Pool Room and Barber Shop as his small daughters, dressed in sausage, dodged falling flames. "Oh, God, such girls, and I should be looking after them. . . ." Midstride he pulled off his jacket, pulled it over his head. Just one sensible son. He leapt onto the boardwalk.

Ines ran beside her father, eyes ahead on her sisters—Dozalina drowsing in the light of the fire, Vera and Elsa inside the burning building. He wrapped his jacket over his head. Behind Elsa and Vera, the roof caved in. A sheet of flame. Tears streamed down her father's face. Ines fisted her hands. If she could wipe his tears, Jesus cries for all children. As he leapt onto the boardwalk, Ines grabbed his arm with both hands. "No, Poppa, don't."

SOUTH OF MAIN, Angela Toleco stood with her arm through Norm Honeymoon's. The north wind blew cinders, heat and stench into their faces, into the faces of the crowd gathered to watch their town burn. But the flames leapt eastward, tossed high into the air from one building to the next, down both sides of the street. Each time the flames landed on a new building, leapt with new fervor at the blackening clouds, Norm patted her hand. Such big pale hands, that Norm Honeymoon, responsible hands.

Cool hands. Warm heart, they said. Norm Honeymoon has a warm heart, a heart of gold just like his dad. Would give you the shirt off his back. Burnett's store and post office leapt into flame. Angela stiffened, watched through heat waves and flames black figures run at the fire, tossing buckets of water that made no difference. Norm's hand cool on hers. Could she tell from here if Rocchio Lazaratto ran into the flames? Rocchio Lazaratto, his olive thighs, olive oil, oh, her skin burning where cloth pressed against her nipples and thighs. Norm's hand patted hers, so cool, his kisses cool on her cheek when he said goodnight, but his breath warm. "I respect you Angela." Her mother and father in the kitchen, "No need to worry Angela, Norm will make you a good husband." Their eyes looking over her left shoulder the way they look over Norm's.

The black figures ran at the fire. Angela tensed her shaking thighs. Jesu, Jesu, mother of God . . . Rocchio Lazaratto, olive oil on his breath, his hands hot on her neck. "You know me, Angela, speak the same language, eat the same food, and I know you . . . " Rocchio Lazaratto maybe now burning in flames . . . "Come with me, Angela. You'll be lost with Norm Honeymoon, won't know what he's saying. In the name of Jesu, you don't even have the same God, can't have the same hell. . . ." Rocchio Lazaratto, a butcher's son—"Don't say his name around me, ever." His lips hot on her neck. . . . "It's not too late, Angela. . . ."

Hail Mary, mother of God. Angela shook her head, squeezed Norman's arm. He looked down at her, so tender, but the fire reflected in his eyes, and in that fire, Rocchio Lazaratto. She closed her eyes, squeezed Norman's arm.

ON HIS BACK in his hospital bed, old man Mannon chuckled to himself. So this was it, eh, the big deal at the end of life. You take a fever, and the next thing you know, you're crossing through the flames to the other side. And it was getting hotter, no doubt about that. Despite his shivering bones, he could feel sweat running down his chest. Now, if his mother were here, she'd rub his skin with onion and cover his chest in flannel. Where was she, anyway. Probably out milking the damn cow. He opened his mouth, felt the word in his throat, Mother, but damn it if you aren't daft Mannon—she crossed over years ago. He shut his lips, so dry they stuck together like paper. You have a fever, you old coot, but no need to go delirious. If Marion were here, she'd run her tongue down his breastbone. . . . "You're the salt of the earth, Mannon," she said, "that's why I married you. . . ." Marion, you chose me didn't you. You did the courting. Mother didn't like you, said you were like the Chinook wind, a lot of blow. But she wasn't there when you delivered the Coutts' dead baby, a girl wasn't it. Wrapped her in a tea towel and sang her a lullaby, your arms cradling her and Dora Coutts at the same time. Hey, where are you, Marion? Your old man's burning hot. I don't think I've seen you for a while, Marion. Where you been? My skin is thirsty, Marion. Can hardly sleep nights it's so thirsty. Marion. When was the last time I saw you? Let me think. Is this the way God comes for you? Muddles your brains? Where the hell are you, Marion? I was walking up the hill from work, swinging my bucket, and there you were, gathering my frozen long johns off the line, hoisting them like flattened corpses onto your shoulders, and you were laughing. No, that wasn't the last time. I was trudging up out of the tunnel. The whistle was blowing. They were bringing up the bodies on top of the coal they'd just dug, didn't want to waste any, by God. When I saw you there, your face white among all those women, I knew I was still alive. "What the hell took you so long?" you said. "What took you so long?" Damn it, Marion, where did you go? It's so damned hot here, I can't stop shivering. The women here wear white. You never wore white—"Not practical in a coal mining town," you said. Had that notion wiped out of you when you were a kid. Not here, though, not this town. We come here when we were already old, an old man going down the mine. Marion, if you could just put your hand on my forehead. . . . You appreciate me don't you? "Don't matter to me, Mannon, if you aren't a talker and a go-getter. Too many of them around." But, Marion, when was the last time I saw you? I didn't lose you in my memory, you just aren't in order. I was walking up the hill through the deep snow when I heard hoots coming from way up. Strangest hoots I ever heard. I stopped to listen. Then you come flying out of the trees in half a barrel, going this way and that. Almost knocked me over. You and those Duncan kids laughing so hard tears froze on your cheeks. "Wanna ride?" you said. "Beats the train." Marion, your cheeks went magenta in the cold. It wasn't your fault we didn't get kids. They just didn't come is all. Your lips turned magenta. If you could just lay them here on my temples. In the mine, we stripped to the waist when we were hot. Nights, when the mine creaked and breathed around us, so black you were alone with your thoughts, your partner right there next to you, I thought of you, Marion. I'd crawled inside you where I always wanted to be. "I want a child inside," you said. "The closest I can get is helping them out of someone else." You always left water in the heater on the stove, there was always hot water. In the morning, I filled the big tub, right there by the stove where you left it. Watched you sleep, the bed in the middle of the room—"Has to be here, Mannon, or we'll freeze in our sleep." Wind blowing through the walls, I sank into your hot water, shivering, scrubbed the coal out of my skin, you there in the grey dawn, big and sleeping. All night, I'd been inside you, yet there you are sleeping. So hot, but I can't stop shivering. Could you get up, Marion, cross back over, pour cold water on my head. No, no, Marion, don't get up. I'll come to you. Isn't that what you said—"If I cross the river first, Mannon, come and find me?" I'll just finish scrubbing here, make myself clean for you, Marion.

SUCH WARMTH. Such odours. Dozalina turned her face toward the Boston Café, closed her eyes. Inside her dark lids, she watched Mah Ki walk between his smoking tables, shaking his head. He crossed behind the counter, pulled open the long drawer, pulled out a piece of paper. With the palm of his hand, he pressed the paper out flat on the counter, ran a finger down the edge of the page. He looked at his smoking tables, the candy melting under his glass counter, the swinging double doors back into the kitchen. He shook his head, pressed his finger hard into the paper, clicked his tongue against the roof of his mouth. Flames danced across his tabletops. He folded the paper into the sleeve of his jacket, held it against his wrist with one hand, slid his other hand up the opposite sleeve. He walked between his tables, licked black by the fire, pushed through the swinging doors into the kitchen where flames ran along the floor ahead of him, out into the back alley.

DR. MCKENZIE RAN down the back street, his heart pounding. Didn't matter whether the wind blew east or south. Behind him, cinders landed on his roof, burst into small fires. He ran toward the crowd gathered beside the open-air rink. "I need help . . . as many men as . . . roof's already . . . eight inside . . . " He had time to make out Norm Honeymoon squeeze Angela Toleco's shoulder and leave the crowd, before he turned and ran back toward his home and hospital, Norm's running footsteps behind him.

NURSE GUNN SLID her hand down her patients' sweaty backs, hoisted those who could sit into a sitting position. Eight patients and only one could walk. Two broken legs, a broken back, three surgery, one black lung and old man Mannon. Along the walls, white paint blistered and burst, left brown smoking scars. A bucket under her arms, Nurse Gunn sprinkled water on her patients' gowns, hair, casts. "Here, hold these over your faces." She dipped cloths into her bucket, handed them to her patients. Leaning over his bed, she touched a wet cloth gently to old man Mannon's papery lips, daubed at the incomprehensible language of death.

She filled her bucket again, with her hand sprinkled water on the paint blisters smoking on the walls. Around the two public infirmaries, around the small private ward. So many walls. The blisters hissed, steamed, filled the rooms with the stench of sickness and sweat. Through the open windows, flames snapped. Below, running feet marked time. Nurse Gunn glided past Ithamar Comfort on the edge of his bed, his cast stuck straight out. His fingers caressed his open bible—"Yea though I walk through the valley of the shadow of death . . . " Past Gus Kinnear, his cast resting sideways on his bed, head in hands. Past Vladislav Svoboda, flat on his back, his eyes black underneath though she has soaped there everyday for three weeks, three weeks from the morning they hauled him out of No. 1 on top of the car that broke his back, his eyes wide open and bloodshot. "Please, Miss Nurse, wipe it away before we bring him home," his wife had said. Catherine Gunn sprinkled water on Vladislav's forehead, into his mouth, avoided his eyes. Outside, snapping flames and feet running up the dry road. Nurse Gunn dipped her finger into her bucket, traced death across old man Mannon's temples, around his eyes staring in different directions, over his papery lips murmuring. She rested her finger on the steady pulse in his throat. "You've worked hard to live, and you're working hard to die. I'll do what I can."

DR. MCKENZIE RAN. His lungs burned. There were his home and hospital at the end of the street, his roof in flames. "Eight," he shouted over his shoulder. "Have to . . . helpless . . . broken . . . fever . . . "

IN THE HALL outside the women's infirmary, Nurse Gunn stopped between the door into the infirmary and the door open to the outside. Nine in the morning and the sky was turning black. Sweat trickled between her breasts. Four more. How can I go in there, sweat and sick flesh and ether? I am trained, but women's bodies give forth children and blood. Women give and give and give. How can I give to women? I could have gone overseas. Someday the soldiers will come home, they will need me. My body has never been seen, never been touched in the dark. Men shoot each other, their limbs snap. Women see through my uniform. I know, hold the cone over their mouths and noses, watch them drift away.

Catherine Nichols Gunn watched flames lick the bottoms of the clouds black, watched the clouds roll, shift. A horse limped through burned stubble. A soldier lay on his back, his arm over his face, mud up to his elbows. A little girl curled on her side under a tree, her belly bloated. A woman in a white gown, a white starched veil falling to her shoulders, bent over the girl.

Catherine Nichols Gunn pressed the palm of one hand against the door frame, ran the other over her eyes. Tired, I'm just tired. She looked up at the cloud. The woman straightened up, looked straight at her. Her face expressionless, eyes on Catherine, the woman turned sideways. Two beautiful white wings. Eyes still on Catherine, she reached back over her shoulder, pulled on one of her wings, pulled it away from her shoulder blade, from the bottom up. Drops of blood fell through the clouds, fell into the red and yellow flames. Without turning her head, she turned her body the other way, ripped off her other wing, tossed it into the air. Spinning slowly, down through the clouds, the wings burst into brilliant flame.

"How?" Catherine Nichols Gunn lay her cheek against the back of her hand. "Show me how." When she looked up again, the woman was already melting into black cloud.

MMMMMM. Smell of hot toffee, roasting onion. Dozalina let her feet turn her all the way around to the Bellevue Café. Through half-closed eyes she watched Mar Ling untie his apron, use it to beat at the flames licking down his walls. His apron burst into flames. Mar Ling ran through the double doors into his kitchen, ran back with a stack of cloth napkins. With both hands he beat them at the flames. Fire licked his fingers, singed his knuckles.

Mar Ling stared at the fire devouring his tables, his wall. Slowly he turned, crossed behind his counter, fiddled with the lock on his small safe, pulled out a stack of papers tied together with string. Eyes on the flames dancing across the floor toward the counter, he gripped the string, broke it apart. One by one, he tossed the papers into the fire. One by one, words rose in the smoke-choked air. *Certify. Owner. Oriental. Mar Ling. Statute. Insured. Partial. Agrees. Limitations.*

Fire at his heels, Mar Ling walked slowly into his kitchen, grabbed a sack of flour, a bag of onions, a meat cleaver. He slit the sack, heaved the flour onto the flames. It exploded. Mar Ling covered his eyes, heaved the onions. Their papery skins flaming, they spun, fiery balls in the air. He raised the cleaver, swung through the flames into his walls. He swung again and again. He turned to his tables, swung his cleaver over his head, sank it deep into wood. One after the other, all seven tables splintered and burning.

NURSE GUNN DID UP the buttons on Euphemia's dressing gown, her fingers steady. She brushed Euphemia's hair back, looked into Euphemia's fevered eyes. "You must walk down the back street, toward the river, someone will see you and help." She lead Euphemia to the back door, Euphemia's wrist vaporous under her fingers. "Go, and do not look back." She pushed her out into the back street, watched her shuffle through the dirt toward the Oakleys' and the Tolecos' houses way down at the end, barely visible in the darkening day. Where her hand rested on the door, paint sizzled and bubbled, pulled like rubber when she lifted her hand. On her palm and fingertips, paint melted into cracks and swirls, her skin underneath throbbed red, white, red, white. She cupped her hand, blew softly, glided into the women's infirmary.

HER SLIPPERS FLOPPING, Euphemia shuffled toward Turtle Mountain shimmering on the horizon. Water, water everywhere; water, water in the air. Above her, the sky grew thick and dark. If he builds his ark there on top of Turtle, we'll be saved. She blinked through the heat waves. There he is, waiting on top. "Wait for me, Noah, the rain is falling. I'll find her and bring her, my guardian angel. She put me here on this dry earth, said 'Don't look back.' I'm coming, Noah. Rise above the flood, hallelujah, hallelujah."

DR. MCKENZIE'S LUNGS BURNED. He coughed as he ran, tight coughs. "Patients . . . black lung . . . T.B. . . . " Behind him, running feet. Ahead, his home and hospital shimmered in the heat. Through cinder and ash raining, a woman in a blue dressing gown emerged from the back of his buildings, raised her palms—"Hallelujah, hallelujah." Dr. McKenzie shouted over his shoulder, "Eu-phe-mi-a . . . fever."

NURSE GUNN HEAVED the whole bucket of water onto the smoking walls. The taps stinking of hot metal, she used her burnt hand, felt paint melt deep into her skin. A trickle of water thrummed the bottom of her galvanized pail. She shook her head. August and the reservoir's low, if I'm to do your work, Lord, I need resources. Think, Gunn, think. She closed her eyes. Through the smoking walls, Mrs. MacDonald's Scottish burr.

O thou who camest from above
the pure celestial fire to impart
Think, Gunn, think.
Kindle a flame of sacred love.
Don't listen, Gunn, think. Mrs. MacDonald flat on her back in a metal bed, metal bed, bed, bed, pan.
On the mean altar of my heart.
Leaving her pail under the stream of water, Nurse Gunn gathered bed pans from under beds, from the cupboard. "As much as you can," she said, sliding them under her patients.

As Dr. McKenzie rushed through the door, Nurse Gunn handed him a stack of sheets. "Stretchers," she said, and handed sheets to all of the men rushing in. "Move the women first. If you can, carry them across the bridge to the flat beside the river." Dr. McKenzie took the sheets, headed for the women's infirmary. "Can't," he said over his shoulder, "Bridge, burned, can't, cross."

YOU HEAR THAT, MARION? Now they say I can't cross the river. How do they expect me to get to the other side if I can't cross? Marion? Where did you go? You had to break that baby's arms, he wouldn't come out otherwise, and they both would have died. You had no choice, you know that, Marion? How do they expect me to find you if I can't cross?

NURSE GUNN TOUCHED the wet cloth to Old Man Mannon's papery lips. She couldn't understand his words, but they smelled so sweet. "Mr. Mannon can't stop shivering," she said to Norm Honeymoon hoisting Ithamar Comfort onto a pile of opened sheets on the floor. "Perhaps we should move him last."

Ithamar Comfort bounced gently up and down in the sheet stretcher.

I will fear no evil.

As they passed out the door, Nurse Gunn sprinkled water the length of his body, and on Norm Honeymoon and his partner holding the sheets by their corners. She sprinkled water on Gus Kinnear smiling in the depths of his stretcher. "Thanks kindly, Nurse Gunn." She sprinkled water on Vlad Svoboda's dead arms and legs—How can they keep growing such thick hair?—avoided his eyes as they passed. All gone, at last. Mrs. MacDonald's burr reverberating with the heat waves down the road.

There let it for thy glory burn
with inextinguishable blaze.

Catherine Gunn lay her fingers on Old Man Mannon's throat. Keep fighting, old man. Some have to fight hard to die. Felt the throbbing in her own.

ANGELA TOLECO WATCHED Norm Honeymoon sprint down the

street behind Dr. McKenzie. He knew what to say, his family spoke English everyday at home—"Have some more roast beef, Angela. You do eat roast beef at home, don't you, dear?" Norm would lay his cool hands on Dr. McKenzie's patients' heads. Angela smoothed her hand down her side where he'd stood, so cool. She would never again be called wop. Angela Honeymoon. If she didn't look at the fire, she might not think, but the flames blazed in the corner of her eye, Rocchio Lazaratto in there with his long lashes and full lips. "Why do you speak English all the time, Angela. You think you're gonna trick your heart to think English?" Angela watched Norm Honeymoon disappear into cinders and falling ash. He would lean over Dr. McKenzie's patients and breathe minty words. "We'll have you out of here in no time." Hurry, Norm Honeymoon. Keep me from running. Rocchio Lazaratto can burn in the flames of hell. She turned to the fire licking the sky black. Onto the blackness flickered a man with long lashes and full lips. He looked right at her, smiled slowly, and between his lips a round plum, this one black and white, but she knew those plums, dark purple in deep red wine, jars of them in the cool cellar. He balanced the plum on his tongue. Angela stamped her foot. "Don't, please don't." He sank his teeth into its plump skin. Her skin hot where her clothing pressed against nipples and thighs. Angela swore at him in Italian. "You fornicator of angels and virgins, you pig of the devil, you—"

MAR LING CARRIED his cleaver and sharpening stone out into the nighted morning. His hands stroked the cleaver back and forth over the stone, one side then the other. "Aaiiiii," he shouted in Toi Sahn to Mah Ki, who spoke only Cantonese, "what do you read in the sky?"

"YOU VIRGIN'S TIT." Angela's voice rose. The vowels rolled out so round, the consonants clipped and pure. "Italian's for singing and lovemaking, Angela. What are you gonna do when Norm Honeymoon whispers along your neck in English, like this?" "Never speak Rocchio Lazaratto's name around me again. You Satan's asshole." Angela shouted at the wall of flames. Around her people shifted, look at poor Angela Toleco worried sick about Norman Honeymoon gone to help Dr. McKenzie. "You pisser of Sacramental wine." Angela shouted over Slavs and Russians and Finns and French and a few English with their strangled language, her throat open wide. So what if the Italians tell Poppa. So what. Angela laughed, lay back her head. "You—" She sucked in. A figure struggled through the flames toward them. Angela closed her eyes, her heart pounding.

NURSE GUNN CARRIED Old Man Mannon to the back door. "I can't let you burn, and we're running out of time." She leaned against the door frame, Mannon's neck heavy on her arm, his eyes wide open, unseeing. Tears ran down his temples onto her uniform. She pressed her cheek against his temple, let one of his tears run down her cheek. "Please believe me, I'm trying. I've seen them decide to die before, I've seen the body refuse." She slid her back down the frame until Mannon rested on her knees. "Time is heavy, especially when it's running out. You could be a baby. I could be your mother. I could be your wife." Under his neck, her arm shook. "But I am a nurse, trained as a nurse, paid as a nurse. If I were your mother or your wife, they wouldn't pay me, so I wouldn't be a nurse." She shifted his weight, his flesh hot on her wrists, her knees. "Who would think bones could be so heavy. But here they come." She pushed her back against the door frame, hoisted herself up, carried Mannon to the end of the garden where Norm Honeymoon ran with the stretcher ahead of his partner. She lay Mannon, eyes staring in different directions, down into the deep folds. "He's the last." She straightened, her arms tingling. "Take him—"

From his shroud, Mannon looked directly up into her eyes. "Wait a minute, here, where are you letting them take me? You promised." She opened her mouth, "I—" but his eyes, one staring over her shoulder at Turtle Mountain, the other at the flames on the hospital roof. Catherine Gunn watched the dirt shimmer around the toes of her white shoes. Take a deep breath, Gunn, you trained hard. "Please take him," she looked up into Norm Honeymoon's eyes, Old Man Mannon shrouded in their blue, his eyes wide open, staring, his mouth murmuring. "Please take him down to the river, lay him in the

grass. I must go tend the others." She turned down the street, Turtle
Mountain's gouged face barely visible through smoke. Cinders fell
onto her uniform, smouldered tiny black holes. Nurse Gunn took
long strides, swung her arms.

WITHOUT CEASING HER PUMPING or pushing bunches of white
cotton under the thrumming needle, Mrs. Toleco spat on the cinders
that landed on the cloth. "Please, don't make holes. Saturday my
Angela marries the son of an Englishman. He's a good Englishman,
this one. No boss in the mine. Works in a bank." Her spittle bubbled
on the dead cinders, popped, left faint brown rings. Her hands guiding material into the shape of Angela—who should know better than
her mother how her arms curve at the shoulder? Mrs. Toleco prac-
ticed English between spits, her four little ones curled asleep among
the beets, their bellies swollen. "Good afternoon, Mrs. Honeymoon.
How for are you? Would you like whale bone corselet? Finest combi-
nation of corset and brassiere, only one dollar ninety-five. Order now,
page twenty-four. I hear your husband, he like hair tonic. Guarantee
grow hair on baldest spots. Order now, twenty-five cents, page fifty.
Your son, he like fine English hand lace kerchiefs, ten cents each,
page thirty-six. So much I like for talk to you, wooden buttons, four
eyes, two cents apiece. Good day, madam, finest cotton bloomers."

EUPHEMIA STOOD at the end of the garden, watching a woman
materialize out of the fog. The woman sat at a treadle machine,
pumping. Around her sprouted pea vines, potato plants, zucchini
leaves, kohlrabi stalks, a strange plant bearing tiny children. Euphemia
shook her head. This was not how the story went. Everyone should be
running two by two to the ark on top of Turtle. She blinked through
the thickening rain. "Noah, make room for plants, we need to eat."
Now the woman treadled a house, a fence, another woman in another garden making loaves. "Blessed creator. Hallelujah." Euphemia lay
back her head, felt the drops on her face. "You have treadled me a
world, Lord, you have shown me your face. Hallelujah." She raised
her hands to the black clouds, felt drops hit her palms.

"TO BE SURE, you come for dinner our house. Baby's pram linen-lined, page forty-six." Mrs. Toleco sewed the inward curve of Angela's waist. The needle thrummed up and down, but there was a new sound, shouting maybe. She glanced sideways. Her tiny daughters lay curled in the warm dirt. She looked the other way. Mrs. Oakley next door held a freshly baked loaf of bread up to her ear, tapped its golden crust. Mrs. Toleco glanced down her garden just as Euphemia pushed open the gate, dropped to her knees, began walking on her knees toward her. Euphemia's hair sparked around her head, her face glowed scarlet.

"Mother of God. Hail Mary. Uncle Doc's elixir cures what ails you. Ten cents a bottle." Mrs. Toleco pumped faster, sewed the long outward curve of Angela's hip.

Euphemia walked on her knees toward the woman sewing another in white. She raised her palms. "I've come from one of yours. She sent me here, said 'Don't look back.' Now I see you are making another, holy angels every one. I'm afraid I've fallen, but please don't turn me away. We'll all drown in this flood. She sent me here, unwashed though I am. But of course you know all that. I've waited a long time. Please don't turn me away."

INES TOLECO HUNG ONTO her father's arm with both hands. Inside the Italian Pool Room and Barber Shop, flames engulfed pool tables, barber chairs. Fiery beams crashed to the floor. Corks and lids popped off bottles, flaming alcohol spewed—green, lavender, purple, gold. Somewhere in there her little sisters, she could not say the word. Jesus climbed up on the cross, but she wasn't there to wrap her hands around his bare arms. "No Poppa," she shouted, "it's too late for them." He pulled and pulled. She hung on.

Frank Toleco jerked his arm as hard as he could. Two daughters inside a burning building, their soft flesh. "I won't ask for a son if you help me save them, Lord." His second daughter gone crazy hanging onto his arm. Where did she get such strength? "Oh, Lord, help me save them. I will go underground everyday, I will forgive the drunk eye doctor, stupid Englishman, for cutting off my eyelashes to make my glasses fit, when it's not me but Dozalina who has weak eyes. Don't forsake me, Lord." With his other hand he pried at Ines' fingers. She hung on. Frank Toleco looked at the dripping tendrils on his daughter's temple. With his free hand, he made a fist. "Forgive me, Lord."

THROUGH HER CLOSED LIDS, Dozalina watched Ines and her father struggle, watched Vera and Elsa behind them move through the flames. Such wasted energy. Such sausages. Her mouth watered as she waited.

NURSE GUNN STRODE down the street toward the two miners' cottages at the end. Her veil fluttered against her shoulder blades. Behind her, Norm Honeymoon and his partner carried Mannon toward the river. Ahead of her stretched time and thousands of patients and herself, Nurse Gunn. She waved at Mrs. Oakley pulling a fresh loaf out of a crude brick oven. "Have you seen Euphemia by any chance?" Mrs. Oakley pointed with her loaf into the Tolecos' garden. Among the vines and stalks and leaves, Mrs. Toleco pumped a treadle machine. On the ground beside her, eyes bright, knelt Euphemia. While Mrs. Toleco sewed, Euphemia flicked cinders from the white dress taking shape. Every few minutes, legs still pumping, hands guiding material, Mrs. Toleco nodded at Euphemia. "I am so pleased to meet you." Euphemia glowed.

ELSA AND VERA SLITHERED through the flames, buoyed by heat waves.
"Are we in Heaven or Hell?"
"Where would we find more sausage?"
"Has there ever been a woman—"
"In a man's pool room?"
Behind them the whole roof crashed. A terrific flame. The blast of heat pushed Vera and Elsa out the long vestibule, smack into their father pulling his fist back and Ines pulling his other arm. Elsa and Vera nodded at each other, swung a loop of sausage over their father's

raised arm, slid a thin Pepperoni into Ines' hand furiously crossing herself.

They laughed, pushed past their father and sister looking after them, sausage hanging from their father's arm, clutched to Ines' breast. There stood Dozalina, eyes closed, smiling. Into her mouth, a chunk of smoking Chorizo, around her neck a coil of Garlic. They ran on. There stood Mr. Burnett as close to the white-hot coals of his store and post office as he could. Smoke rose from the coals of the mail bin, formed words of unread letters in the air above him. *Dear Mother. Mud up to my groins. Tinned rations. Lost both legs. Mortar mors mortis. Love. Don't worry.* Mr. Burnett clenched and unclenched his hands. Elsa and Vera nodded silently, slipped into each of his hands a warm Salami. On down the street they ran, silent now except for groans and sighs from the smouldering ruins. Past Mr. Johnson patting his head through the burnt out crown of his hat. His shoulders shook. They nodded. Into his pockets, thin Pepperonis, around his shoulders, a heavy coil of Garlic.

North behind Main. On the edge of the hotel ruins, the proprietor's son rocked back and forth, hummed through his magnifying glass to the galloping horse corpses. Vera and Elsa held a thin Pepperoni in front of his glass. He laughed his cow moo, pulled the Pepperoni so close he could make out peppercorns and globs of melting fat. He laughed and laughed. At the end of the block, his parents looked up from the list of items their insurance agent held before them. Beer glasses, beds, cutlery, barrels, sheets, blankets, bottles, chests of drawers. Looked up from tables, mugs, ashtrays, mirrors. "Do you hear a calf bawling?" Bent closer over the list. Kegs, cellars, sacks, straw.

Under Mr. Excoffin's dripping chin, they stuck a round Capicola. Down the street Elsa and Vera ran, where Mah Ki and Mar Ling watched the fine cinders rise from the ruins of their cafés. Mah Ki held his arms crossed, hands up his sleeves. He shook his head. Mar Ling stroked his meat cleaver over a sharpening stone, made it sing. Vera and Elsa crept up to the men who gave them houndstooth toffee and warm root beer, placed at their feet a pile of hot sausage. Then ran south toward the open air rink.

There ahead of them trudged the black jacket and pants of Rocchio Lazaratto. They ran up beside him, his face black and tired as when he came off shift. Still running, they slipped into his back pockets a Chorizo. He smiled as they passed him, his teeth white between heat-blistered lips. "Hey, what's this, sausage for the butcher's son?" They ran toward Angela staring ahead at Rocchio Lazaratto, Norm Honeymoon rising above her shoulder, his hand gentle on her arm, Rocchio Lazaratto reflected in Norm's blue eyes. Around Angela's waist and Norm's waist, Vera and Elsa wrapped coiled sausages. On they ran down the hill toward the river.

They stopped when they saw Mannon in his shroud in the deep grass, murmuring. They stared down at his wide running eyes.

"Is he in Heaven?"

"Is he in Hell?"

They squatted beside him, smelled his sweet breath.

"How long does it take?"

"How does it taste?"

They squeezed a sizzling Mortadella, ran their fingers over Mannon's papery lips until they shone with grease. Then one at his feet, one at his head, they lifted him in his shroud, rolled him face down into the Crowsnest River.

Back up the hill for home. At their gate, they passed Nurse Gunn watching their mother on her treadle machine. Under Nurse Gunn's arm they tucked a sizzling Mortadella.

At last, their mother. Elsa and Vera lay a crown of tiny sausages around her head, kissed her on the neck. She laughed, pumped her treadle. They lay a crown around Euphemia's head, pieces of Salami and Pepperoni and Capicola under their sleeping sisters' noses.

In the garden, they flopped down among vines and stalks and leaves.

IN THE GARDEN of the house on the edge of town, flop down on the grass. Cold water droplets mix with the sweat dripping down your arm. Try to find a quiet spot among the voices on the wind, coming from the mountains. Try to think of the green handwriting beside the description of the fire.

Not a trace. Not one trace of the fire, as if it never happened. Walk down the alleys. Look behind the café, the dairy, the inn. Try to find the old hospital. Not a trace.

Sweat evaporating from your body, you begin to shiver. Wrap your bag around you. Look at the garden—beanstalks, pea vines, kohlrabi, lettuce. Dressmaker's mannequin. Corset. Treadle sewing machine. Look at the back of the house you are camped next to. Cottage. Wooden scrolls above the door. Shake your head. What year is this? What are you doing here? Who is telling you these stories? Try not to listen to the voices teasing along the back of your neck toward your ears. Focus on the green handwriting you remember, think you remember, in the book you bought. The book. Where? Yes, here. Against your thigh. Pick it up. Solid. Flip it open, sniff the paper. Dust. Ink. And the green words.

There are always voices missing. There should always be more voices. And more questions.

VOICES
FROM
TOWN

HENRY REED, yup, I remember Henry Reed. Had features like the boys from down on the Blood reserve. Long between the cheek and jaw, high cheekbones, eyes reddish-brown, slanted a bit. Had the habit of staring at you too long without saying nothing. Made you feel like looking over your shoulder, the way you feel when a coyote stares you down. And he always wore them jeans and boots, and that checkered shirt.

He helped out on the ranch, hell, he was his father's oldest son. Only kid for the longest time. He must of been, what, ten or so when the next one come along. Old enough to ride by hisself up to Bellevue where Samuel kept his bulls. No people in the Pass yet, nothing to bring them here. Mines didn't get going till the railway come in. Must have been 1900 or so.

Nope, them were the days of running cattle all over this country. No fences. Cattle run everywhere, up the mountains, in the trees. Took the place of buffalo, only you couldn't hunt them. Run wild, but they were branded, by God.

Now Henry, he rode out to check on his dad's cattle, not 'cause he cared about cattle, but 'cause it gave him an excuse to ride a horse. We never seen a man sit a horse so natural. He rode like them Blood, only with more, what do you call it, finesse. Yeah, finesse. Course, they had them cayuse ponies. Henry got hisself some thoroughbred blood there somehow. His horses had a wild look in their eyes, like they was always surprised. Could run like the wind. You couldn't tell man from horse.

No one wanted to steal Henry's horses neither. Too damn fired up for anyone else to ride. That's how he liked them—fired up. They'd stand still while he hopped on, but take off before he was seated. He was right there, bent low over their necks, smiling like the by Jesus. Must have been the Indian in him. Then again, it mighta been the English. His dad, there, Samuel, he was odd as they come. Always movin' in a hurry, like he wanted to be somewhere else. And that funny English way of talking. You'd think he learned a different alphabet. But he could ride like the devil. The whole damn family could ride.

Henry was a quiet man. He didn't say much, had a soft voice, kinda like rubbing tanned hide. Always wore a cowboy hat, even inside. When Samuel died, back in '96, same year Charcoal raised hell down here, Henry took over. Sold the cattle, the ranch, everything except the horses. Bought a bunch more, too. He was a shrewd horseman, that Henry. Could look at a foal and know how the bugger would run.

Was easy for him to sell everything. His mother wanted out. She hardly saw Samuel laid in his grave before she was back with her people. Remarried that same fall.

There were three or four girls in the family. Henry had brothers, two, but he was the oldest, so he was in charge. That's the law of the land, oldest son takes over. We thought he'd marry, move his wife onto the ranch. He never seemed interested. Next thing you know, he sold the place. Moved his horses out into the mountains, in the Upper Oldman area. Lived alone there with them. Guess he figured horses made more sense than people.

That wasn't so unusual in them days. Some guys couldn't live in town. But they usually took a woman with them. Kept the bed warm at night. Some guys couldn't stand even a woman. We thought Henry was one of them guys, bit of a lone wolf. We thought we knew him pretty good.

He was just a young cub when he went back up there, nineteen or twenty. Lean and fierce looking. But he was a gentleman. Come into town twice a year for supplies, early spring and late fall. Brought three pack horses, loaded them up with flour, tea, sugar.

He could tell stories, Henry. Didn't swear or nothing, but he knew how to make you listen. His favourite, we never got tired of hearing it, was about the time Bill McIntosh rode back with him to his cabin. On the way, somewhere up by Dutch Creek, Bill seen a wolf den and said he would sure like to get a couple of wolf cubs. So he got off his horse and crawled into the den. Figured the mother must be out hunting.

Now when Bill was young he had quite a paunch on him, and a wolf always makes a mound in her entranceway to keep bigger animals out. But Bill really wanted them cubs. He's a stubborn SOB, too, so he squeezed his belly over that mound. There he was, his bum stuck between the mound and ceiling, when he come face to face with the she-wolf. He was in there a hell of a long time. Henry got to wondering, so he got off his horse, and went and looked down the air hole in the top of the den. What did he see but the wolf's pointy nose this close to McIntosh's pug nose. Neither of them moving or saying nothing. So Henry takes a branch and sticks it down between McIntosh's nose and that wolf's nose. Then he comes up behind McIntosh, his bum still stuck up there, ties a rope around his feet and drags him out with his horse.

McIntosh stayed up there a week, and he didn't see nothing unusual. Gear on the table, saddle on the chair but nothing strange. Henry didn't do nothing strange neither. Same as he always was.

He was a real gentleman, Henry. Always bought boxes of candy before he saddled up. Told us to take them home for the wife and kids. He never stayed in town.

He died up there alone. He must have been eighty-four or five. A bunch of us helped him round up his horses in the spring. He let them loose in the mountains all winter, except for a couple he rode.

They came back wild, kicking and snorting. What a sight, Henry in his eighties, low on his horse's neck, his herd thundering down the valley ahead of him. Had eighty or ninety head when he died. Always grinned when he rode.

He was grinning when we found him. Should of left him alone, but no, we had to go check on him a couple of weeks after roundup, see how he was doing with all them wild horses around his place. Bunch of us guys rode off up there early in the morning, got there late afternoon. We could feel the heat blistering off the mountains.

When he didn't answer the door, we went inside. His place was empty, but how far can a guy in his eighties go unless he saddled up one of them horses and rode off.

We crossed the river and headed up the valley behind his place. We let our horses wander up the creek, into the meadow below Thunder Mountain. Scared a few sheep, saw a grizzly turning boulders up in the bowl there. Maybe we hoped we wouldn't find him.

Saw his horse first, in the evening, the sun making the peaks around us golden. A rangy black with one white eye. He whinnied as we approached, but didn't move. When we got closer, we could see why. Poor bugger was tied to a tree, so dehydrated he could hardly stand. Been there a week or so. Couldn't figure out why a fellow who practically slept with horses done such a cruel thing. You can never tell what gets into a man raised half and half. His parents, they didn't speak the same language. Samuel never learned Blood, and she hardly spoke nothing. Must have been something there, though. They had a hell of a lot of kids.

We smelled Henry before we seen him, sweet like leather moulding in the dirt and moss. We looked around in the trees, but couldn't see him nowhere. Then one of us looked up. "What the hell is that?"

A platform up in the trees. Two poles strung parallel with short poles running across. Jesus, he must have worked hard getting it up there, an old man like that. Poles were fresh, too. We should've left then. We could tell by the stink he was dead.

McIntosh went up first, shinnied up a tree. When he come down, his face was white. He didn't say nothing. Then Tom Coutts went up. Same thing. Come down whiter than the Virgin Mary, didn't say nothing. We all shinnied up, one at a time. No one said nothing.

Maybe the birds ate it off, or squirrels. They eat meat, but they hadn't touched any other part of him. And there was no mistaking, he had breasts and lips kind of shrivelled like where his prick should've been.

No one said nothing.

DOLORES DIVINE

THE STRIPPER was coming all the way from Vancouver. That's what the poster said, Dolores Divine from Vancouver. The poster tacked up beside the door of the Michel Hotel, Dolores pouting into the camera, her cleavage pouting over her sequined top. All the way from Vancouver.

Donna Wisachuk had never been farther west than Kimberley where the sign outside town says WILKOMMEN, and the buildings look like something out of Heidi. Thirteen years ago already, after grad.

"ALL THE WAY FROM VANCOUVER. Can't wait to see this broad." Donna and the other beer slingers whisper for weeks as they pass each other between tables, trays balanced on one arm, close to their bodies or over their heads when they feel like showing off.

THIRTEEN YEARS AGO, ALREADY. Kimberley. WILKOMMEN. The sign bleared out of the dark at her. "Wilkommen, you bet I will." She said the words and laughed, squeezed Wayne's thigh. Must have said them out loud because the other kids jammed in the back seat of Wayne's old white T-Bird laughed, and the car smelled like beer and that goddamned pine freshener dangling from the mirror. Thirteen years.

"ALL THE WAY FROM VANCOUVER. Can't wait." The beer slingers whisper through clenched teeth, slip by each other, swing their hips automatically around each other's hips, men's shoulders, terry-covered tables. Not one of the beer slingers comes from Michel or Natal. Nobody comes from Michel or Natal except a few grimy kids and grey housewives. Who would want to live with a mine in the backyard raining soot every goddamned hour? Good place for a hotel, though, right under the tipple. Beer. Best cure for coal in the throat.

Already the miners in their home clothes, black around the eyes no matter how much soap in the washhouse, taste the foam on their tongues dissolve the dust in their throats and watch the new stage George just built. Turn their whole heads to look, as if they still have lights on their heads, batteries on their belts.

DONNA WISACHUK PARKS her '68 GMC truck in the sooted lot, hikes her tight jeans up the steps. Beside the door, soot clings to Dolores Divine's pouting lips and cleavage.

"Your mouth looks like an asshole, but I love it." Pouting her own lips, Donna swings into the dark bar.

"Hey, did I ever tell you about the time me and Wayne went to Kimberley?"

Four of them on, thudding clean ashtrays onto the tables, counting bills and change into their apron pockets before the shift whistle blows and the men head for the washhouse, then the bar. Donna's voice husky from smoke and talking with the men and yelling at her kids.

"Bunch of us drove out in Wayne's big old T-Bird, you remember that one, what a pig. So drunk we could hardly see the road. Been partying all night up behind Coleman, grad party. Wayne stood in the middle of the fire, his goddamned sneakers melting. What a stink. Said, 'Let's go to Kimberley.' So we piled into his car. Kimberley, supposed to be some kind of romantic ski resort, all the stores done up like chalets. Alls I remember is puking down the side of one of those chalet places, Wayne holding my head, me hornier than hell."

"That where it happen, Don?" Cindy with her skinny ass and tight little thighs, banging ashtrays in the empty bar, permanent stench of beer. Cindy with her high heels and sexy walk and long straight hair, but her voice like a rough motor on a cold morning.

"Wouldn't you like to know, kiddo." Donna winks, crosses the empty dance floor, her ass jigging in her jeans.

ALL THE WAY FROM VANCOUVER. The men shouting over music, their breath hot in Donna's ear, eyes black rimmed. "Jesus, how long does it take to drive from Vancouver? How long it take you to drive from Coleman, Donna?"

"Not long enough." She laughs. She always laughs, bangs a circle of draft on the table in front of them. "Haven't you seen a woman take her clothes off before? Three-fifty, I'll put it on your tab. Come on, Ernie, you're a married man. Haven't you ever seen a woman take her clothes off?"

And they blink at her, their eyes pale inside their black rims. "Course I have. But not a woman who dresses up just to take her clothes off."

She swings her full tray over their heads, swings her heavy hips, snaps her gum on their beer and smoke and man talk.

"It's the clothes, them little sequin things, that g-string sitting where you can't never touch."

"It's not the tits and snatch. Hell, I got those at home."

"It's the dancing that does it."

"It's watching till your eyes cross and not being able to touch."

All the way from Vancouver.

AT THREE IN THE AFTERNOON in her dinky house down by the tracks in Coleman, Donna Wisachuk feeds her three kids, drops them off at her mother's, drives west past Crowsnest Lake into B.C., laughs and jokes all night with men in the smoky bar, swings her hips around the other slingers—Cindy, and Edie, her front teeth punched out by her man but tits to stop a train, and Norma, allergic to smoke, husband run off to Montana with a young chick, by the end of the night fighting for air, shoulders up around her goddamned ears.

Donna eases her tray onto the bar, shifts her weight from the ball of one foot to the other, shouts at Bernie behind the bar.

"Four draft, a pitcher, two Blue, an Old V., and, Jesus Christ, my feet are sore."

Bernie pops the beer caps off, steam foaming out. "I know a good cure for sore feet."

"Yeah, cut 'em off, right, you old asshole, Bernie."

"Give me a break, eh. Nope, my cure works better and gives you a hell of a lot more fun." Slams the beer, three glasses on her tray.

"Sure, I seen you look at that picture outside. Dolores Divine, eh, Bernie."

Bernie pulls the tap on the keg, beer swills into the tall glasses. "Look who's been looking." He winks. "If you didn't have kids and an old man, you'd be out like a shot. Straight to Vancouver."

"Cut the shit, Bernie. How does your cure work, eh? You get it up back there, and it takes a load off your feet?"

She laughs, snaps her gum, swings her full tray over heads, between tables, dodges an elbow, brushes past Norma.

"How can you tell a miner at a strip show?"

"Hell if I know."

"By the slack in his pants."

Bends into the smell of miners, carbolic soap, Brut aftershave, machine oil. Donna hoists glasses full of beer from the back of her tray first, bangs them into their talk.

"Seen a stripper in Kalispal once, professional dancer from Saskatchewan."

"Saskatchewan, no shit?"

"She could dance, man, could she dance."

"Heard she grew up Mennonite. I'll tell you I had a religious conversion."

Donna leans over, her tits and the beer lined up on the edge of her tray tipping her forward. "Five sixty-five," flexes her biceps, swings her tray up and around.

All the way from Vancouver.

GRADUATION NIGHT. Fumbling in the back seat of Wayne's car, an itch between her legs. Straddled Wayne in the back seat of his car, the air thick with evergreen deodorant. His face and long stringy hair swimming in and out of focus. Her jeans and panties dangled from one of her ankles. His pants around his knees, his thighs thin and narrow under hers. Spread her naked knees on either side of him, the upholstery squeaked. Urgent between her legs. Brought herself down on him, ground her teeth into his teeth swimming in and out of focus.

"I'm getting outta this hole." Ground her pelvis into his. "This goddamned stinkin' hole." Pumped her thighs, the hair-sprayed bubbles piled on top of her head squishing into the roof.

In Wayne's mouth, the taste of cigarettes, beer. "I got an uncle in Vancouver. He's got a fishing boat." His teeth grinding against hers.

JUKE BOX THROBBING music up the backs of her legs, Donna swings her tray through smoke.

> I wanna tell you all a story
> Bout a Harper Valley widowed wife,
> Who had a teenage daughter
> Who attended Harper Valley Jr. High.

Brushes past Cindy, face to face, trays balanced on their forearms, Cindy's arms skinny and knotted. Cindy, eyes always wide and surprised as if she can't believe the tough voice that comes out of her, is as surprised as the men who come home with her to her dinky apartment above the auto supply shop expecting to ride her all night, fingers wrapped in her sweet fusty hair, to the beat of the bass guitar in the Greenhill Hotel across the street. The bass frets the nerves along her spine, she arches, whispers her rough engine voice in their ears, "You wanna fuck me, you gotta sing."

> I beg your pardon,
> I never promised you a rose garden.

Donna whispers into Cindy's ear as she brushes past. "All the way from Vancouver. That's all the bastards talk about."

Cindy's lips like a child's against Donna's ear, her hard voice. "I asked that Bill what's-his-name if he'd like a beer for his little friend there, the one sharing his chair."

"What did he say?"

"Nothing. Crazy bastard didn't get it."

"Probably too pissed."

"Gas got too many of his brain cells."

"What do you expect from a guy who can't even get the goddamned coal off his face before he comes for a drink?"

Through the beer and smoke and men's voices, Donna glides her tray like a bird on her palm, swoops it onto the bar, shouts at Bernie over the music, "Two jugs, a Pil, two Old V., six draft." Shifts her weight foot to foot, sings with the juke box.

> Blue sky
> Shinin on me,
> Nothin but blue sky,
> Do I see.

THIRTEEN YEARS AGO. Vancouver. Stanley Park. Tulips in April. "There's a nude beach, man. I got an uncle in Vancouver. He's got a fishing boat." Wayne's teeth ground into hers, his thin thighs heaved off the seat of the car, shuddered.

"We'll get married," he said when she told him. "I got an uncle wants to sell his place in Coleman, down by the tracks."

He cut his hair, took a job at the IGA in Blairmore shooting price tags onto cans and boxes with a silver sticker gun.

"Watch out, bud." Donna sidesteps a man stumbling backward to the can, the cleavage of his ass sticking out the top of his pants, still talking to his buddies at the table. "Twat from Vancouver smells like fresh cod. I know, I been there. I'd pay a hundred bucks to sit up front and sniff."

The plastic shuffleboard rocks click. In the juke box's blue light a man in tight jeans presses buttons. The juke box whirs, clicks.

> Your love is lifting me higher
> Than I've ever been lifted before.

Donna sweeps her tray around a brylcreamed head, bangs glasses and bottles on the table. "Six-ten." She drops the ten dollar bill into her apron, counts out change. Her hips sway to the music.

So love, build my desire

And I'll be at your side, forever more.

Across heads and shoulders, Edie's hips, and tits that could stop a train, rock to the beat. When Ron knocked her teeth out, Edie stopped smiling, unless she had a hand free to cover her mouth. When she has enough money, Edie is going to buy new teeth. Ron is going to help. Donna swings her tray to the music.

Your love keeps liftin me

Keeps keeps liftin me

Higher and higher.

Whispers over Edie's shoulder. "Hey, are they going to shut her down?"

Edie shrugs, speaks with her top lip pulled down. "Who knows. Ron says there's something funny going on. They're cutting back shifts."

"They should go on strike."

"What's the use?" Edie shakes her head. "Strike, shut down, it's all the same."

"Like hell it is. At least if they strike, they got some say."

"Yeah, but no more money."

Donna eases her tray onto the bar. Not a clink from her ashtray full of tips. "Hey, Bernie, what's your cure for sore feet?"

"Ask Cindy."

"What do you mean, ask me?" Cindy's wide eyes and sweet face, her rough voice. She rests her tray on top of the jars of pickled eggs.

"Come on, Cindy, I seen you. This is what she does. Puts the beer on the table, stands real closelike, so her thigh rests against the edge, then turns around like she's looking where the next beer goes, lays her ass on the table, right there where it folds. Gives you a rest and a thrill, eh, Cindy?"

"Bloody rights. Gotta get 'em where you can. We sure the hell ain't getting 'em from behind the counter."

Donna sways her hips to the music. "Christ, if I did that, they'd have no place to put their beer."

Every day except two days off, she wipes jam off her kids' faces, shouts at them to shut up, pries their fingers out of each others' hair. At three, she drives them to her mother's, says, "Be good for Gramma now, or no fishing on Saturday," and escapes. West, as far as Michel.

"Last call, fellas." She sings it out, standing over them. Shifts her weight from foot to foot. "Looks like Dolores ain't comin' tonight. Guess you'll just have to wait."

After the last miner steps out the door, shouts to the sooty stars "Dolores, Dolores Divine," they turn the lights down, sit in the dark bar, each one at a different table saying, "Goddamn, my feet hurt," then swinging them up on a chair. Bills laid out with the queen's head in the same direction, coins in piles, they count out their cash. Donna, Edie, Cindy, Norma gasping for air. Then they count out their tips. "You think you deserve ten percent, eh, Bernie?" Pocket the rolled bills and loose coins. "A good night, eh. If it weren't for the tips, I'd pack it in, work at Philips' Cables. Some good jobs there, eh, running twelve machines if you got the biceps."

Cindy flips her long fine hair over her shoulders, her eyes surprised before she speaks. "Need a ride, Donna?"

"No, I got the truck tonight."

"Good night, kiddo."

"Sleep tight, if you know what I mean."

"See you Monday."

The door shuts behind her. A gust of warm beer and smoke blow across her neck. Donna flicks her butt into the black sky. For a minute it shines with the night lights on the tipple, flickers over pouting Dolores Divine and falls.

She kisses the poster smack on Dolores' sooty lips. "G'night, Divine. All the way from Vancouver. Bet you don't got a box boy for a husband. Bet you don't got stretch marks or saddle bags." Donna turns, gives her the hip. "Bet you fly, too."

She sniffs the air. Sulfury smoke and rain. "Damn rain again. I just wanna sit out in the yard, put my feet up, suck on a beer." She flips up her collar, races across the parking lot.

The truck starts first pop, rumbles under her back and thighs. She pats the dash. "Nothing like an old GMC, eh. Yeah, you're a hell of a truck." She breaths in evergreen air freshener, sighs. "Still makes my heart speed up. What a place for your first lay, the back seat of a souped-up T-Bird, puke on your breath. All you hear is the zip, then you feel it pushing against your hair there, and you're breathing in air freshener.

"Jesus, I gotta tell Sarah never to get in a vehicle with one of them Christmas trees hanging around. Check the mirror, check under the dash. If you see one, run, or I'll break your bloody neck. Thirteen ain't too young to worry about."

She presses the clutch to the floor, lifts the gear shift up, back, down. "Three on the column, Jesus, I love it on the column. Give me a standard anytime. Wouldn't know what to do with an automatic. You don't have no control in an automatic."

She noses the truck onto the highway, revs her up to second, third. Except for a line down the middle, she could be driving on water. Her lights shimmer across the black surface. Rain pours down her windshield, too fast for her wipers. She holds the nose to the centre line.

Around tight bends, sharp curves, climbing. "I can't see you in the dark, mountains, but I know you're there." She presses the gas into a long curve, lets her slide into it. Through her hands, up her arms, the engine throbs. Against the wheel, her palms sweat.

She wipes her palm on her thigh, flicks on the radio. Nothing but static. "Damn mountains, let a little radio through, eh. Bet your sweet ass Vancouver has its own station, three or four. Dolores Divine, bet you can get music anytime, sweetheart."

Into another curve. Cranks the wheel, gives her gas. Beneath her, the truck surges, swoops into the curve. Clicks the radio off, sings.

> Pass me a jimmy in white
> Passin everything in sight
> Six days on the road
> And I'm gonna make it home tonight.

She beats time with her clutch foot. The truck surges into the straight. Donna gives her more gas, pushes back against the seat as they climb the summit. Way below in the blackness, the light of Shorty's bar flickers. "Jesus, I could be a pilot. I'll bet you fly, Divine, fly from Vancouver to little shit towns like this, pick up a bit of money, then fly off again." She pushes in the lighter, sucks on a fresh smoke. "I love you truck." On her right a giant wild rose looms out of the dark—WELCOME TO ALBERTA.

She presses the pedal to the floor. The truck picks up speed. She makes the whirring sound of the juke box, clicks her tongue behind her teeth.

Through the streaming windshield, the centre line wavers, disappears. "Christ." She grips the wheel, lets up on the gas. "I know this road like the hairs on my old man's ass."

The line reappears. "Get a grip there, eh, Donna. You're almost home for Christ sake." High on her left, a single light flickers through the rain running down her window. "Okay, kiddo, the communication tower. Now comes the fun part." She gives her more gas. "Hey, how's this one, Divine, a song from one of our very own cowboys."

> Guess I'll go out to Alberta
> Weather's good there in the fall
> Got some friends there that I'm lookin
> For to see.

"Divine, if I had a body like you, I'd take it all off. Strip the coal and shit. Move my ass in little circles, 'Look here fellas, I don't have to give you nothing.' Move it in little circles, legs apart, slide my pants off. 'Look here, I ain't a mother no more. I ain't a wife. I'm a stripper.' Up on that stage, I'd wear high heels, spikes. Just touch them to the floor, dance my way outta this shit hole. Yeah, move my ass in circles, hook my thumb under my string. 'Look here, only I can touch this baby. You want to fuck me with your eyes, man? Course you do. I'm a stripper, see. I ain't your mother. Ain't your wife. Ever seen your mother strip, man, really strip? Ever seen her dance outta coal grime and beer, and hauling your old man outta the bar? Ever seen, really seen your wife naked under shitty diapers, macaroni and cheese, your friggin' weight? I'm a stripper, man. Don't have to give you beer, new shoes, supper on the table, nothing, man, nothing. See these heels? I dance on your eyeballs and you don't even know it.'

"Then I'd fly off. Tell you what, Divine, I'll lose weight. I wasn't always this beefy, you know. We can be partners, do a steamy number together. I can sew, I'll make us a bunch of those little sequin bras. We can live in a city, Vancouver, Calgary. Think about it, eh. Dolores and Donna Divine, Dynamite Duo. All the way from Vancouver."

ON BOTH SIDES of the road, the Crowsnest Lakes, black as coal. Bottomless everyone says. Divers from Calgary came, couldn't find the bottom.

AHEAD, THE ROAD RUNS straight for a rock wall, veers at the last minute. Donna wipes her palms on her thighs, gives the truck more gas. It picks up speed, shoots through the dark for the rock she can't see. Any minute, any minute, faster into the dark. Any minute.

Limestone, her headlights pick it up. She cranks the wheel, hugs the corner. Perfect. Around the corner, a clean arc.

She pushes in the lighter. Holds it to her smoke, sucks. Red glow. The road lurches sideways. She shoves the lighter back in, grabs the wheel with both hands. "Son of a bitch." The truck fishtails, spins, throws her against the door.

Spins, tilts.

Flies through the black night.

She crashes forward, full weight into the wheel. "Jesus Christ." Breathless, and the truck sinking, black all around. She yanks the door handle, throws herself against the door. "Look, I got three kids at home, a husband. Shit." She slides across the seat, hurls herself at the other door. "Three kids, I make the money. Open, goddamn it, open." She wraps both hands around the window handle, leans all her weight. "I know this road. This can't happen. Open, damn you, open." She jerks, yanks. Slides behind the wheel, tries that window. "Help me, for Christ sake. This don't just happen. Get me outta here." Her chest leans against the horn, blasts the water pulling her deeper and deeper.

The truck floats down gently, pulses up and down when the tires hit bottom. Her headlights shine into water thick and black. Bottomless, people say. Hands on her lap, she slides into the middle of the seat. Peers into blackness. The only sounds, a ticking under the hood, her breathing using up air.

The headlights flicker.

In complete darkness, she slides behind the wheel, pushes slowly, evenly on the window handle. The door she knows will never open, tons of water sealing it shut.

The window handle will not budge. She presses the gas pedal. Water. In complete blackness, sloshing inside her shoes, swirling around her ankles. Unable to see a thing, not even her own hands, she slides to the passenger side, finds the window handle, half stands in the water rising around her calves. "Please, God, help me," and plunges down on the handle. Nothing.

Back to the steering wheel in complete blackness, water up to her knees, her jeans soaked and heavy.

Forehead on the wheel, she pants. "Look, I don't wanna leave my life. I love my life. Lord, get me outta here." In utter darkness, water seeps behind her knees, wicks up the backs of her legs against the seat.

"Christ." She makes a fist, pounds the steering wheel. Water bubbles around her crotch.

She pushes in the lighter, "Jesus, make it work," closes her eyes on darkness until the lighter pops out. "Help me breathe, God, help me breathe. Help me. Breathe." She props the lighter on the dash, here, no here.

There, a face watches her through the window—a small child's face, black around the eyes. Donna smiles. The face smiles back. Donna purses her lips, half closes her eyes. "We have an audience, Divine, a live audience." On her knees on the seat, she rolls one shoulder, then the other, slides her blouse off one arm, the other.

Guess I'll

Go out

To Alberta

Splashing in water up to her thighs, beating time with her knees.

Her arms heavy, her head heavy. Slides her blouse over her breasts. Through the window, the child watches, eyes wide open. Donna moves her ass in tight circles.

> Got some
>
> Friends there
>
> That I'm

Her ass in circles, easy and weightless, brushes the backs of her heels. "Oh Divine, we're a pair." The child does not blink. Swivelling her hips, Donna slides her zipper open.

> Lookin
>
> for
>
> To see

Pulls her jeans down over her hips, tight circles. She pants. The child raises her hand. Something in her fist. Water eddies around Donna's gyrating hips.

> If
>
> I
>
> Asked
>
> You

Her panties down. To her knees. Her hair. Floating. Look.

> One
>
> More
>
> Time

Look.

ON YOUR BACK, in this strange place behind this strange cottage, in this strange garden, looking up into the sky. As if you are floating face down in a bottomless lake. Your book open under your head, holding you this way. Below you in the lake, green writing swirls through the water.

Is this the only ending for a woman who strips, really strips? Is this just showing the way it is, or is it a failure of our culture to imagine that she could make her own choices, have a life after?

Below you in the bottomless lake, the letters fan out, float.

LOOK, DIVINE. A crayon. The kid's holding a crayon.

One

More

Time

The child holds her crayon to the windshield. Draws. A woman, round thighs and arms. Green. Floating backward. Back.

Donna tips her head back. Air. Breathes in. Open. All along. Her hair slides out first. Her face. Looks up and up through water. Clouds. Mountains.

Her neck. Shoulders. Skin naked, slippery. Ribs. Hips. Thighs. Knees. Toes.

Air expanding in her lungs, she rises through the cold water. Lungs burning.

YOUR LUNGS BURN. Your body slippery wet, and cold. "Who," you start to ask the wind and the mountains, "who was the child?" But the voices wrap around you, pull you under.

BONES

SAMUEL SCOUTS the river bottom for a flat spot. "Here," he says and drops his pack, "a tarp over my head, a basket of fish and my son by my side. What more could a man want?"

Together they pitch their tent, spread their bedrolls. While the sides of their tent snap in the wind, Henry goes to the river for water and Samuel makes a fire. While the fire burns down, Henry goes to the river for poplar saplings, peels them there. She brings them back to Samuel, who has already wedged the bannock pan among the coals. Samuel lays the poplar saplings parallel on the coals, lays four fish across, one Cut-throat, one Dolly Varden, two Rainbow.

While the sky turns green, orange, purple, Samuel and Henry suck fish flesh between their fingers. While the sky blackens, Henry takes fish bones down to the river. She throws them overhand. They sing past her ear, disappear into the river black as coal.

Inside her bedroll, Henry strips naked. The wool scratches her skin. She smiles. Inside his bedroll, Samuel strips naked. His blanket scratches his thighs and he thinks of Coyote Woman tracing horses across his skin.

"Fish moving water," he mumbles as he falls over a steep bank into sleep.

On her back, Henry listens to her father thump the ground, then his quick breathing. In the dark above her, the tent flaps in the wind. She closes her eyes, feels herself slide into cold water, opens them. Water rushes in her ears. The ground lifts and falls beneath her. She rolls onto her side, pins the ground with her hip and elbow. The blanket scratches her cheek.

In Samuel's dream, two Coyote Women walk toward him, one beside the lake, the other upside down in the deep green water. The woman on shore rubs her face with her hands, rubs until her cheeks turn white. The woman in the lake covers her face with both hands. She pulls her hands away, stares upside down at him from a brown face. As White Coyote Woman walks, her flowered Dolly Varden dress billows out from her waist, bells around her deerskin leggings and moccasins. Her skin turns pink, then scarlet in the hot sun. Afraid, Samuel looks to her reflection. The dark soles of her moccasins float just below the surface. Looking down, Samuel looks up her legs, straight and bare, down into the lake, down to her belly swollen under a deerskin dress pulled taut as a drum. Down to her hair floating among weeds in the bottom mud. Suddenly, she jerks forward at the waist, grabs her belly. Between her fingers, the deerskin rips open. Across her stretched skin gallop tiny horses, their hooves drumming her flesh. Samuel looks up just as White Coyote Woman pulls her burnt flesh from her nose, exposes the white flesh of cooked fish. She rolls the skin from her cheek, uncovers a fish eye. He groans, drops his gaze to her brown reflection. Drumming, the horses' hooves make red fissures that widen, strain, rip up and down. Samuel looks up. White Coyote Woman peels back her Dolly Varden dress, hooks her fingers under the inside of one breast, swollen brown under the sun, peels it slowly back. No, he covers his eyes with his hands, no.

The wind sighs. Henry rolls her blanket down, lays her cheek against the ground, wiggles her head until her ear cups a flat spot.

SAXOPHONE AND SNAKE

A LLYN DAVIS doesn't know her da from a hole in the ground.
Allyn Davis doesn't know her da.

Allyn Davis does not know.

She knows that a man came in the night and touched her on the head. "Look after your mother there, miss." Then went away.

Allyn doesn't know if she closed her eyes.

She knows she heard grunting from her parents' room at the back of the shack. Heard it through the blanket separating the room where she sleeps between the coal stove and the galvanized tub. She knows she smelled mud and gunpowder.

In the morning, she watched her mother draw a red line around her mouth. "Keep your eyes in your head, you little bugger. I'm going uptown. Don't know when I'll be back." Then her mother left, marched across Bogusch's field, heading for town.

Allyn watched the square lines of her mother's shoulders disappear over the hill, then cut a jagged piece of bread and sat on her bed with a slate and chalk.

She drew a stick man in baggy pants with a hat on his head, smudged him until he was a shadow.

After that, Allyn Davis didn't know her da.

HER MARRIED SISTER GWEN lived in Calgary. "Allyn should live with us," her sister said, tears curving around her mouth. Their mother stood up from her chair, pulled Allyn against her legs. "I always knew you were a thief."

Her next older brother, Wynford, went to live in Vancouver with their other married sister. Allyn and her mother walked with him across Bogusch's field, down the main street of Bellevue, down the long hill to Hillcrest station. Everything that day made triangles—the mountains, trees, shops, train cars, people's heads. Then everything made triangles with everything else. Watching her mother put a lunch sack in Wynford's hand, forming a triangle within a triangle, Allyn wished she'd brought her slate.

At home, she kept her slate beside her dinner. Her mother jabbed at her potato, chewed quickly, stared out the window at the black hump of Turtle Mountain across the valley. Allyn stared and stared at the potato on her own plate, picked up her chalk, drew a line, rubbed it out, drew another one.

Wynford's train snaked away from Hillcrest station, up the valley to Blairmore, then out of sight into mountains. Allyn turned her slate face down.

AFTER WYNFORD LEFT, Allyn Davis followed her much bigger brother, Owen, and Owen's friends, wherever they went. Owen and his friends made circles.

"Her?" Owen squinted through his cigarette smoke. "She won't tell nothing." His freckles turned copper in the sun. "She knows better." Beyond him, the gouged face of Turtle Mountain, hazy across the valley.

Owen turned his back to Allyn. "Come on. We got business." His squint reflected in the Bellevue Café window.

Down the long hill, Owen and his friends with their hands stuffed in their pockets. Their feet sent puffs of hot dirt swirling up the hill to Allyn's bare knees. Allyn jumped from side to side down the hill behind them, sent puffs of hot dirt up to the Catholic Church on top. The crowns of their heads, round and shiny.

Past Hillcrest station, along the Frank Road, along the tracks, Owen and his friends ahead of her.

"Why'd your old man join up, Owen? Don't he know miners don't got to go?"

"What if he gets shot, eh, Owen? Then you'll have to put food in their mouths. I hear it takes a mouthful to satisfy your old lady."

"Hey, Owen. I hear it's quiet around your place these days, real quiet."

Past the lime kiln, three towers blowing yellow smoke, into the Frank slide, their voices rising damp around her.

"I'm going over." Owen's voice echoed among the rocks. Allyn sniffed limestone and river grass, cold in the shadows.

"You can't shit us, Owen. You gotta be eighteen, and you ain't even seventeen."

"Yup, taking the train to Calgary and signing up. Not buying a ticket neither."

"Listen to the bullshitter. Joe Petroni said you just about pissed yourself when a few rocks come down."

"Yup, me and the old man, fighting in the trenches. I'll send you a postcard."

"C'mon, Owen. The only fighting you'll do is fighting your own piss down No. 2."

Their laughs shivered back to Allyn hopping from one boulder to another. She picked up a sharp stone, heaved it high into the air, into the green lake tucked against Turtle Mountain.

"Race you to Big Rock. Last one there's a rotten egg."

Owen and his friends broke into a run down the curved road. Allyn turned away from the road, turned toward Big Rock. She jumped from one boulder to another, leapt one jagged fissure after another, dank rock breath on her bare legs. Owen and his friends disappeared down the twisting road. Allyn jumped straight toward Big Rock rising grey out of the green lake.

Her feet landed on the hard flat ground beside the lake. She gazed into the green water between her and the rock, taller than Owen. Turtle Mountain taller than anyone, looming dizzy on the other side.

Behind her, crashing leaves, twigs, feet. Sunlight broke over her shoulder, broke across the green surface of the lake. Deep in the green water wavered rocks dizzy as Turtle's face, and under the rocks, the old town of Frank—women and their miner husbands and their children crushed in their beds. She squinted into the water. Rocks wavered down and down into green-black. If she started way back, ran at it. In the bushes behind her, Owen and his friends. If Allyn took a giant leap, she could clear the water and the rocks going down, down. If she used her arms. Behind her, Owen and his friends crashed through bush.

"I dare you, Owen."

"Don't stop."

"Jump."

"Look out kid."

A sting across her cheek. Through watery eyes, she saw Owen land on all fours on the big rock in the lake, bounce, roll over laughing. The other three shuffled circles on the shore.

"I can't believe it. The big shitter did it."

"Dare him anything."

"Hey, Owen, you got any smokes?"

Allyn swiped water from her lashes. Owen held up a can of tobacco, shook it. "Plenty more where this comes from. You just gotta jump." His freckles pulsed in the sun.

Alone on shore, Allyn scratched with a twig in the hard dirt. Broken water, broken sun, a big rock, four shadows on top, spirals of smoke twisting upward. With her feet turned out, then pigeon-toed, she stamped her picture into dust. Bent her knees, jumped onto a rock jutting over the lake.

What was that on the water? Green. Flicking.

Allyn Davis squatted above the water flicking side to side toward her. How? She held her breath, sat still. Underneath lay rocks, and underneath rock, a dead town. The green water flicked from side to side. Allyn let her breath out slowly, held her elbows still on her knees. Almost below her, flick, flick, flick. Sssss coming toward her. Allyn held her head still, moved only her eyes. Sssss.

She saw the flat head first, raised out of the water, flicking side to side, then the body snaking after.

From the big rock, Owen's voice and his friends' voices. Allyn focussed on the thin green snake, its head stretched out of the water, its tongue darting in and out toward her. Sssss. Allyn slid one arm down her knee. Her fingertips touched cold rock, her chest pressed her thigh. The snake swam below her, its head raised, tongue in out, in out. Allyn slid her other arm down. Her heart beat against her knee. She leaned into her fingertips, unfurled her knees behind her. Below her on the green surface, the snake's body whipping slow curves. Allyn pressed her groin, her stomach, her chest into stippled rock, reached over the edge. The snake's tongue flicked. Allyn reached down, down, rock biting into her armpit. The snake's tongue flicked for her hand.

Over her shoulder, a bigger hand, black-knuckled, brushed Allyn's hand aside.

"Jesus, the kid's charmed a snake. Your kid sister's a charmer, Owen. Must run in the family."

The black-knuckled hand grabbed the snake behind its head, held it whipping the air above Allyn's head. Owen's friend snorted.

"Look at this, eh, a real live snake."

He slid his other hand down the snake's thrashing body, dropped its flat head. The snake's tongue flicked in Allyn's face. Its yellow eye stared upside down into hers.

"Don't you know not to play with snakes, kid?"

Owen's friend raised the snake over his head, his black-knuckled fist closed around the end of its body. He snapped his wrist. The snake spun slow circles over his head. Whip, whip, whip. Its body straight out. Faster. The snake flew over the water.

Owen's friend wrinkled his nose, held his hand away from his body. "Christ, it stinks, the damn snake stinks. Must run in the family, too, eh, Owen. A family of stinkin' snake charmers."

Owen's freckles copper, his face red. He looked at his friends, down at Allyn, at his friends. His big round Adam's apple crawled up, dropped. He nodded his head toward the road. "Come on, we still got business." His hand hovered in the air over Allyn's head. "You gotta be tough, kid." He jammed his hands into his pockets, turned, skipped across the rocks.

IN THE SOFT DIRT beside the Hillcrest Miners' Hall, Allyn Davis waited for Owen and his friends. From the vent over her head wafted beer and smoke and men's voices. She scuffed in one direction, then the other, the dust she raised turning to meet itself, until the whole square billowed in dust.

At last the door whoofed open, whoofed smoke and beer. Owen and his friends staggered out into the afternoon sun. Owen squinted at Allyn through a thin spiral of smoke. Behind him, his friends wove on their feet, hands in their pockets.

"C'mon, Owen, ya big shidder. Get goin', Owen. Ya shouldn'a tol' 'em 'bout the trenches. They were laughin' at ya, Owen."

They took exaggerated steps down onto the street, brushed past Allyn, headed down the road to the edge of town. Allyn Davis followed their weaving backs past the edge of town, down the hill toward the river. Swished through long grass. Their voices slurring over their shoulders.

"Ya can fight inna gazebo, Owen, but you'll never see the trenches. Prob'ly never see your ol' man again."

Owen stopped, squinted down at a steaming cow pie, squinted at his friends. He crouched, lifted the round steaming pie into the air, the whole sky round, plopped it over his round head.

"At least I ain't chickenshit. At least I know who I am."

Across the bridge, Crowsnest River, cool and dark underneath, cow shit dribbling down Owen's temples, around his ears, into his eyes. Along the bank, past the mine tipple and six stacks smoking the valley black. Crunch over the slag pile, coal slag filling their shoes.

Down by the deep green swim hole, Owen dropped his clothes into the grass. "Dare," he shouted, his mouth wide open.

"Dare you," his friends shouted.

Owen dove straight down. Widening circles around his bum disappearing like a bull's eye. With her fingernail, Allyn drew circles on her arm. Her skin erased them from underneath.

Bubbles burst through the circles rippling around the swimming hole.

"The guy's crazy."

"No one can hold his breath that long."

"Shit, let's get out of here."

They disappeared up the cliff into the bowl of sky. Allyn turned three circles one way, three the other.

Owen's round head broke the surface of the water. Bull's eye. He looked around for his friends.

In the long grass at the edge of the river, Allyn held her hand out to Owen naked, dripping. Owen stood over her, his head blocking the sun. "Here." He lay a wet coin on Allyn's palm. "Remember, I'm the best diver in the world."

"OWEN WENT OFF to bloody war." Allyn's mother's brows made a black V. "Lied about his age, so he could find his bloody da." Her mother's lips, two thin lines. "Serves him right if he gets shot, it does. Thirteen pounds when he was born, and him the first. Ripped me wide open."

On her slate, Allyn drew a circle. Then she drew a line straight up the middle, like Owen's ass, then she drew a line straight across the middle. With her finger, she erased the curved lines. She erased the crossed lines, but their imprint stayed on her slate no matter what she drew and erased overtop.

AT NIGHT, A SHADOW CREPT into the shack, sometimes through the door, sometimes through wall cracks. It drifted about in the dark, in and out of the coal stove, the galvanized tub, cups and bowls and glasses, into Allyn's mother's room. Smells of mud and sweated wool and tinned meat and gunpowder wrapped around the walls.

On her slate, Allyn drew a bloated cow floating down the Crowsnest. She tried to draw the shadow of her da, but she couldn't get the shading right.

Days when it did not rain or snow, Allyn Davis watched her mother's square back march away across the long rectangular field until she disappeared. On her slate, she drew squares and rectangles, smaller and smaller.

On the days it did not rain or snow, Allyn Davis took her slate to the base of the ridge behind Bellevue. She lay on her back, drew dark pine, round sky, white poplar. The top of her head pressed against the base of a cliff, she drew dark stone cascading into blue sky. Allyn Davis erased everything she drew.

In the graveyard tucked between two firred ridges, she drew sepia faces under oval glass, plastic flowers in glass jars, spider webs between the fingers of a stone baby, kneeling lambs. She erased them with her fingers, her shirt, strands of grass that made her slate smell cold and green.

Lying on the rocks above town, she drew the roofs of Bellevue, people's heads among them. Somewhere down there, her mother did what she did when her square back marched away from Allyn. With a swipe, Allyn made them all disappear.

Down by the mine works, she drew a wide-open mouth belching rusty water out of the earth, six stacks and a tipple blowing smoke.

When the poplars turned bright yellow, Allyn drew a blind pony, then marched across Bogusch's field to school, her slate tucked under her arm.

ALLYN DAVIS KNOCKED on the principal's tall door. She hugged her slate under her armpit.

The principal's head floated above his neck. His neck floated above his shoulders. His feet hovered above the floor.

Allyn Davis squeezed her slate tight to her side. She stared out the window, at the dark spruce waving in the wind.

"You do know why you are here, do you not, Miss Davis?"

Boughs heavy with needles moved up and down, up and down.

"Mrs. Bell tells me that you refuse to learn the alphabet."

Up and down, whhoooshhh, whhoooshhh.

"Mrs. Bell tells me that you refuse to listen."

Each bough, each needle swayed in the wind.

"She tells me that you refuse to speak."

Each needle each bough, up and down, around and around.

"Tells me that you can't even dress yourself properly."

A green-black magpie shrieked on a green-black bough. Up and down, up and down.

The principal's hands reached for the binder twine holding up Allyn's pants, threw it in the garbage.

The strap, a red welt across her palm.

UP THE HILL, across Bogusch's field, Allyn Davis placed her feet in big round tracks in the snow. They walked ahead of her to the door of her shack.

Her toes pinched. Her breath frosted her slate.

Before she could stamp her boots, her mother tiptoed through the hanging blanket, her finger pressed to her lips. "Ssshhhh. You don't want to wake the boarder now, do you."

Allyn breathed in baking bread, stewing meat and a sweet musty smell she did not recognize.

She sat on her cot, slid her slate between the covers until the frost melted. All afternoon, stomach watery, she drew tiny squares. She leaned close over her slate, did not look up once as the light softened and the new smell wafted around the walls. She pressed hard with her chalk, concentrated on each square.

"Allyn, shake hands with our new boarder now. His name is Mr. Yurek."

"Now, Bran, Mrs. Davis, you must let your daughter call me by my first name. If she calls me 'Mr.,' I won't know who she's talking to. The name's Stan, Stan Yurek."

Allyn Davis poked at her meat. Across from her, her mother ladled potatoes onto Stan Yurek's plate. Their backs and her mother's arm, a triangle. Allyn Davis pushed her meat around her plate.

"You'll not be sulking in front of our new boarder now. Off with you." Her mother's arm whisked Allyn's plate away. "I said off with you."

By the warm stove, Allyn Davis drew triangles and dots. She placed dots inside triangles, outside, at the tips, along the sides. She erased them, erased the whole lot. But she could not erase the new smell.

Allyn Davis knew that in the night she heard panting and groaning and laughing, and the moaning of a saxophone on the Crowsnest wind.

She did not know if she saw a shadow slip through the wall cracks, turn this way and that, bump into the stove, the galvanized tub, the blanket separating her room from theirs. She did not know if she smelled gunpowder.

She did not know.

"WE NEED COAL, Mrs. Davis. Allyn can come with me. Two can carry more than one." Stan Yurek wound his muffler around his throat.

"Come on, Allyn, put your slate away and put your muffler on. You have one, don't you?"

Allyn Davis watched the blue muffler wind around and around Stan Yurek's thick neck.

Her mother handed her Owen's old wool jacket, her mother's red mouth pursed tight. "Don't ask her what she has and doesn't have, Mr. Yurek. The only thing she knows is that damned slate. Now come on, you're getting to be as lazy as your da."

Allyn Davis drew a thick line, rubbed it out with her elbow, drew a soft line going around and around.

Her mother shook Owen's jacket. "I said, come on now. Do you hear me?"

Soft blue, around and around.

"Do you hear me? If you can't answer, at least show that you hear me."

Around and around and around.

Owen's empty jacket snapped the air.

"God damn you, you little bugger. Sitting there judging me. Where the hell do you think the coal in this house comes from? Where the hell do you think the meat and the bread and the tea come from?"

Allyn Davis pushed her chalk in spirals off the top of her slate.

Owen's jacket whipped the air, landed on Allyn's pillow.

Allyn Davis dropped her chalk onto the mattress between her knees, clutched her slate. But her mother's arms, strong and square, reached into Allyn's lap, yanked the slate out of her hands.

Her mother raised the slate over her head, brought it down, crack, against the corner of the stove. Swung her foot. Pieces of slate rang against the stove. "Get out, get out of here."

Stan Yurek tiptoed across the room in his big boots. His arm around her mother's back. With her chalk, Allyn Davis drew squares and zigzags and half-circles on her thigh, over and over.

STAN YUREK WOUND his muffler around and around Allyn Davis' neck, tucked it under Allyn's sweater. Allyn sniffed soap and talc and a new smell that made the back of her throat ache.

"In Poland in the first big war, I had two daughters and, of course, my wife. My daughters were small like you. Six and eight when the war started."

Ahead of Allyn, Stan Yurek tracked moonlit snow.

"We lived on a farm, had chickens, eggs, milk. My wife used to get up in the dark, make sour cabbage, fat dumplings, soup, boil milk. When the sun came up, she already had milk in a bag hanging from the porch for cheese. Come, she told the neighbours, come get eggs, cheese. You want dumplings? Pretty soon, we had no more milk, no more flour, no more eggs, no more chickens. The neighbour children crawled out in the field on their hands and knees, ate grass. Their stomachs stuck to their backbones. Pretty soon, they swelled up. From our big window, we watched them curl on the ground like seeds, their mouths too dry to cry.

"My wife stopped eating, fed our daughters one egg between the two of them, one spoon of sour cabbage. I stopped eating. At night we listened to stomachs crying for food, couldn't tell whose. My wife put her hands on her ears. 'If I die first,' she whispered, 'feed me to the children.' I held her until she slept. 'No, no, we will be all right, you'll see.'

"In the dark, I sat by the open window, played the saxophone so she couldn't hear stomachs crying. The wind blew the hair and clothes of dead children curled on their sides in the field. I played for them. Played dumplings and torte and eggs with dark yolks. The wind made them dance in the moonlight, all those children. All night, dancing, hair fine like yours, dancing, until the sun came up.

"In the morning, no eggs, no cabbage, no torte, no wind. My wife poured water on our daughters' lips, red like yours, said, 'Go sit under the tree and watch the clouds.' In the big pot, she boiled water, stripped flowered paper off the wall, threw it in the pot. Our daughters opened their red lips, swallowed, stomachs stuck to backbone. My wife kissed them on their lips. In bed at night, she turned to me. 'I smell death on their breath, Stan. I must die first.' All night, I held her, her breath on my cheek. She died after, Allyn, after our daughters ate grass, swelled, curled up and died."

Stan Yurek walked ahead of her. The steam from his breath spread his words over the field, hung in the air for Allyn to catch up with.

"I never wanted to marry again, Allyn, never wanted to be around children. Until now."

IN THE NIGHT, Allyn Davis listened to thumping through the blanket, guttural sobs. She listened to the tenor sax on the wind.

When the shadow slipped through the wall cracks, bumped into the stove, table, galvanized tub, hung onto the hanging blanket, Allyn Davis pulled the sheet over her head. The sick smell of gunpowder and rotting meat filled the room, leaked through Allyn's sheet, mixed with the chalk smell coming from her own body, the new smell she could not name coming from her mother's bedroom.

Without her slate, Allyn Davis did not go to school. After Stan Yurek ate his porridge, drank his coffee in the dark, slipped out with his bucket into darkness, before her mother stretched and yawned and pushed through the hanging blanket, Allyn Davis went back to sleep. When grey light came in the window, Allyn dressed, ate the porridge Stan Yurek left her, drank a cup of coffee. She filled her trouser pockets with bread, cheese, Welsh cakes, slipped outside.

A pair of wool socks on her hands, Stan Yurek's blue muffler around her neck, Allyn Davis breathed grey light until she floated grey and light across the field for the dark ridge sleeping against the sky. Farther up, behind town, miners' lamps flickered higher and higher up the hill.

At the base of the ridge, Allyn slipped into cool pine. She climbed through the trees, straight up the ridge behind their shack. She could hardly see anything, including her own hands and feet. Behind her, grey light floated in the valley. Her hands shimmered in front of her eyes. If she had her slate, she would draw her sisters walking, Gwen across the prairies to Calgary, Meinir through the mountains to Vancouver. She would draw Wynford riding a snake through the mountains to the sea. She would draw Owen chasing a shadow.

She would draw Stan Yurek playing his saxophone.

Allyn Davis wiggled her toes, looked back over her shoulder at the flushed tip of Turtle Mountain. Steam rose from the cracks in her boots.

Along the rocky ridge, one cheek growing warm in the rising light, the other cool. Ahead, the ridge dipped, but she could not see over the rocks to what she knew lay below. She breathed in deeply.

At last. Allyn Davis stood on the edge of a rock. Below her a deep green meadow and budding poplar. And horses.

Horses.

Allyn's heart beat fast. She shifted her boot against the rock. Horses. Thick dark manes, and red and black and white, and the toss of their lifted heads, their nostrils flared.

Allyn placed one foot quietly in front of the other down the steep hill. Snorts and stamps, and their leg muscles twitching. If she could make no noise, no quick moves.

She stepped, let her foot down slowly. Slowly. She breathed in deeply through her nose. Grass and poplar and horses. Horses. She breathed slowly in and out, in and out. Hot and oaty, and her fingers tingled.

Manes hanging in their eyes, blowing in the wind, their ears pricked forward. Allyn stood still, hands at her sides. Horses. Manes and tails, fine lower legs and thick haunches twitching, bunching.

A hand.

Heavy.

On her shoulder.

Hot wetness down her spine.

"Shake like this, and they'll come." A tobacco tin, blue, in front of her face, rattling.

Allyn cupped both hands, numb around the tin, and shook.

Horses. Hooves, ears pricked forward, nostrils quivering, legs and shoulders and flared nostrils towering over her. Black and sorrel and white, and a whinny rising, shaking the air, the mountains, the bones in Allyn's chest.

"Put some on your palm."

Two hands reached over Allyn's shoulders, one took the tin of oats, the other cupped Allyn's hand palm up. The tin tipped, and oats tickled Allyn's numb skin.

"Watch your thumb."

The hand tucked Allyn's thumb into her pointer finger.

"Hold your hand up in front of you."

Allyn reached her hand forward, and a rangy black dropped its head. Allyn held her hand still as the black nuzzled her palm, its breath moist on her wrist.

"Your other hand."

Allyn raised her other hand, stared into their eyes, velvety brown shapes deep inside. The black turned its head. A milky white eye, black in the middle.

"Walleye. She can see you."

The hand tipped more oats onto Allyn's palms, lifted them up for the horses' lips, their face bones long and angular, and soft veins under tight skin. Their lips moved back and forth, moist and soft over her skin. She closed her eyes, her hands throbbed.

"Put your hand under her chin. Blow in her nostrils."

Spoken softly over her head. Could have been the horses breathing. Allyn opened her eyes, lifted her hands slowly, slowly slid her fingers along the horse's round hard cheek, down under her chin, pulled the horse's head, nostrils quivering, toward her, drank her hot breath, blew into her quivering nostrils.

Hands under her armpits, lifting her into the air, her legs sliding over the horse's black back, her pants bunching up, hair brushing her bare ankles. Soft hard warmth inside her thighs.

She looked into the long face of an old woman.

"The name's Henry, Henry Reed." The woman extended a hand.

Allyn shook the woman's hand, dry and warm, Allyn's other hand tracing on her thigh the woman's high cheekbones, wide-apart eyes. Allyn opened her mouth, wordless air over her lips. The woman nodded.

"It's okay. I know who you are."

Her fingers wrapped in coarse dark mane, Allyn Davis rode the black horse around and around the meadow behind Henry Reed taking long strides through grass. Footbeats and hoofbeats echoed among the rocky peaks. The horse's mane rose and fell. Henry's back, checked shirt crossed with twine suspenders, rose and fell. "Now they know you."

Henry's palm on Allyn's head. Allyn slid to the ground, her legs watery. She looked up into Henry's face, extended her hand.

"My name is Allyn Davis."

ALLYN CLIMBED the steep hill, legs shaking, the pressure of the mare's back still warm between her thighs. In the meadow behind her, Henry Reed and horses.

At the top of the Livingstone Ridge, Allyn turned and waved. Blowing grass and shivering poplar. But no Henry. No Horses.

She turned toward home. On the other side of the valley, shadows and light trembled across the face of Turtle Mountain. She wiped her eyes with the back of her hand.

"I spoke to a woman. I told her my name."

BESIDE THE WARM STOVE, Allyn Davis curled into her pillow. Horses flew through the dark. Muscled, tails and arched necks. Their hot skin. If she had a slate.

In her pajamas in the dark, Allyn Davis drew her chalk over the top of the stove. Nostrils, manes, hooves.

Allyn Davis knew someone came in the night, stood over the warm stove. She smelled icing sugar and almond and lemon that made her throat ache.

In the grey dawn, Allyn Davis ran her fingers over the cover of the sketch pad beside her bowl. Pebbly cardboard. She flipped it back. Ran her fingers over a sheet of unmarked paper, grey in the grey light. She picked up the stick of charcoal beside the pad, drew a square, a circle, a half-moon.

Allyn Davis took her pad to school. While the other kids drew A and B and C, Allyn Davis drew horses, little girls with spun sugar hair, a girl fishing in the Crowsnest River.

When the poplar buds burst green, Stan Yurek bought a '37 Packard, drove it across the field right to their door, two tracks of crushed grass.

Allyn Davis' mother stood in the doorway.

On her pad, Allyn Davis drew a square inside a rectangle.

"She's a nice car, eh, Mrs. Davis. Her name is Branwen. You can't refuse her now, can you. I took off one week. Maybe you and Allyn and me can make a trip to Calgary, visit Gwen."

Allyn Davis drew a mountain falling in the night.

"I borrowed a tent, Mrs. Davis. Thought your daughter wouldn't mind a tent in her yard."

Allyn drew a boulder falling on a miner's shack.

Allyn Davis' mother disappeared inside. "You're quite right, Mr. Yurek. A boarder should sleep in a tent."

Allyn Davis drew a pit pony with white eyes.

IN THE BACK SEAT, among quilts and baskets and rolled canvas, Allyn Davis turned and knelt, crossed her arms on the dusty cardboard panel below the window.

Across the valley, Turtle Mountain jounced up and down into clouds. Allyn Davis turned in her seat, lay her pad sideways across her bare knees. She lay the tip of her charcoal in the centre of the page, pressed lightly upward. The car bounced, her charcoal dipped, jumped. She guided her charcoal up the side of Turtle, kept it on the page as it fell and climbed. Across the top, over Turtle's humps, her charcoal falling and leaping. Down the other side, into the valley, her charcoal slashing, swooping up.

Turtle Mountain. Goat Mountain. Crowsnest Mountain. The Seven Sisters.

WRAPPED IN A QUILT by the side of the road, Allyn Davis watched orange and red and green leak out of the sky, watched black leak down on her and her mother and Stan Yurek.

In the black, Allyn Davis knew she heard the rustling of clothing on dry grass, knew she heard panting in the wind, smelled sage spiced with that smell she could not name.

She did not know what brushed her cheek in the night.

IN THE BACK SEAT, Allyn nibbled a Welsh cake. Crumbs fell onto her pad. Allyn pushed the crumbs around and around. Greasy translucent stars.

"Why don't you sing us a song, Mrs. Davis. I hear you sing when I play the saxophone. Such singing."

Allyn held the stars to her eyes.

"Go on, Mr. Yurek, with your flattery." Her mother lowered her voice. "That's no way to make a woman sing."

"All right then. Mrs. Davis, you have a voice like an old crow."

Her mother threw back her head, laughed deep in her throat. "You've heard right, then, Mr. Yurek, a crow I am."

Allyn Davis peered through the shiny swirls at her mother's hair, black, swept up off her neck.

Stan Yurek looked over his shoulder. Through the swirls, the hairs straying out of his nostrils jiggled.

"You know what a scholar is, Allyn?"

Allyn Davis shook her head.

"Well, time you knew, in case you want to become one. Don't you think she should know, Mrs. Davis?"

Allyn Davis' mother twisted in her seat. Allyn Davis dropped her charcoal between her knees, hugged her drawing pad to her chest.

"Mr. Yurek, as far as I know my daughter hasn't bothered to master the alphabet."

Stan Yurek nodded, his ear red.

"You see, Allyn, according to English, a scholar is a person learned in English. Makes sense, no? Doesn't that make sense to you, Mrs. Davis?"

"Mr. Yurek, she won't even print her name. All she does is draw pictures."

"So you see, Allyn, a person who speaks another language cannot be a scholar here."

Allyn Davis' mother pushed her shoulders into the seat. On her pad, Allyn drew a truck on the bottom of a lake.

"Mr. Yurek, she understands English, she will not write it. She does not write anything. She does not write to her bloody father overseas."

"Some day, Allyn, I'll teach you Polish. I'll teach you music. You teach me drawing."

Allyn Davis' mother smoothed the swoop of hair lying against her neck. "Mr. Yurek, some day this war will be over and boarders will leave."

ROLLED IN HER QUILT beside the road, Allyn Davis listened to the tenor sax ruffle the dry grass, dip into dark coulees, listened to her mother's wordless song chase the wind. Grass fine as hair tickled her cheek, and she smelled Henry Reed's horses.

The tenor sax sang her name over and over. Allyn, Allyn, Allyn. Through grass, down coulees, up hills, over rills.

Beside the road in her quilt, Allyn Davis did not know her da from a horse. Did not know her da from an old woman in a checked shirt crossed with binder twine.

Bent over five flat tires in two days, her mother's hum rolling over the prairie, Allyn did not know her da from a grey-haired man blowing a saxophone.

"I'LL SLEEP IN THE HOUSE with Allyn. Mr. Yurek will sleep out in the tent." Allyn Davis' mother pursed her red lips, lay her hand on Allyn's shoulder. "After all, he is our boarder." She squeezed hard.

Allyn Davis drew a crow on top of Crowsnest Mountain.

She lay on her back in the house surrounded by houses farther than she could see. Walls, walls the wind could not blow through, walls that shadows could not drift through.

Allyn closed her eyes. The walls whispered in her ear.

"But Daddy is still alive."

Daddy, daddy, daddy. In the dark, Allyn Davis smiled at the wall. Gwen was grown up, and she had a daddy.

"What business is it of yours if I take in a boarder?"

Here in the city, the wind moaned in the wires. Allyn listened for the tenor sax outside the closed window where Stan Yurek went out to the tent after cards and laughing and goodnight, sleep tight, but all she could hear was the wind moaning. Boarder, boarder, boarder. And Gwen's voice.

"What if the man's a resident alien?"

Her mother's voice low and sharp. "You keep your bloody mouth shut, or someone will go to your in-laws and tell them she happens to know what their name was before the first war."

"But all these men. You're confusing Allyn."

Allyn. The walls whispered her name around and around, flat, whispery, not open and clear and up and down like the tenor sax. Allyn Davis curled into the pillow, flipped open her drawing pad.

ALLYN DAVIS DOES NOT REMEMBER seeing her mother unbutton her blouse, step out of her skirt, pull her slip up over her head, slide her nightgown over her breasts beginning to droop. She remembers the smell of lilac, talc, cigarette smoke, whiskey and the dark scent of armpits, groins and hollows secret under cloth sliding under the covers beside her. She remembers her mother's sigh.

She does not remember her mother slipping out of bed, slipping through plastered walls. She does not remember the wind dying in the wires.

Allyn stood on her pillow, still warm, leaned her elbows on the window sill. She traced the hanging walls of the tent, lit from inside, onto the pane. She traced her mother's shadow and Stan Yurek's shadow inside the tent's lucent skin. She traced an immense arm reaching, hair flowing down the sides of the tent, arms twirling up, a breast a nipple, legs wrapping around legs around legs.

WHILE THE OTHER KIDS WROTE "Canada is a country, Ottawa is our capital city," Allyn Davis drew on any paper she could find. A saxophone blowing out of its brass bell the Crowsnest Mountain and Turtle Mountain, Crowsnest River cutting its way from green bottomless lakes through Coleman, Blairmore, Frank, Bellevue, Passburg, Burmis, Lundbreck, out into the prairie.

The other kids wrote "La Verendrye was an explorer," and traced his route on a map they traced from *Explorers of America*. Allyn Davis drew Stan Yurek blowing into his sax in the smoke-filled Bellevue Legion, dancers throwing money, socks, toques, scarves into the box for refugees, orphans, prisoners and striking miners. She drew her mother's red lips pursed around a cigarette, her face flushed with whiskey. She drew Stan Yurek's daughters twirling among all the sweating dancers, their hair flying.

The other kids wrote, "The First Great War started in 1914, ended in 1918. This Great War to End All Wars started in 1939 and will continue until peace is won." Allyn Davis drew two tiny skeletons curled on their sides in a field, horses' eyes from the side with women's breasts deep inside.

She never drew herself.

She never drew her da or Owen or Wynford or Gwen or Meinir.

At night, the smell of oranges, garlic, whiskey, talc, grass, sweat and that smell she could not name filled the shack. The shadow and the smells of gunpowder and rotting meat no longer slipped in through the cracks in the walls.

Sobbing and laughter swept through her blanket wall, and the wind howled in the trees. Allyn Davis rolled her face into her bed, wrapped her pillow over her head, pressed her groin into her mattress. All night, she felt the horse between her legs.

BRANWEN DAVIS DRAWS on her roll-your-own, paper so dry it clings to her lip. She flicks with her tongue, tobacco scratchy and dry. Jesus, nothing like a cigarette for a lover, inhale in in in, shrouds of blue smoke in the Legion air, she floats, smoke and whiskey held in her lungs, floats above the tables just below the ceiling, hot and dizzy, hold me, Jesus, floats above Mary McNab, stupid broad with a chair on her shoulder, playing the legs like a bagpipe, face redder than her hair. Keep me up here forever above pickled eggs, sausage rolls, all those feet don't know how to dance, lift one-two-three, one-two-three, around one-two-three, one-two-three, through air blue and smoky, here, here, here between heads and ceiling, keep me here, Stan Yurek, don't look up, your lips pursed softly blowing in your sax, blow softly, your lips blow music out its round brass bell, blows me softly, keep me up here blue smoke, someday the man, my husband, will come home, I had to get away from Wales, the valleys too narrow, his fingers rough between my thighs, I spread my legs, felt the sea lapping, lapping and wide open space, I, Saskatchewan, trapped by space, spread my legs, between my thighs blowing dust, keep me here in the whiskey warm space between heads and ceiling, Saskatchewan, my legs spread wide, prairie eating me inside out, mouths pulling my nipples, pulling, pulling, but the horses, I loved them, velvety muzzles, not once did I ride, his head between my thighs, skin over skull I could crack like an egg, watch his yolk run out, his children's skulls, membranes between my legs, I tore the sheet with my fingernails, I knew how to wring a chicken's neck, blow hot, blow blue, your music floats me here, up here above heads, he will come home, there were others before you, I paint my lips whore red, float on smoke, run your music down the fine hairs on my belly, yes, with you I'm happy, there were others before, there will be others after, there's a half-breed, red-brown eyes and mapped hands, rides into town on horseback, smells warm and oaty, someday him, too, yes, I love you like whiskey, like coal, like smoke, blue smoke, like love, the man, my husband, will march across the field to our shack, there will be no haze, no smoke between us, I will look and see his green uniform, his skin underneath white, waterlogged, and underneath his skin, bones

and sinews and pumping purple organs, there is nothing left in him I
do not see, in the horses' eyes brown velvet shapes like starfish
drowning on the prairie, a windmill spun on the horizon, but I did
not, could not, ride across space, in Drumheller, the coal man beat his
pony, a pit pony brought up shying at the light, my husband ran out
from sleep, his white skin glaring at the sun, hit that horse again and
I'll kill you, ran his fingers short and square up the pony's neck, the
pony snorting eyes wild, easy boy, easy boy, ran his fingers down the
pony's cheek, easy there, easy, under his chin, blew in his nostrils,
easy son, all day the pony followed him delivering coal, but my husband would not stay underground, he came up into the light, washed
darkness from around his eyes, when I looked into them I saw the
light side of the moon, the dark side gone, I could not stop my fist,
there was nothing between it and the smack when it hit his cheek, I
have smacked a raw breast of chicken, the skin bunches under knuckles, he looked confused when his fist rang against my ear, the men in
my family are boxers, you don't know about boxers with your sax
against your lips singing for you, ah blow hot, blow hard, sing me
your dead wife and daughters, all those notes playing my skin, music
wafting in blue smoke, my fists smashed his flesh over and over,
bones and cartilage underneath, that's all, bones and cartilage, he
looked surprised when his fist cracked my jaw, flesh and bones and
organs and cartilage that's all, I must turn my head to see you through
all this smoke, this music, your notes hum between my thighs, Gwen
ran for the policeman screaming, I could not stop my fist, my hands,
my hungry knuckles, blow smoke, blow whiskey, never let me see you
soaking in the light, your dead wife and daughters, aching sounds,
someday he will walk across the field into our shack, I'm home, I will
see the sinews along his neck, the insides of his calves, yes, I love you,
Stan Yurek, blow smoke, blow whiskey, blow music, blow death, blow
love, and if he lies rotting in some trench, I must never see you clearly, there will be others, I will wear a black satin dress, pull back my
black hair, paint my lips red, spread my legs dreaming of your notes
humming my thighs, your dead wife and children, ah, aching
sounds, I will laugh, I will cry, I will hum, I have seen his skin soaked

in the light, must never see you clearly, and if you come back I will take you down earth rent by giant ice claws, floating on smoke and whiskey we will dance the hoodoos orange, grey, black, all night your sax echoing among them, blow music through dinosaur bones, make the hoodoos sway like monks dancing, play my thighs, when the hoodoos flush pink you must go, must never see you clearly, you must never make me see, keep me blue, keep me smoke, keep me here, up here between skull and ceiling. Yes, I love you.

LYING ON HIS BACK in the tent, Stanislov Yurek felt Bran's hair flick the length of his body, his face, chest, stomach, penis, thighs, legs, feet. She nibbled his big toe.

"I must go in before they send the moral brigade." Her voice husky.

The flaps on the tent rustled, burst open onto a triangle of city lights, flapped shut. She was gone.

He breathed in lilac, talc and whiskey. His wife never drank, his skin raw and already aching for more. He concentrated on the wind moaning through the electrical wires. His fingertips felt for the cool brass of his saxophone, he pursed his lips without having to see, breathed out more natural than talking. Under his fingers, she moaned like the wind. Back in Bellevue, propped in the dark back room among musty wool blankets, sticky whiskey glasses, Turtle Mountain silhouetted in the window, cold air breathing through the walls, he would finger his sax and blow, and she would moan for Bran, and Bran would laugh and roll toward him her body under her nightgown dark and secret, and after, he would ache and ache and pray for his dead wife while Bran slept, her face turned away.

FOR BREAKFAST, Gwen served them cold cereal and cold milk left by a milkman in a cupboard by the back door. Stan watched Allyn spoon flakes into her mouth, her face narrow and delicate. Cold cereal for a growing child. If they'd had enough to eat, his daughters would be older than Gwen now, and Stan would be a grandfather. Cold cereal. He shook his head.

Allyn lifted her gaze from her bowl, looked directly at Stan. Her eyes green like grass growing out of her pupils, specks of brown, old eyes. His daughters' eyes were pale blue, and old. Stan reached out, smoothed a strand of hair over Allyn's forehead.

"You want to grow big and strong like a horse?"

Allyn nodded.

Stan met Bran's eyes, black and cold. Yet, where her hair had flicked, his skin ached for more.

"Then maybe your sister can give me an egg, no?"

Allyn held her spoon halfway to her mouth, stared at Stan, her hair so black, not like Stan's daughters' pale brown, but her eyes old like theirs.

"An egg?" At the counter, Gwen rubbed at their reflections in the toaster, he and Bran and Allyn around the table. Gwen rubbed and rubbed. "I don't see why not." She leaned into the ice-box, her hand on the handle polishing up and down. If his daughters were alive now, here, they would have an ice-box with a motor on top like this one, full of eggs, white and brown.

Gwen stood with the egg on her palm, her cloth poised above it, looked at her mother. "How do you want it cooked?"

"You'd best ask Mr. Yurek." Bran's lips hardly moved. She licked her finger, jabbed at crumbs on her plate, her eyes black and vacant. "He's the one keen on eggs." Her finger dabbed her tongue between her lips. In the morning, his wife was soft and warm. She died in the morning, looked out the window at the yellow sky, like lemon, Stanislov. But where Bran's tongue had tasted, his skin ached.

"No, raw. Allyn needs a raw egg, to make her strong and healthy." He balanced the egg on his palm, leaned toward Allyn, the egg reflected in Allyn's green eyes.

"Now, if you please, give me a pin. I will make Allyn a perfect raw egg."

Three sets of dark eyes on his hands. His daughters would turn his hands over, squeeze the pads, you have pillows on your fingers, Poppa. Stan Yurek jabbed the pin neatly into the pointed end, circled the pin to make the hole bigger, spun the egg around and jabbed into the round end.

"It's easy, Allyn. I hold the egg, you put your mouth over this end, see, then you suck hard as you can. The egg will slide right out this hole, not even break the yolk. When it slides into your mouth, you swallow it whole."

He held the egg up to Allyn's mouth. Allyn opened wide. He slid the egg between Allyn's lips, red like his daughters', a tiny crust of dry skin where the top lip dipped. He used to rub goose fat on their lips when they played in the wind. One egg a day and they would not have eaten grass, curled on their sides in the field around blown-up bellies. One egg. His wife watched them dry up and blow away. She would not have faded into a yellow sky. She would make cheese in a bag in the sun, boiled cabbage, torte. Allyn's lips tight around the egg, Stan pursed his own mouth. Back in Bellevue he would play a deep sliding melody on his saxophone.

He looked up at Bran across the table, her eyes like coal burning deep inside.

His skin ached, ached for more.

THEY STAYED WITH ME for a week, a week of my mother glaring at Stan Yurek during the day, sneaking out to his tent at night. They never blew the lamp out. Anyone could see what they were doing.

I covered all the upstairs furniture in clear plastic. The orange flowers on my couch gleamed in the sun. The glass bluebird on my coffee table fluttered in its plastic cage. Allyn skated over her face reflected in my hardwood floor, touched her cheek and nose warped in floor wax and plastic. But she never talked, never, not even when we were alone.

They sat in the kitchen at my white arborite table or in the basement on a wooden bench, Mom and Stan and Allyn, while I cleaned and cleaned for my mother, who could care less.

We couldn't get many eggs in the war, but I got half a dozen the week before Mom came, carried them up the hill in the crook of my arm.

I cracked an egg into a bowl. "Mom, I want to make you a cake."

My mother drew on her roll-your-own, blew blue smoke at my white ceiling. "Are you sure?"

I nodded, leaned over the bowl. My hands turned cold. "The yolk's green, it's the only egg left." My hand shook as I tipped the bowl over the sink.

The whole week, Stan Yurek took Mom's dirty looks and sharp words. He'd look out the window or ask Allyn if she needed more milk. He was always asking Allyn if she was hungry, always offering her food from his plate.

He leapt over Allyn in her chair, roared. The veins in his neck stood out purple. One step and he was at the sink, scooping the egg out of the drain, the white hanging down through his fingers. He grabbed the bowl out of my hand, slid the egg gently inside. "Never," he shouted at me, his face pulsing red, "never, never throw away an egg. Never."

He looked at Allyn, his eyes wild, back at the green egg, tipped the bowl over his face and swallowed the egg whole. My mother sat there and smoked her cigarette, a light deep behind her black eyes. Later his lips swelled dark blue. He spent the evening in the bathroom vomiting.

My mother spent the whole night out in the tent with him.

MONDAY MORNING Stan Yurek got up before the sun, tied back the tent flaps, sat cross-legged on his wool blankets, his sax cool between his lips, brass under his fingertips, played the sky yellow. His notes rose in flats up the electrical wires stretched across the sky like music bars, hovered above the top line until the sky was completely lemon.

He tucked the sax into his blanket, tied the tent flaps shut. Inside Gwen's house, he filled a pot with water, put it on the stove to boil. Moving on the balls of his feet, he found the cold cereal in a middle cupboard, shoved the cereal box as far back into a high cupboard as he could reach. He bent over the cupboard beside the sink, lazy Susan, Gwen called it, pulled the folded door straight out, spun the wooden shelf through his thumb and finger. Quaker Oats *rapidement*, the Quaker stared at him from under a black hat. "Don't stare, it's a sign of aggression." He poured enough oats for four into the boiling water. While the porridge bubbled, like gas and water in the mine, Stan Yurek ran a trickle of water into the kitchen sink, shaved in the cool yellow light.

He ate facing the dark hallway, the room where Bran and Allyn slept at the end, Bran's dark moist smells seeping under the door, down the hallway, into the kitchen. Careful not to clink his spoon against his bowl, Stan swallowed big mouthfuls, rinsed his mouth at the sink.

Under the balls of his feet, the floor groaned. He stocking footed for the back door, hoping Bran would appear hot and musty in her flannel gown—where the hell are you off to so early, Mr. Yurek, her voice sleepy. He would play it back to her in Bellevue. She would laugh up onto her toes, close her eyes.

He stepped out into cool morning, closed the door gently behind him. Thank God she slept in her own darkness.

He walked slowly past the sleeping houses, rolled his feet from heel to toe, as if he could not wake them asleep in their yards. Yard, what is a yard, such a small piece of land. What kind of garden can you grow in a yard? He shook his head.

Past house after house after house, the sun beginning to glint in windows. He fingered the letter in his pocket.

> *Canadian War Office*
> *Calgary Branch*
> *421 8 Ave. S.W.*
> *Calgary, Alberta*
>
> *May 10, Year of Our Lord, 1940*
>
> *Mr. Stanislov Yurek,*
>
> *It has come to our attention—*

No, on the streetcar he would read it again. He ran his fingers over the folds furred already with reading, made his hands swing at his sides the way they swing through dawn or dusk in Bellevue down the hill to the mine or uptown to the Legion.

Past house after house, streets and avenues crisscrossed in straight lines. Numbers for names, imagine having a number for a name. 25th Street, 37th Avenue. 23rd Street, 34th Avenue. Gwen says the streetcar goes down 14th Street, turns on 8th Ave.

Past a school yard, a church, more houses. Around a corner, 18th Street, 33rd Avenue. He looked down a long straight hill. Shops, parked cars on both sides, sunlight gilded onto rounded fenders, at the bottom a right-angled street. Already cars were moving. The wire arms of a trolley reaching straight up as it buzzed and sparked through the intersection. Too far, but he heard it. Sometimes lightning electrified the rails in the mine, surged over the hairs on their bodies. They hugged the cracked wooden handles of picks and shovels, swung them into the dark. In Bellevue, he would make his sax vibrate between his lips, under his fingers, blue sparks charging the black hair down Bran's belly.

Past a bakery. Maybe later he would buy a plum torte for Allyn, fork the plums for her, plump and purple.

He stepped into sunlight. On the corner, a vacant lot with a long white tank abandoned on its side. Stan Yurek strode for the corner, spun at the last moment, one foot off the curb. He circled the tank, placed his hand on its belly. Cool. He sniffed. Gas. He banged the tank with his fist. Hollow. Didn't they know fumes were enough? Underground miners lined their rooms with brattice cloth, gas seeped cool along it away from their lights, and here they put a gas tank in full view, close to a school.

Stan stood on the top rung of the ladder welded to the tank, peered into the open chimney on top, round as his head. Black. Stench of gas. He banged. "Sonofabitch. Stupid." Inside the tank, his words rumbled. "Stupid, stupid."

At the end of the street, trolley cars buzzed downtown, the sun climbed above the Bow River. Stan Yurek clanged down the ladder muttering, hunted among broken glass, gravel. Kicked through long grass.

Tin, red and orange. Stan tapped it with his toe. It spun, clanked to the gravel—*Queen Anne Shortbread, Finest from Scotland, Only the Freshest Highland Butter.*

Fingers familiar with metal underground, Stan smoothed the orange and red Tartan lid over the hole, crimped it around the chimney. Thank you Queen Anne.

Down the hill he ran for the trolley.

Mr. Stanislov Yurek,

> It has come to our attention that while you speak the Polish language, you are in fact a citizen of Austria. It is urgent that you report to our office immediately. If you do not report by the end of June, you may face orders of deportation. You are responsible for arranging your own interpreter, should you need one.

Sincerely,

Harold Chalmers

STAN YUREK CLIMBS stairs that creak and groan like the mine. In the mine, he cannot see, merges willingly with her moist blackness. Here, the stairs have sharp clear edges. The smell of burnt dust on radiators makes his eyes water. He hunches his shoulders down a narrow corridor, flinches past wavery glass in office doors. In the mine, darkness drips on your shoulders, soaks your stiff woolen clothes. When you enter her black mouth, you sit or lean while your eyes adjust.

Stan Yurek checks the room number on his envelope. In the mine, rooms have darkness for doors, every room has a number, but you know in your head, no need to write what you can't see. At the end of the hall, his footsteps creaking hardwood behind him, Stan ducks into room 214.

Into a narrow waiting room, metal chairs along both walls so that no matter where they sit, people waiting cannot help but look into each others' eyes.

Stan sits, the metal chair icy through his trousers. On the wall opposite, a faded reproduction of Van Gogh's *Potato Eaters*, a paint-by-number of a cowboy on a bronc throwing its genitals to the sun and

a ration coupon taped above a sign: NO MATTER WHAT LANGUAGE
YOU SPEAK, STEALING A RATION COUPON IS TAKING FOOD FROM
THE MOUTHS OF CHILDREN.

Stan Yurek cranes his neck, cannot see what hangs on the wall over
his head.

Across from him, an old woman, head wrapped in a black babush-
ka, stares over his left shoulder. He cannot see her eyes, only sockets.
Three chairs to her right, a young woman in a faded flowered dress
chews on the ends of her hair. Her skin the colour of boiled potato.
To his right, a man with flat Slavic cheekbones leans his elbows on
his knees, drags on a cigarette, holds the smoke for what seems forever, the whites of his eyes nicotined.

On his thighs, Stan plays quarter notes, eighths, sixteenths, taps his
foot. Smoke jets out of the man's nostrils. The backs of Stan's legs, his
bum, burn against cold metal. He shifts. In the mine, men together in
shafts of weak light sift through darkness to the surface, sift blackness
to their rooms between pillars.

Above the door at the end of the room, a clock. 8:30. A crack
under the door at the end of the room leaks light into Stan's waiting.
Motes of dust spiral, flicker. On the other side of the door, a man
coughs. Not one of them in the waiting room moves, except their
eyes. The young woman's potato eyes follow the clock's second hand
around and around. The man's nicotined eyes count the yellow
moons of his fingernails. Darkness in the old woman's sockets.

Stan Yurek clears his throat, phlegms language into a ball. Holds it
on his tongue. In the mine, he is a champion spitter. Works haulage in
the main entry, a boy's job, but his body has learned the invisible
dance of whipped cables, maverick cars as he hooks and unhooks
them in the moving dark, each vertebra, each nerve alert.

Stan looks at the old woman in black, the young woman gnawing
the ends of her hair. Women in a war office. He has loved two
women, one in this morning's moaning dusk, but here in the light in
this office, he has lost time. This morning, that morning, the other
morning—he has lost the language of time. Their names sit on the
end of his tongue, roll with the phlegm in his mouth. He is a cham-

pion spitter underground, can hork twenty feet sitting down, easy to measure on coal. Every day he cleans spit out of his sax.

He looks sideways at the young man. They must be with him. He must be with them.

Click.

The door swings open.

The old woman holds her eyeless gaze over Stan's left shoulder, the young woman gnaws her hair, the young man snorts. A stream of smoke curls around his cupped fingers.

Squeak of leather. Stan Yurek grips the metal chair. Here in the Canadian War Office, he has lost time. Hears German boots marching across his burned field, frozen under a dusting of snow, probing with shiny toes his daughters curled on their sides. Canadian boots marching in the dark damp to the drip, drip, drip of water on coal. His daughters' boots when they learned to walk across the wooden floor, a sausage in each fist making them believe they could not fall.

He has lost time.

The ball of phlegm in his mouth melts, flows over his tongue. If he were underground, he would spit, his spittle arcing through beams from head lamps like a falling star. He would aim his single eye of light, find his spit foaming on coal, measure distance stepping three feet to the step, exactly.

"Mr. Yurek."

Stan rises, takes three steps, looking neither left nor right. His boots squeak on tile. The muscles in his throat refuse to swallow.

"Please be seated, Mr. Yurek. I assume since you did not bring an interpreter that you have some grasp of the English language. Am I correct in my assumption, Mr. Yurek?"

Stan Yurek stares into the clear blue eyes of a boy in uniform. Phlegm blocks his throat, he cannot swallow. He nods.

"Good. Then we can proceed. Please, Mr. Yurek, take a seat."

The boy in uniform moves behind a desk, sits erect in a large wooden chair. Stan lowers himself into a chair in front of the desk. As if Stan has disappeared, the young man studies an open file. Looks up suddenly, aims his blue eyes directly at him.

"We have cause to believe you are an enemy alien, Mr. Yurek."

A laugh foams in Stan's throat. German, Polish, British, Russian, Canadian, Czech. He cannot find the language of answers. He tenses the muscles in his throat, says nothing.

"Mr. Yurek, there is no point pretending you do not speak the English language. We are well aware that you do. Furthermore, it has come to our attention that you also speak German. Is that correct?"

Stan balances the ball of language on the tip of his tongue, nods.

"Our sources tell us, Mr. Yurek, that you do indeed speak Polish, as you yourself claim on your entry card, yet you have entered our country on an Austrian visa. How do you account for this discrepancy, Mr. Yurek, or should I call you Herr Yurek?"

Stan searches the boy's blue eyes for the joke. Laughter flattens in his throat. He swallows.

"My mother spoke Polish, my father spoke Polish, my grandparents spoke Polish, their grandparents spoke Polish. I am Polish."

Eyes so young, so blue. The young man smiles. A frown creases his forehead. Stan searches the eyes of a boy in uniform, cannot find time. His daughters' arms jerked under the soldier's probing toes, jerked and jerked, and Stan covered his mouth with his hand before the sound like a laugh burst from his lips. How could they dance so crazy, his daughters? When the soldier turned to smile at him, the fine hair on the soldier's upper lip lifted in the breeze. "*Tot,*" he said, "*ja, sie sind tot,*" his mouth stretched in a smile. Stan licks his lips.

"Mr. Yurek, you are obliged to answer my question. My question was not what language your parents spoke, but how do you account for the fact that you claim to be a Pole, yet you are here on an Austrian visa and you speak German?"

Stan Yurek leans forward in his chair.

"Mr. Whatever-your-name-is, if this is a question of language, I also speak Russian, Czech, Latin, Canadian English, British English, and I read music."

"Mr. Yurek, this is not simply a question of language but a question of security and truth. You are not helping your case any by refusing to answer my question directly. We have had no choice, Mr Yurek, but to intern cases like yours until this war is over. Now, Mr. Yurek, yes or no. You arrived in Canada on September 22, 1921?"

"Yes."

"You arrived in Montreal alone?"

"Yes."

"You rode the Harvesters' Excursion to Saskatchewan where you took work with a farmer of German extraction?"

"Yes."

"Did you say yes, Mr. Yurek?"

"Yes."

"You left his employ in the spring, hopped a boxcar to Alex, Alberta, where you took work with another German farmer?"

"Yes."

"You discovered shortly after your arrival that he was bootlegging, yet you stayed on with his family."

"Yes."

"You felt a certain loyalty, Mr. Yurek?"

"He took me in as a worker."

"Perhaps the loyalty of a man for his countryman?"

"He asked me to help him with the harvest. Not once did he ask me to bootleg."

"Yes or no, Mr. Yurek. You felt a certain loyalty for this farmer, this Herr Braun?"

———

"Mr. Yurek, you realize your silence only further implicates you. Yes or no—you felt a certain loyalty to Herr Braun, a loyalty that kept you on his farm even though you knew he was bootlegging, knew he was using his foreign language to help him break the laws of this land? Perhaps you spoke this language with him in his home, occasionally on the street in town?"

"Not once did he ask me to help him bootleg."

"Yes or no, Mr. Yurek."

"His family came from Russia by the Volga River. Before that, they were starving in Germany. 'Come to Russia,' the government said to his grandparents, 'we have lots of land.' In Russia, his mother and father and sisters and brothers and aunts and uncles and cousins worked all the time but never had enough food. On the side they sold extra wheat instead of making bread for themselves. They sent him to Canada. Every one of them born in Russia. Not one of them speaks, reads, writes Russian."

"Yes or no, Mr. Yurek."

Stan Yurek looks into his boy face, not one wrinkle, the skin over his temple smooth. He looks at the stone paperweight on the desk, the cool blade of a letter opener, his own thick hands. On the other side of the door, he hears silence. Waiting.

"Yes."

STAN YUREK HANDS his coupon to the driver, walks to the back of the trolley. The car jerks, clacks, edges onto 14th Street. Through intersections, picks up speed. 12th Avenue, 13th, 14th. Bars of sunlight and shadow play across Stan's hands, folded between his knees. At home in Bellevue he will blow this city foreignness hot and cold down Bran's spine.

Bellevue.

Home.

His fingers ache.

Ahead, the 14th Street hill, vertical from this perspective at the back end. The trolley noses up, its wired arms straight out front, metal rolling metal, labouring gravity.

Stan Yurek fingers the new letter in his pocket. Working haulage, you know the danger in jumping track, crushed between cars or underneath, bones ground into coal. He shakes his head, laughs out loud. Polish, German, English, Russian, he doesn't care what language.

War Office
Calgary Branch
421 8 Ave. S.W.
Calgary, Alberta, Canada

The 20th of June, Year of Our Lord, 1940

To Whom it May Concern,

> Be it known that Mr. Stanley Yurek has been thoroughly inves-
> tigated by the War Office, and it is felt that despite the suspicious
> circumstances surrounding his arrival in Canada and his suspi-
> cious actions prior to his arrival in the Crowsnest Pass, Alberta, his
> occupation as coal miner in said area is deemed to be of aid in the
> Canadian war effort. As long as Mr. Yurek remains underground,
> his status remains that of Displaced Person, until such time as
> further investigation is warranted.

Sincerely,

Mr. Reginald Attwater
for Mr. Harold Chalmers

STAN YUREK LAUGHS deep inside, sprays his hands with fine spittle. Stanley. Stanley Yurek. D.P. Saved by coal. His laughter climbs the
aisle, shakes the shoulders of the woman in front of him, jiggles the
hat of the man next to her. Laughter booms from his lips. They turn
in their seats. He shrugs, rocks himself back and forth. The Canadian
Underground. Stan Yurek laughs himself silent, his throat emptying
itself. The woman covers her mouth, the man chuckles, Stan's throat
empties itself—*Tot, sie sind tot, ja,* if I die first you must eat me, not a
matter of language, Mr. Yurek. Yes or no.

Tears stream down his cheeks.

At the bakery he uses the rest of his coupons, points to a plum
torte, a lemon pound cake, a poppy seed roll. The girl points also.
"Ja," he says, "ja, ja."

He carries them in boxes against his chest. Ducks past the empty
lot, runs through the maze of city streets, runs for Allyn's red lips
flecked with sugar.

No one should stop eating, ever.

AT THE END OF THE STREET, trolley cars buzz past. Up and down the steep hill. The sun climbs over the trees, glints in the pieces of broken glass that Allyn crunches under her feet. She shades her eyes at the white tank in the middle of the lot.

Allyn Davis climbs the white ladder, straddles the tank fatter than Henry Reed's horse. Metal sucks heat from her bare legs. She squeezes her knees, clicks her throat, rocks forward inch by inch. The skin inside her thighs sticks, squeaks.

She closes her eyes. Easy up there, easy up. Her legs burn. Hyah. Her horse muscles forward. Allyn leans over her neck, drinks Crowsnest wind. They gallop over the ridge, down the mine road, her horse's hooves drumming to the miners underground who stop digging, aim their lamps at the coal ceiling. Must be Allyn Davis. She's tall on that horse, awfully tall. Past the graveyard, angels and sleeping lambs and faded photos swivelling their heads. That Allyn Davis flies on her horse, positively flies. Crashes through the bushes into town, along Main Street. Dairy, bakery, Green's Garage, Joe the Chinaman's. Streaking colour on both sides of the street. Allyn Davis on a horse. On her left just ahead, the Legion, grey and dozing in the sun. People flood out. She looks for her mother's black hair. Her heart drums.

She heels the hollow tank. Cold pressure between her legs, up her belly. She opens her eyes, sees the red and orange cookie tin overtop of the chimney between her thighs. *Queen Anne Shortbread, Finest from Scotland, Only the Freshest Highland Butter.* She traces the Tartan pattern bright in the sun, wraps her hands around the cool white chimney. She looks at her legs straddling the tank, her feet almost straight out to the sides.

Sun hot on her head, Allyn wedges her fingers between the crimped edges of the lid and the white chimney. The red and orange lid spins through the air, clatters to the ground. Allyn leans over the chimney, peers into a black hole. Like the mouth of Bellevue mine yawning black, men disappearing, their lights growing smaller and smaller, then, poof, gone. Not once would they let her inside to see where they went.

She leans her face into the hole, hears breathing inside. Except for her hair waving in the wind, Allyn Davis sits absolutely still. As if in slow motion, she lowers her face until blackness circles her sight. In one flowing motion, she reaches in her back pocket, runs a wooden match along the tank behind her, draws the hissing flame past her ear.

ALLYN DAVIS DOES NOT REMEMBER whether light shattered darkness or darkness exploded light.

Allyn Davis does not know how long she lay on her back in hospital, light and dark kaleidoscoping her bandaged sleep.

Does not remember twirling through space inside her new infinity, while nurses needled her arms and doctors tubed her throat.

They spin her from her kaleidoscope into a foggy room, baskets of yellowy brown fruit, nuts, cakes heaped around her bed, a woman in a yellowy brown coat seated by the door.

The woman stands, tips toward Allyn, arms out. "What colour is my coat?"

Allyn Davis blinks. "Yellow."

Midstride, the woman wheels away from Allyn, flaps into the dense fog. "She's blind. My sister's blind. Black, my coat's black."

Gwen's voice pulses through Allyn's fog, each word arcing colourless light onto the backs of her eyes.

WHEN LEAVES TURNED bright yellow and other children tramped to the schoolhouse on Bellevue's main street, bright red and purple and orange lunch buckets under their arms, Allyn Davis sat propped on her pillow, drew the explosion she couldn't remember in the only colour she could see. Yellow-brown.

When the other children snapped hands in the air, "Ask me, Miss, ask me," Allyn Davis scratched the puckering scab under her chin. Her mother smoked at the table, her smoke mingling with Allyn's fog. "Don't pick, you'll get infected."

Crisp and sweet, the leaves fell, crackled under other children's feet. Yellow-brown snow drifted from the west, blanketed the leaves, drove past the window above Allyn Davis' bed.

Allyn Davis lay on her back beside the coal stove. Eyes open or closed, brown swirls licked chimney, washtub, icebox, Stan's trousers and shirts and long johns hanging upside down around the room.

From their bedroom, wild music flicked the hanging blanket, flicked the brown swirls. Allyn Davis half-closed her eyes so she could see inside and out. Horses' heads curled out of the fog, arched necks, shoulders, chests, haunches, legs. They trotted in time to the music, lifted their hooves high, their manes rising and falling with Allyn's breath rising and falling.

The music climbed higher and higher and higher.

Allyn Davis sat straight up in her bed, watched silence, yellow-brown spaces around the stove, inside the tub. But she had heard blue, blue sky over horses' heads. She strained forward, listened to the yellow fog, the backs of her eyes aching.

Voices, low and wavery. People or horses, she couldn't tell. Laughter or neighing. Feet or hooves. Drumming closer and closer. Allyn strained to the edge of her yellow-brown fog. Blue, what would blue sound like outside her head? Her blanket curtain twitched. She strained her ears, her eyes. What shape would blue sound outside her head? The backs of her eyes ached.

Her hanging blanket shuddered, whipped the air. Stan Yurek burst into the kitchen.

"Did you see him, Allyn, a mouse as big as a mountain lion? He was drinking from your mother's glass, I saw him. A big bugger of a mouse taking food. Here, you help."

Stan Yurek stark naked except for rubber boots flopping his calves. Stan Yurek hopping around the galvanized tub, his prick dancing. Stan Yurek raising a broom over his head.

"Come out, you coward mouse, come out and fight."

Stan Yurek's lips blue, the first colour in Allyn's yellow-brown fog.

"Look out you mouse, stealing food. Here Allyn, you help, take your pillow and chase that way, see. We'll get you mouse."

Allyn Davis swung her pillow over her head, swathed the thick fog. But she had seen blue, blue around Stan's lips. She laughed until tears muddied her vision. Tomorrow she would draw Stan Yurek starkers, broom aimed at a giant mouse. Under Stan's skin, all over his body, under his temples, down the insides of his arms, around his belly button, along his dancing penis, Allyn will draw blue veins.

BRAN DAVIS PICKED the letter up at the post office in town, a thin blue envelope, thin blue writing. She said thank you to the postmaster, gave him a curt nod, the corners of her red mouth pulled down. She stuffed the envelope into her handbag and fought the wind whistling down Main Street to the Bellevue Legion.

She pushed, the door flew in, wind funneled ahead of her, blew the women's skirts against their shins, ruffled the men's hair, twisted and twirled blue smoke.

At home Allyn sat on her cot, tried to draw on her sketch pad, light and dark exploding. Her eyes made out lines and shapes, could not make out violet, red, blue, green, indigo in the light, in the dark. Yellow-brown. Her only colour. She rubbed her eyes with her knuckles.

Bran ordered whiskey. "Neat," she said. "I like my whiskey straight up. I like my whiskey warm."

She tipped her glass back slowly, her little finger in the air. Over against the wall, a table of men hunched inside their wool jackets, hunched inside the black frames of their eyes, watched the whiskey roll down the side of her glass into her red lips, watched her full white throat swallow, watched her tongue slide over her bottom lip. She did not look at them, not once.

She stared somewhere over the stage, over the piano and drums. They saw her black hair and eyes floating in blue smoke, framed in black, black as the coal they chiselled and blasted every day.

"Have you heard from the old man or the boy yet?" They knew they could not trust their hands, trust their groins. Not one of them could play music.

She tipped her glass back, let the whiskey roll warm and amber into her mouth, licked her lip, set her glass slowly on the table. "Haven't heard a word, thank God." She did not turn her head to look at them. She drained her glass, reached into her bag for a bill, her fingers brushing aside the letter. "Here, buy yourselves a drink." She tossed the bill onto their table, turned and floated through blue smoke.

She floated into their shack in yellow-brown light. Before she took off her coat, she shook tea leaves into the tea pot, poured boiling water from the kettle on the stove. "Keep your eyes in your head," she said to Allyn, "they're beginning to water. I can see from here."

Then she took her coat into her bedroom where Stan slept before night shift, came back with the letter, placed it on the table among the cups and plates.

"It's blue," she said, "blue paper."

She poured hot water into a basin, washed two cups and plates, poured dark brown tea into the cups, cut yellow cake onto the plates. She put Allyn's cup and plate on the stump of wood Stan Yurek had placed beside Allyn's bed when they got back from Calgary.

"Don't be dropping crumbs now, or we'll get bed bugs."

Bran sat with her back to the window, ripped open the letter with a knife, held it at arm's length, her face in shadow.

Allyn watched her mother's cup float through the yellow fog, disappear into darkness, heard her swallow.

Bran folded the letter over and over into a small square. Allyn drew her, a yellow-brown woman looking out of an old photo, sepia eyes with lights inside.

Without a word, Bran poured water into a pot, gently lowered two eggs into the water, put the pot on the back of the stove. She disappeared into her room. Through the brown curtain, Allyn heard her rummage.

"White." Bran waved a piece of paper as she floated back through the hanging blanket.

"So's this." She flicked an envelope back and forth.

While brown steam curled out of the pot, she sat at the table and wrote on the paper Allyn saw as yellow. Then she lifted a lid off the stove, dropped into the hole the folded letter Allyn saw as brown.

Bran floated among the shadows for the icebox, drifted past the window with a chunk of amber ice in her hands, cracked it over the sink. Slivers of ice she put in a bowl of water, then scooped the eggs into the bowl. "They need eggs at the front. The land is as scorched as your eyes."

She dried the cool eggs on her skirt, lay them in the envelope. "I'm going uptown, to the post office." She drifted away through the yellow-brown fog.

SCORCHED
EARTH

RHYS DAVIS LAY on his back in a bunk hardly wide enough to hold him. He squeezed his elbows into his sides, crossed his hands over his chest.

Blackness heavy on his eyeballs. Blackness creaked and groaned, rocked him side to side. He could be back in Bellevue, coal solid under his back, solid above his head. Until she shifted.

He could be back in Bellevue. "Miners don't have to go. Look, take it easy, Rhys, you're forty years old, for Christ sake. The rest of us want to go, too, but hell, this war is making us money. I'd go, too, if I didn't have this damn silver plate in my skull."

The Hilary creaked and groaned. Her belly sliced the North Atlantic. Belly in the sea, darkness in her belly, boys bunked in darkness.

That was it. There was always that layer around the one you could see. There was always something else out there.

Four years in England. To sea at last.

Where?

Hell if I know, but God I can't wait.

And now, men, a special message from General McNaughton.

By now you are heading for Sicily, the Mediterranean Theatre of

> *War. This is a most significant stage in our fight for democracy.*
> *Secrecy has been our most effective weapon. Each one of you has*
> *trained hard and trained well, and now you all have the opportuni-*
> *ty to use that training to stand you in good stead. Good luck and*
> *God bless.*

Sicily. We're going to Sicily.

Who would've thought Sicily?

At last, we're gonna meet the enemy face to face.

I can taste it already.

A special message from General Montgomery.

> *I would like to take this opportunity to use the authority vested in*
> *me to welcome the Canadian Division and Tank Brigade to the*
> *Eighth Army. We, Gentlemen, are a force to reckon with, as our*
> *enemy shall shortly discover when he faces us in Sicily. Best of*
> *luck, and again, welcome.*

Eighth. Christ, that's the cream of the crop.

Almost makes waiting four years worth it.

Best kept secret of the century.

> *ATTENTION: Do not, I repeat, do not unseal the bag we are about*
> *to give you until told to do so by your commanding officer.*
>
> *We land on the west side of Pachino Peninsula on the night of*
> *9–10 July. Our landing operations must take place in the dark.*
> *The arrows on your maps indicate our route. Maucini to Pachino*
> *to Giarratana to Vizzini to Grammichele, where we reconnoitre*
> *with the 2nd Brigade. We launch assaults during the day, but*
> *much of our movement will take place at night.*
>
> *Notice the air photo. This is mountainous terrain, men, tough,*
> *mountainous terrain. I want you to memorize every gully, every*
> *valley, every outcrop. We'll be taking much of it in pitch black.*

Somewhere in the dark, the Hilary's engines throbbed. He could
be back in Bellevue, inside the mine. Inside Bran's dark hatred. He
could not thrust deep enough.

Forty years old. He could be back in Bellevue, picking, blasting,
shovelling, loading, mining darkness. He could be moored in sweat,
horse shit, oats, ammonia, wet wool, leather, jam, black powder.

But here, there was another layer. There was connective tissue, stinking feet, meat breath, boot-black, bilge fumes, rope, salt.

There was the enemy. Forty years he'd waited to see him face to face.

RHYS DAVIS PLANTS one heavy boot in front of the other in a long line of men planting one heavy boot in front of the other. They march in time, left right, left right, let's fight, let's fight.

White dust mixes with the sweat under their arms, drips down their chests, backs, behind their knees, into their boots. Dust coats their necks, faces, limes their hair white and fierce in the midday sun.

Rhys Davis looks ahead up the endless line of marching warriors, over his shoulder down the endless line marching back to the second century, which he cannot see trapped here on this road in Sicily, 1200 hours, 11 July, 1943.

Past lemons and oranges hanging obscene after four years in England, look at those oranges, can't wait to sink in my teeth, they march into battles that don't exist, won't exist until after they are fought, until someone points to a spot on a map and says, "That was the Battle of Ortona, see," and Rhys Davis who was there will not see anything except rubble crashing around him, dust, his coated hand heaving what looks like a metal lemon.

Rhys Davis breathes through his nose. Somewhere out there, the enemy watches.

Somewhere up there, General Montgomery will click his heels, salute—"Men, I have perfect confidence."

Somewhere across the hills to their left, his son Owen spits on his boot, rubs a shine into its toe. Rhys Davis does not know Owen is here in Sicily.

Somewhere in the Crowsnest Pass, Italian families kneel around the wireless waiting for news of their other soil. "The Allies struck a remarkable victory this morning," a fast English voice tells them. "In the early hours of dawn, Allied infantry completely demolished the village of ——, after which Italian soldiers cheerfully surrendered."

In Bellevue, the Polish pilots kiss Bran's hand, hug Stan Yurek, reel out the door of the shack in Bogusch's field, point themselves east by the North Star, head on foot for Fort Macleod, thirty miles away, where they are stationed. Bran lifts her glass to Stan Yurek. *Sto lat.*

Rhys could be in Bellevue, blacker than black, negative to this stark positive marching in the naked hills of Sicily.

He could be in Drumheller before that, blasting and burrowing into badlands, while overhead wind and sun sculpt clay ripped out of prairie by a glacier that retreated centuries ago.

But Rhys is here, marching, left right, left right, let's fight, let's fight, 1200 hours, 11 July, 1943.

His feet ache.

ALLYN DAVIS SITS on her cot while the Polish pilots throw back Stan's whiskey. *Prosit.* Yellow-brown, their eyes are yellow-brown.

Allyn draws eyes without lashes flying through fog.

The Polish pilots watch her mother drift about the room, piling cabbage rolls on plates, cutting cake. They slowly chew each mouthful, swallow, sigh. "*Sto lat,*" they say, "*sto lat,*" and raise their glasses and jam jars and tea cups of whiskey to Allyn's mother.

Allyn draws hands with featherless wings, textured like plucked chicken.

Stan Yurek wipes the mouthpiece of his sax, closes his eyes, croons in a language bluer than Allyn has ever heard him play. The Polish pilots close their eyes, lean back in their chairs and on the overturned tub. Tears roll out of their lashes, flow openly around their noses and mouths.

Allyn Davis holds her charcoal on her cupped palm. She closes her eyes, slides into Stan's music. Blue and yellow and fine hair and plums and a thin, thin hand and sausage and bellies caved in and fat baby legs and couples holding each other, swaying, and the stench of scorched earth.

She keeps her eyes closed after the music stops. For a moment, silence, then a flow of words she cannot understand, laughter. She squeezes her eyes, afraid to open them, afraid what she has seen will fly out before she is ready, afraid of colours she will not see.

"WAIT. WE NEED CANDLES. There's too much light from these electric bulbs."

The blanket drops behind her, blows cool darkness on the back of her neck. Turtle Mountain hulked in the window, Bran swishes the dark for her bed, her shins goosebumping. She kneels. Cold draft up her dress. Her fingers fumble paper, cloth, glass in the box under the bed, grope for wax. Hard and soft. Her nails sink into it.

"You must each hold a candle so you have the right light." She hands candles—Christmas, birthday—to each man.

"You need the right light to fly by." Bran hands each of the Polish pilots a stick of smoldering kindling, turns off the white light.

Red stars. In the dark. Swoop. Circle. Fumes of melting wax flow through blackness. Bran leans her hand on rough wallboard, ice frozen into slivers. Poof—nine candles burst into flame. In folded shadow, Stan Yurek cleans his mouthpiece, cleans his mouthpiece, cleans his mouthpiece.

Bran Davis tips her glass. Whiskey, the tip of her tongue, her throat.

She watches Stan Yurek purse his lips around his mouthpiece. They have played moist circles over the soft white skin inside her arms, her thighs. His full lower lip. He closes his eyes. Bran washes back whiskey, scrapes her nails along the iced wall. Deep furrows between his brows. Whiskey fumes.

The first note so blue, so melancholy, hot down her spine. Nine Polish pilots in candlelight around her table, their thick men's fingers printing her glasses, balancing her forks, gently combing their hair in candlelight. She sways on the balls of her feet, her groin aching.

Men, halved by shadow, multiplied in darkness. The second note reaching long, wavering candlelight, men swaying in flickering shadow, reaching. She arches her back, nine flames arching, the note wavering.

Bran twitches, her shadow twitches across walls, ceiling, in thick gold light. The saxophone moans. Bran holds her breath, lifts onto her toes, spreads her arms.

Music under her skin, her instep, her shins, thighs, under the shadowed hair on her belly, the undersides of her breasts, her nipples, her throat.

Stan Yurek blows, sucks in. She rises on her toes, spreads her arms over the whole room, lays back her head, spins and spins and spins.

THE LAST NOTE WAVERS in his head, sweet like his daughters when they crawled under the down quilt, begging, "Play for us, Poppa." He sucks candle smoke, holds it burning in his lungs. He could close his eyes forever, he should have died first, he meant to play them cake and sour cabbage and sausage. The sweetness wavers in his head, he opens his eyes. Millions of skeletons stare at him from eyeless sockets. A million children sway in candle shadow, skeletons rubbing their flesh thin, eyes shut tight. "Play for us, Stan Yurek, keep us alive." His sob bends the flames, they flicker. Across the ceiling, down the walls, Bran's shadow swoops, folds him to her shadow breast. "Keep your eyes in your head, Stan Yurek. It does no good to see too clearly."

IN THE DARK, the boat opened its stomach. First the tanks like prehistoric beasts rolled down the bridge the engineers built. Only the men in her black gut, rocking their rifles in their arms, having dozed standing up across the Strait of Messina, could not see the bridge, so saw tanks that night roll on water black as the sky.

Then artillery, guns mounted on a magnificent suspension system. A technological feat men, these guns, twenty-five, hundred-pound shells. Rolled across water, aimed at stars hidden in cloud.

At last the men, two by two, clomped along the bridge, rising and falling with the sea, marched out of the scent of bilge oil, metal, gunpowder. So black when they turned around, they couldn't tell if they were inside or out.

Disgorged onto a beach in Italy, they waded heavy with rifles, shells, canteens, tin hats, through wet sand. Inland, from the black mountain tops, the enemy stuck his million eyes to a million precision-ground ocular lenses. On the beach, every muscle tensed. Not even the curtain of blackness could protect them from falling shells.

ALLYN DAVIS FEELS their hoofbeats strum the earth long before they reach town, feels their vibration run underground through the centre of the ridge, across Bogusch's field, up through the floor of the shack, into the soles of her feet. Horses. She has been drawing on her browny-yellow drawing pad, horses without flesh or muscle, bones flying. Allyn slides her pad and charcoal under her pillow, slips out into thick yellow sunshine.

Scrambles straight up the hill, fir and poplar caressing her bare legs, in and out of thick cool shade. She lopes along the top of the ridge, sharp limestone through her boots. Through thick fir, across Old Baldy, past the hoist. Trunks and grass and rock and coal distilled to shades of yellow-brown. Her legs churn, her arms piston, she draws cool wind over her teeth. At the saddle, she stops long enough to see the woman, Henry Reed, astride one horse, leading another.

Down the hummocky slope, her heels slicing clumps of dirt and grass, Allyn rehearses in her head, It's me, Allyn, Allyn Davis. She leaps, suspended in gelatinous air, lands on both feet, jarring trees and Henry Reed below, leaps almost before she lands.

The first horse turns uphill, its head bobbing as it climbs, Henry Reed's head bobbing in time. The packhorse follows. Both horses the same colourless yellow-brown. Allyn sucks in, blows out, sucks in.

"It's me, Allyn, Allyn Davis."

From limestone, her voice bounces back at her—Allyn Davis, Allyn Davis, Allyn Davis. She stops. How do you draw your own voice?

She laughs, shouts again.

"It's me. Me, me, me. How do you do, Henry Reed, Reed, Reed?" Henry Reed's horse stops downhill. Allyn looks directly into Henry Reed's mapped face. She extends her hand.

Only when Henry Reed leans to shake her hand does Allyn see the colt behind the packhorse, its nostrils trembling.

"Sorrel. Someday you will see." Henry's voice soft, her mouth barely moves. She swivels, smiles at the colt.

"Small and graceful as a deer, strong as a bear, stubborn as a moose, wild as a wolverine."

She turns, smiles at Allyn.

"Can you help? In town, he will be afraid. Can you ride him, meet me here when the sun goes down, ride him all day?"

Heart thumping, Allyn Davis breathes into the colt's quivering nostrils, lays both hands on his trembling shoulders, vaults onto his back. Poplar leaves quiver, the colt's sides quiver, the air quivers. Allyn squeezes her knees. "Steady, boy, steady." Still and calm between her legs.

Henry Reed disappears over the ridge, her checked shirt, brown and yellow.

The colt's head drops, he bawls. Trees and mountains heave. Allyn lurches back, lurches forward, her body snaps, her head snaps.

The colt's head snaps back, smashes Allyn's nose. The earth shifts, and they are flying up the hill, Allyn's hands wrapped in the colt's mane, her stomach banging its withers, her legs sliding back. The colt's shoulders bunch, spring, pound the wind out of Allyn's chest.

The earth crashes up at her, falls away, and they are flying down the other side, down the mine road, past hoist, trees, trucks, meadow, abandoned coke ovens. Air slams into her chest, in and in.

The ground swells behind them, and they are flying across a flat meadow, Allyn hanging onto the colt's mane rising and falling, the colt's body rising and falling beneath her. She rides and rides until the sun sets deep brown, and she rides the colt over the ridge into an empty meadow, around the meadow, through the trees long after dark, and, Henry Reed not there, rides him stepping fast across the field to her shack, sweat foaming the colt's coat, her legs.

Before she can grab a tea towel to rub the colt down, Allyn's legs trembling, her mother drifts through the yellow-brown curtain, a cigarette in the corner of her mouth. "See any colour today?" Allyn shakes her head, flicks the towel behind her back. Her mother reaches for her, both hands, grabs her shaking leg. "Nothing like the smell of horse. Go rub him down before he gets stiff."

ORTONA. Italy.

Italian soldiers with their hands behind their heads stream out of town. Some wave white flags. "To you, we surrender."

Rhys Davis palms his rifle butt. Italian. His neighbours, Italian, families clustered in shacks by the Crowsnest River—Il Bosc. Bushtown. Boxcar doors on their shacks. "What do you think of my door?"

Drank chokecherry wine, dandelion wine, red currant. "You like the vino, huh? You sure you don't got Italian blood?"

Us. Them.

Flexes his fingers, joints swollen.

Dark hair, dark eyes, like his own. Not the enemy, not these. At home in Ortona, peering at him out of windows and doors, the enemy has moved in.

Home. Bellevue.

A hundred yards back, artillery fire smoke-shells over their heads. Midair, the shells rip apart. Canisters rocket from their base plugs, thud somewhere out there, hiss smoke, smoke between them and the enemy. Italian soldiers cough through smoke. Rhys Davis points his rifle. Not the enemy.

Powder sizzling full burn, their own base plugs hail down on them, explode. A hundred yards back, artillery check wind velocity, topography, Xs on maps. Must be the enemy, as far as we can see.

Ten yards ahead of Rhys Davis, a plug lands on one of their own. The soldier turns, runs toward them, screams, "Help me, help me, somebody help me." Falls. No one turns him over. Rhys Davis cannot for the life of him remember the man's name.

No. Rhys Davis flexes his aching knees. Not now, another time, another place. He will take this smoke, these bodies bursting, falling, this flesh stench, he will take home. Bellevue. He will take his arthritic connective tissue.

"Ortona," he whispers out loud. "Home. Enemy. Bastard."

There is no smoke.

High cloud.

Run.

Shells pound. Feet pound. Dirt. Wide open. The enemy. Soft thud, bodies not men.

Rhys Davis ducks down a side street, he and three others. Stone walls, the enemy inside. Rhys Davis runs through open space. His heart hammers, his shoulder slams stone, shittin' stone.

His hand coated in rock dust heaves a grenade. The top floor of a house that the enemy has moved in blows flying rock and dust everywhere.

"Go for it, Davis. Stay low. I'll cover."

Crouches, rifle cocked, finger hooked around the trigger. Hurls himself across the open doorway, flattens against the wall. His heart hammers. He pants.

A shell ricochets off stone to his right. Bastard. He aims his rifle at the stairway, squeezes. Sweet recoil against his shoulder.

"Got you covered, Davis. Go."

Over his head, shells shower the stairway. He hurls himself across the open floor, ducks under an alcove. Hanging pots, spoons, plates, somebody's home.

The enemy moves upstairs.

Rhys Davis slides to the bottom of the stairs, shattered stone, fires straight up. Thunder rolling around inside, shatters his eardrums. His mate's breath rasping in his ear.

"We'll get him, the bastard."

Up the stairs two at a time, knees bent, thighs flexed. An open door. He thrusts in his rifle, empty, ducks in.

Thunder cracks in another room, shakes walls. A shell ricochets off stone. He flattens against the wall, shouts to his mate's helmet rising up the stairs.

"Can't see the bastard. He's there, behind you. Try to cover."

Aims his rifle down the hall.

His mate flat on the floor, rolling for the wall, shells chipping stone behind him.

Rhys Davis squeezes, squeezes, squeezes. Forty years. The son of a bitch.

Thunder cracks, shakes the walls, rolls, echoes. His eardrums flutter. He squeezes the trigger. Burnt black powder. He licks his lips.

Except for soft thudding outside, silence.

Rhys Davis slides around the corner, back to the wall, slides for the door at the end. Down the long hall, two open doors, one on each side, gaping at him.

"Cover your ass, Davis, for Christ's sake."

His shirt rubbing stone, his feet hardly touching, his breath even. Past one gaping door, silence, the other, silence.

The enemy has moved in.

Forty years.

Face to face.

Rhys Davis presses himself against the wall beside the door, listens. Scraping wood on stone. He takes a deep breath, spins into the room.

"Jesus Christ. Don't."

Rags on her feet, on her head, a tiny girl slides a wooden box out from under a soldier slumped on his stomach, shit spattered buttocks raised to Rhys Davis, on his arm a swastika.

"Don't touch, don't touch, don't touch."

Rhys Davis waves his arms. The girl looks from his waving hands to the window where there are mountains and trees, slides the box to the window, lifts her foot.

"No," Rhys Davis shouts. "No, a bomb, it's a—"

The explosion slams him head first into stone. His teeth sink into his tongue. Blood and dirt fill his throat. In the rubble, he hears the child's gurgling breath. Afraid to look. In the mine, you are afraid to shine light on men you know were digging darkness when it exploded. Rhys Davis hunkers toward the rasping gurgle. Out of stone, her eyes watch him lurch through the smoking rubble. He feels them dark and brown and liquid. His hands sweat along his rifle butt, he feels her eyes looking, cannot raise his own. Underground, you beam weak light over rubble, ignore the feet and fingers that, severed, could be anything, anything not human taking refuge in darkness. It is the eyes, jumping out of darkness into light, your light, that make the groan rise to your lips. Rhys Davis eyes shattered stone, glances over splashes of red. Grey, stone is grey. His palms squeak over his rifle butt. He knows where she is, her eyes dark and scalding, refuses to look. In the mine, you can do nothing for them—hold their hands, listen to prayers, tip your water to their lips, avoid their eyes.

Rhys Davis raises his rifle, aims for the white spot between her eyes, dark as his own. "Close them," he groans, "for God's sake, close them."

This he will take home to Bellevue.

He rubs his ripped tongue over his teeth.

House by house, floor by floor, room by room, hand to hand, when Ortona has been named a battle, the Canadians will be renowned street fighters.

This he will take home to Bellevue.

And creeping through evening damp on their way back to their trenches, the Canadians will step over bodies of men and mules. A young private will say, "So we commandeered donkeys, eh. We'll go down in history as the regiment that used donkeys instead of tanks." The private, no older than Owen, will kick the corpse of a bloated mule, its tongue hanging out the side of its mouth. "Poor bastard."

And Rhys Davis will drop his rifle, grab the boy by his shirt front. "You cocky son of a bitch."

Lying in water in his trench, Rhys Davis will dream his hands sculpting the mud of Italy, shaping heads in the dark.

This, too, he will bring home to Bellevue.

ALLYN DAVIS WAITED for a moonless night. After her mother and Stan had gone to bed, while Stan's sax laughed on the far side of the curtain, Allyn dressed in deep brown dark, slipped out into Bogusch's field.

Her lungs tasted frost, she skirted the long grass. Tenor, she rubbed her hand up and down his neck, I name you Tenor. The colt snorted, dropped his head, chewed at the long grass. Allyn smelled the green she could not see.

From the west blew thick sulfur smoke. Allyn leaned into the wind, leaned into coal smoke stinging her eyes, tilted across the earth under a dark sky.

Toward the tipple down by the river, the top of its stacks barely visible, Allyn leaned her full weight into the wind blowing her breathless.

Across the field, where the houses started, a dog barked. Allyn shoved her hands in her pockets. Only her in this thick brown fog, the miners underground or at home in bed. "Miners have their ways of seeing," Stan Yurek said. "They listen."

Allyn's feet sure of the earth, swished grass, rolled gravel, skimmed rocks, stopped at the edge of the cliff. Below, mine lights yellowed darkness. In the haze floated tipple, powerhouse, shacks, smokestacks.

Allyn Davis coughed, shifted her weight. Directly below her, the long low building where they stored hay. Allyn crouched, probed the edge of the cliff for the right shaped rock, tipped it over, uncoiled the rope she hid there, wrapped one end around a tree trunk, in the dark tied a bowline.

Her hands prodded darkness for the chute they used to dump bales down, found cold metal, threw the free end of rope down the chute. Allyn ducked into the reverberating dark.

Slid, her spine skimming cold sheet metal. Pure joy of falling in the back of her throat. Pure blackness.

She slammed into solid bales, the wind knocked out of her. Allyn lay on her back, sucked at air. Her lungs burned. She sniffed. Dust, hay, oats. She shoulder-rolled onto the cement floor.

Allyn worked quickly, stuffed her pant pockets, shirt pockets, jacket pockets with oats, peeled hay in one piece off the end of a bale, unbuttoned her shirt, pressed the hay against her skin, buttoned all but the top two. She stuffed hay down her trouser legs as far as her knees. Sweat prickled her stomach, trickled through the hay on her skin, the smell from her open shirt hot and sweet as she moved.

Her hands found the rope end. She grabbed, leaned back, climbed. Her feet slipped on sheet metal. Her arms ached, her thighs shook from crouching. Hay against her sweating flesh.

Feet finally flat on the dark plane, Allyn Davis untied her rope, coiled it into the dank hole under the rock, handled the rock until it fit exactly. She leaned her weight into the tenor sax laughing in the wind.

ALONG THE COASTAL ROAD, a convoy of trucks, lights off, shot around hairpin curves in the dark, flirted with gravity.

Rhys Davis clutched the shimmying steering wheel, riveted his eyes to the pale square of light coming from the differential under the truck in front of him. The prick of light swooped, jounced, veered. Mud spattered his windscreen, wind fluttered and whistled overtop the rectangle of glass.

"Give her gas, Davis, they're speeding up." Simpson's voice in the wind, as if he were far away and not seated next to Rhys.

"Christ. We're already doing 50."

"Do 60."

Hurtling along the twisted coastal road in the dark, the truck falling out from under them, slamming up to jar their kidneys, swaying around curves. Wind overtop of the windscreen whipped their hair. Rhys Davis focussed on the prick of light zigzagging madly ahead of him.

Rhys Davis parked the truck in the ditch with the other trucks and jeeps, the taste of oil and gas in his mouth. Rain soaking his thin cotton shirt, he hoisted his shovel from the back of the truck.

"Where you going, Davis?"

"To bed."

Behind Rhys Davis' eyes, the light zigzagged. He swayed, anchored his shovel into mud for balance. Movement of the truck still in his limbs, he fought the sucking mud, dug himself a shallow slit trench. Fell into a restless sleep.

MIST AND RAIN SWIRLING around his head and shoulders, Rhys Davis waded out of his slit trench. Muddy water eddied around his thighs. A jeep floated past. A bedroll. A tin can. A gun, belly up. Men flailed about in water.

"I lost my goddamn rations."

"Anybody see a grenade float by?"

"I can't swim."

"Bastard Krauts."

"Hey, catch that rifle."

"The jeep's floating away, Jesus Christ."

"We'll freeze to death."

Rhys Davis plunged his aching hand into water and mud, held his wrist against the current. If he could stop. Make it stop. Grab hold.

WADDED IN SHEETS AND BLANKETS, her nightie crusted to her thigh where her flesh tasted Stan Yurek's music, laughing slippery in the dark, Bran Davis hears the door open and close twice, the smell of Allyn's horse under the door.

Bran Davis stretches, her feet plunging into unwarmed space between sheets. Her knuckles brush rough board, she fists her hands, a shiver runs along the fine hairs of her skin.

"Ahhh ahhh ahhhhhhh."

She dresses quickly in the grey dawn, Turtle Mountain's gouged face watching her across the valley. "You can't see my stretch marks, can you, with your eyes fallen out of your head. Serves you right."

In the kitchen, she peels a carrot into the sink, mutters into the dawn wrapped around her. "This is orange." Quarters an apple. "This one's green. What do you want to know for? Hunched over your desk at school, I can just see you, you little bugger, squinting out lines before you draw them. But you could talk instead of drawing."

"Shit." She snaps the carrot into pieces. "You're the last. I wanted them to leave, they left, now you are the last, and I'm not sure." She slides her arms into Stan's overcoat, pulls his collar up to her chin. Into his pockets she stuffs apple and carrot.

Outside, the mountains float. She inhales, crosses the field toward him, the horse her daughter draws over and over. Charcoal sketches that Allyn strokes with her thumb. And Stan Yurek with his saxophone to his lips, sucking in all the sharp objects under the sun, his dead wife's protruding pelvic bones, metal fragments of Polish airplanes, his daughters' jawbones, holds them piercing his guts until night when he blows them raw through his throat, taut lips, out the curved brass bell of his sax, sounding every inch of her skin.

She stands with her hands in Stan Yurek's pockets, thumbs a piece of cold wet apple. The colt nuzzles her wrist. She holds the apple piece to him between thumb and finger, the smooth flesh inside his lips moistening her skin. His teeth graze her nails, sink at her fingertips into apple flesh, his breath hot. "I told them to go away, they did. Someday my husband will walk across this field. His white skin naked under the sun."

The colt nips the soft flesh of her hand. She holds a carrot to his lips. He grabs, tosses his head. "I know my daughter named you sound. I didn't know she could, but I saw her write your name on her pad then smudge it out. She never speaks, always looking at the bones of things. Stanislov Yurek will walk away, will haunt my thighs, and it is too late. I could have ridden away. There were horses in Saskatchewan, but five children. It's too late."

Over the ridge, sunlight greens the grass, reds the hair on Tenor's neck. Bran Davis wipes the back of her hand over her eyes, squares her shoulders. She turns on her heels, Turtle Mountain's missing face pale in the sun, marches for the shack. The colt follows, nips her shoulder, butts the small of her back. She marches past the end of his tether, swinging her arms.

He snorts, she marches for the shack, her back square, her lipstick red, black hairpins.

His squeal knocks the wind out of her, spins her around. He stands still, the wind lifting his mane. She stares at his long face, his dark eyes staring at her.

"Keep your eyes in the sides of your head," she whispers, "and your vision will always be split."

AFTER THE WAR IS OVER, Rhys Davis will limp into the Bellevue Library, pull a red hardbacked book off the shelf. He will stand an arm's length from the desk, hand the librarian the book. As she writes the title in her register, Rhys will pretend to read book spines, breathe through his mouth.

The bad meat smell of his leg will seep through his pants. He will grit his teeth, shift his weight onto his wounded leg. Pain will explode in his head, wipe out his sense of smell.

"Your book, Mr. Davis."

"Ta." He will reach for the red book, avoid her eyes. Outside, he will cough, spit into the weeds along the library wall.

At home, in Bogusch's field, he will sit alone at the table piled with dirty dishes, stare at the red cover. He will look over both shoulders, open the book.

FROM PACHINO TO ORTONA: *The Canadian Army at War.*

Rhys Davis fingers the letters, black on white. *Pachino. Ortona.* He glances over the colour plate on the facing page. Dead trees, dead horse, dead tank. *Ortona.* He fingers the word, feels nothing but the raw pain in his leg.

He flips a page: "The Red Patch Goes to the Mediterranean."

"Red." "Mediterranean." He touches the words, looks over both shoulders, whispers them out loud. Smooth white paper, his voice dry.

He riffles back to front. "Skirmish." "Assault." "Operations."

Words. Black and white. Official.

Rhys Davis closes his eyes. The pain from his leg swells.

"Formation." "Campaign." "Theatre."

"Infant

     try."

He squeezes his eyes shut.

Behind the official black and white.

Behind enemy lines.

RHYS DAVIS AND SIMPSON WALK down a road in the dark. Their boots make sucking sounds. Behind them, their regiment boil tea over truck gas.

"Christ, that tea smells good."

"If we ever get leave, I'm going to find a place where they brew tanks of tea. I'm going to stand under a spigot with my mouth open and my prick out so I don't have to stop drinking when I need to piss."

"They could use you in Rome, Simpson. Statues are starting to look like capons."

"Eunuchs, Davis."

"You said it, Simpson."

"Bugger you, Davis."

Whispering, always whispering. Ahead, their engineers fashion a rough crossing over a mountain ravine out of darkness and a demolished bridge. On their left, a wounded olive grove. On their right, an abandoned farmhouse.

"Do you hear that sound?" Simpson grabs his sleeve. Or he grabs Simpson's sleeve.

A low rumbling. One of them whispers, "Tanks."

"Oh."

They walk on, boots sucking mud. Behind them, the rumbling grows. Faint metal clank.

"Jesus Christ." One of them stops. Listens.

The other whispers. "What the hell's wrong with you?"

"We don't have any tanks out here, not one, not one tank."

"Good Christ, you're right."

"Would they have moved one in without communications?"

They listen to the growl growing bigger, closer. Their faces mere shapes in the dark.

"I don't know."

"How far back?"

"Half a mile."

"Shit."

"That old house."

"Shit."

Across the field, running. Through the door, into cool darkness. They separate, either side of the door.

Rhys Davis crushes each vertebra into the wall. Urges them to fuse with stone. Shoulder blades, elbows, the back of his skull.

He moves only his eyes, sees the outline of Simpson pressed to the wall on the other side of the open door.

Up his spine the tank roars, cancels their muddy footprints. Keep going, he thinks, keep going, keep going.

The tank pivots, he can hear the engine change. It scales the ditch. His bowels loosen. Not yet, not yet. Not until the shell hits.

Stone, only stone between him and the tank circling the farmhouse. It grinds metal against stone, rounds a corner, throws a beam of light past a window.

He flexes the muscles in his throat. Assholes. Can't you see? Why aim your light out there? Get it over with. He bites his tongue.

Through stone, the engine purrs along the back of his neck.

Away from the house. Keep going, keep going, don't shoot. The tank growls, spins around, he can tell by the sound, rolls straight for them.

He can't tell if it's his heart or Simpson's beating so loud. Shoot, you pricks, get it over with. Don't explode, he tells his heart, tells Simpson's heart.

Throw grenades overhand.

Always wear a helmet.

Keep low.

Afterdamp travels the ceiling.

Know which side before you shoot.

Never fire your own blast.

No matches.

No oxygen.

Get me get me get me

out of

The tank gun glides through the open door, between him and Simpson. Glides past his left ear. Metal, gunpowder, exhaust. He moves only his eyes, thirty years underground, catches its dark curve. Outside the open door, the tank clanks to a halt, purrs.

Mine, he thinks, in the mine. Shovel handle, blasting machine.

To Fire, pull up rack bar to full extent, Then push Down with full force, Using both hands.

His hands curved around the sweaty barrel of his Bren rifle, metal sucking his joints dry.

Tank gun. Eye level through the open doorway. Cleaves the air between him and Simpson. Wrap two hands around it, and it would suck the marrow from his bones. Better than warm shit when the shell—

He urges his fingers into stone. Don't move.

Along the underside of the tank's gun, a beam of light no bigger than a miner's bores a hole in the darkness between him and Simpson, illuminates the clouds of their breathing.

Rhys Davis rolls his skull over stone away from the light, breathes into darkness. Along the edge of his vision, the light bisects the room, cuts him off from Simpson, probes fissures and cracks in the far wall.

Underground you see parts. Hands, knees, feet.

No connective tissue.

He moves only his eyes, sees Simpson's face etched in the wall on the other side of the light, Simpson's breath roiling into the relentless beam. At Rhys Davis' sides, his fingers ache into stone.

The light moves toward Rhys, mouth level. He rolls his head back, cold at the base of his skull, breathes overtop of the beam of light. It climbs up his eyes, inches away, slices his vision in half. He holds his breath, rolls his head down, cold against his neck, lets air out slowly.

The beam inches toward his face. He breathes out the side of his mouth. Inches closer, if he licked, he could taste light on his tongue. Closer, his cheeks burn. Closer. He flattens his ear to stone. The beam of light caresses his cheek.

Dies.

Blackness floods his vision. The engine revs, stone shudders against his ear, the gun glides backward out the door.

Fused into the wall, Rhys Davis and Simpson listen to its steady growl recede down the road, caterpillar tracks erasing footsteps they have not yet made.

"How did you do it?" Simpson whispers.

"Do what?" Rhys Davis whispers back. His lips brush stone.

"Disappear. How did you disappear?"

"An old miners' trick."

"Whose tank?"

"The Enemy's."

"Which one?"

Backs to the wall, they laugh across the open doorway, laugh until their knees buckle and they slide straight down, their helmets ching-ing stone.

"Which one?" Rhys Davis drops his face into his hands.

HE AND SIMPSON PASS an abandoned barn. In the shade of the barn, a haystack. Simpson raises his rifle, cocks his bolt.

"Hey, Davis, you ever use mice for target practice?"

"Don't."

"Come on, Davis, you could use the practice."

"I said don't."

"Ever eat mice, Davis? You aim for their heads so you don't damage the meat." Simpson squeezes the trigger. Rhys Davis lunges for him, knocks his elbow.

Near the top of the stack, hay explodes, the rifle butt jerks from Simpson's shoulder, recoils into his ribs. Whine of bullet through air, hollow thud.

Simpson's chapped lips inches from Davis' eyes. "You bastard."

Spurt of red flowing down the hay.

He and Simpson flattened against the stack, chins embedded in pricking stalks, mouths open, wine running down their throats. Simpson gurgling. "Italians, Davis, hide their wine first. Always check the stack. What do you think?"

Rhys Davis' stomach hot, his head floating above the hay stack. "Goes well with mice."

DAY, NIGHT, DUST, MUD, march, march, olive, pine, goat, mule, march, climb, climb, march, mountain, enemy, eye, watch, watch, doze, wake, eye, crawl, run, Italy, Bellevue, home, their, our, body, corpse, flesh, bone, warm, cold, blood, shit, God, God, God.

IN THE DARK, they sit in a circle, heads slumped forward on their knees. In the dark, his hand finds his mouth, crams food—bully beef, hard tack—crams until he has to swallow. His hand finds his mug, finds his mouth. He slurps, cannot tell hot or cold.

Two feet to his left, two feet to his right, chewing, swallowing, gulping. Stench of wet wool, tinned meat. Not a word. Not a word.

Mail.

Instant moonlight. Shadows across half their faces. They bite, chew, swallow, watch their shadows on the ground feed themselves. Let them shoot.

In Bellevue, coal absorbs light and shade. Bellevue.

The CO reaches into his sack, calls out names.

"Hill, MacGregor, Tokarski, Gilroy, Fauville, Panek. Our first mail from home, gentlemen. So you don't forget where you live."

They put up their hands, eyes on the ground, when their names are called. The CO presses envelopes, boxes, parcels into their raised fingers.

Rhys Davis stares at the toes of his boots.

Home. Slit trench. Mud.

"Davis."

Puts up his hand, sees the envelope in shadow descending, feels paper between his thumb and finger. He lays it, bulging at the bottom, on his knees. In the centre in bold print:

> Mr. Rhys Davis
>
> Italy

In the upper left corner:

> B. Davis
>
> General Delivery
>
> Bellevue, Alberta
>
> Canada

Bellevue. He runs his fingertips over two bulges. Slides the tip of his army knife under the top flap, slices clean through.

Eggs. They roll, crushed and stinking, into his crotch. Eggs. He runs his fingertips over their shattered shells. Unfolds the letter, tilts it to the anti-aircraft moon.

> Dear Rhys,
>
> Do you remember in Drumheller Gwen hugging the chicks until their necks broke?
>
> We have shortages here. Sugar, flour, eggs.
>
> You should have stayed underground where you belong. There have been no explosions in the Pass since the war.

The Italians paraded down Main Street in all the towns when they heard they changed to our side, singing and dancing and spraying each other with red wine.

Everyday men come home without hands, feet, legs. They would be better off dead. They should shoot themselves rather than let their families see them like this.

Everyday Poles, Ukrainians, Italians, hold funerals for relatives buried over there.

A neighbour, Mr. Yurek, says the whole lot of us, every nationality, should have one day of mourning for the dead, the hungry, the maimed. He says we should hold services in music because that's our common language.

The wind howls all goddamned night. Miners say the tunnels creak and groan.

If you do not come home, I will know you died for Peace.

In the spring Allyn lit a match over a gas tank in Calgary. She won't say, but she did it so she could see inside. The tank exploded her thirty feet into the air. Only her eyes were burned. She can see, but she has lost colour. The doctors say it may come back.

I showed her your picture. She did not know you.

If Owen is there with you, give him one of these eggs. They were fresh.

As Ever,

Bran

HE HOOKS a fingernail under a shard, flicks shell onto the ground. Black film clings to the white. He peels it back. It rolls like dead skin, clings to his fingers. He wipes them on his pants, squeezes the white, tough and spongy. It breaks open. Green slippery yolk. He scrapes the outer layer with his knife, holds his breath. Pops the yolk into his mouth.

Until he has to swallow, he rolls it around his tongue, unable to breathe.

Allyn, Bran, Gwen, Meinir.

Daughter. Son. Wife. Husband. Father. Mother.

He wraps the other egg in tissue, slides it into his pack. Owen. If he sees him, if he recognizes him, Rhys Davis will give him the egg, will say "Your mother sent this."

COLD, YOU ARE so cold lying here on your back on the ground. And hungry. Fumble in your pockets for a cracker, a candy, one of the eggs you boiled for the drive.

Empty. They must be back in your car, down by the river. Down the hill. Sit up, pull your sleeping bag up over your head, cross your arms over your chest. A sick feeling in your stomach. Breathe deeply, think of the green writing in the margins of your book.

Back and forth. Always coming back to an event, trying to see it differently, trying to crawl inside. Always the need to leave.

Close your eyes, lean forward, put you head between your knees. Your stomach growls.

Beans. Peas. The people who live in the cottage won't miss a few. Drop your sleeping bag. Stand and stretch. Turn toward the vines and stalks and leaves you swished past before you flopped down here, earlier.

Grass. Nothing but long blowing grass.

Turn toward the cottage, the carved wooden swirls over the door. Nothing but a shack, a tiny tilted shack.

Spin a full circle. A vast empty field, grass dipping in the wind. Smell of green. Wind in your nostrils. Smell of horse. Behind the shack.

Swish slowly through the long grass, through the shadow of the shack in moonlight, around the corner. Put your hand out, croon softly. A voice whispers to you through the grass.

Hidden. So many hidden stories. Shape you. Sshhape. Sssshhhhhh ape us. Hidden. Hide. Sssshhhhhh.

Run your hand up the horse's warm neck, bury your fingers in its mane, lean your chest against its chest. Your heartbeat. Its heartbeat. Wrap both arms around its neck. Press your cheek into the warm curve of throat.

HORSES

A LL DAY, Samuel and Henry Reed throw their lines into the Old Man River, brush through cottonwood and poplar and willow so sweet it turns their stomachs. They cast from sandbars, gravel bars, flat rocks, round rocks, from under a canopy of leaves.

Always cool between vertical banks of shale or dirt or limestone. Above them, where they cannot see, Samuel's cattle graze the long grass. In two years, a blizzard will blow down the Pass, run eight hundred head, blind with fear, over the bank.

When they find their twisted carcasses, Samuel will say, "I had less before. If they were buffalo, no one would own them, and we would all have eaten them."

Henry will lean over her horse's steaming neck, stare at the mess below. Her hand will slide down her horse's neck, under her mane. Horses would never let snow sting them blind.

All day, they drop their hooks into deep green pools at their feet, dark water below logs, keepers below rapids. All day, their feet follow the river.

Whoever pulls a fish thrashing from the water, Samuel flicks it off the hook, hands it to Henry. Henry squeezes both hands above its tail, feels through the cool film of slime its crisp scales and powerful muscles. To the nearest tree, she swings the fish swimming in air. She strokes its side, iridescent violet and blue and red, or under its throat, two rust-red lines.

As he hands Henry the thrashing fish, Samuel tells her, "That one's Rainbow, that one's Cut-throat."

Henry kneels beside the basket, river loud in her ears. "Squaw," she has heard the other ranchers say when her mother walks by. "That there's Samuel's squaw." Sometimes they laugh or point at her, Henry. "Ssshhhh, the kid can hear you. Looks just like his mother."

Henry leans her head close to the shining fish. The river had this fish in it. Now I have this fish. She closes one eye, stares into the fish's eye, round and unblinking. Her mother said they must fish moving water. Henry lays the cool body in the basket on top of four other cool bodies.

Even when she fixes on her line in one spot, her eyes see water moving. She closes her eyes. Now the river has me in it, and I have the river moving in me.

ALL MORNING, SAMUEL AND HENRY REED FISH against the current, cast, pull in, cast, all the while stepping through cottonwood, poplar and willow, through sand and gravel and boulders.

They watch their lines hang above the rushing rapid, plop into the keeper below. They pull against the current, upstream. Around the bend roars a rapid they can't see.

Around that bend, then another, casting, pulling in, cutting through flats and foothills, below mountains. Unseen, unseeing, except for water and trees and steep banks across the river, behind their backs.

Hidden by earth, pulled by water, they pass beneath a flat meadow. The year Samuel Reed dies of pneumonia, he will ride sealed in a pine box behind his team, his friend John Willow driving, east along this track to Pincher Creek where they bury him beside the river.

Samuel watches Henry upstream. Watches her look into the fish's eye.

When he dies, his wife will dress him in the deerskin coat she chewed, sewed, beaded beside the fire after dark. She will smooth it over his chest, down his stiff arms. When she has seen him off beside the river, she will go back to her people. When leaves turn yellow, she will marry a Blood.

West along the river singing in Henry's ears,

> *in weeds by rocks*
> *in pools through rapids*
> *slips the cool slips the rainbow*
> *slips the cut-throat slips the fish*
> *slips the woman*
> *slips the girl*

Above on the flats, towns not yet found, not yet built, not yet abandoned.

Down in the valley, Henry throws her hook out into the river.

TWO YEARS LATER, the North West Mounted Police, on horses with fine long legs and deep chests, ride double file onto the flat meadow, pitch four large tents, three for sleeping, one for cooking and eating.

Mostly men under twenty-five. They strip off their tunics, hang them from trees around their tents. "If we're going to stop cattle rustling, we need a structure. Not exactly a fort but a solid log structure."

They pull pots, pans, paraffin candles, sacks of flour, Hudson Bay blankets, straight razors, bootblack, tooth powder, mustache wax and a Union Jack from the bags loaded onto four packhorses dozing in the sun. Throw it all into the tents, no time to lose. "No telling what rustlers are up to in the heat of the day."

They charge into the trees, those privileged by position brandishing axes. A packhorse cranes his neck, looks back at the grassy meadow. An officer yanks on its halter. "Come on up, you lazy bugger, we're all on duty here." Up over the hill, along the creek, where twenty years in the future men will carry picks and shovels and cans of black powder, and a hoist line will sting the trees day and night, the packhorses snatch tufts of long grass between trees.

On her way to her father's bull pasture, her sorrel mare in heat, Henry rides past their camp. Four tents with flaps back, gear piled inside. Scarlet tunics sway in the trees. Twelve bays hobbled in the long grass. She counts them.

Slides her hand forward under her mare's mane, pulls back gently on the hackamore. They swing to face the bays. Against the insides of Henry's legs, her horse's sides heave in and out.

Henry breathes in her mare's smell, hot oats and grass and hair. Twelve. Forty-eight legs, twenty-four haunches. Her mare dances sideways. Henry strokes her neck. "There now, there now. Must be one left uncut."

Beneath her legs, her mare's sides tremble. Henry is prepared when her mare's voice breaks the silence, rings through the meadow. Twelve heads lift. Deep in her mare's chest, a low rumble rolls up, shrill from her mouth. Echoes through the trees. She leans over her horse's neck, whispers. "Listen. Axes and saws. Over the ridge. Wait till they go to bed tonight. Nothing will wake them up." Her horse's sides under her legs, heaving.

One bay, head up, tail up. Between his legs, long and black. Front legs hobbled together, the stallion jumps forward. Henry turns her mare, squeezes her knees. "Hyah."

Her horse grunts, bolts.

The stallion squeals.

Henry lets the reins run through her fingers. Gives her horse her head. "Hyah, hyah." Lying low on her neck, her mare's body stretched beneath her, muscles tight beneath her skin beneath her legs.

Away from the stallion's squeal, behind them shivering the air, the mare's haunches, the back of Henry's neck. Sweat, thick foam along the mare's shoulders, Henry's pantlegs. "Hyah."

Henry keeps her horse walking while she counts her father's bulls, passive without cows and calves, thick necks and shoulders among trees. Henry's horse steps around them, snorts.

"Forty, fifty, sixty." Henry counts out loud, lets her horse find them. Her horse weaves through trees, lunges up hills. "Seventy, eighty." The mare tosses her head. Flecks of foam spray the air, float back, land on Henry.

"Ninety." Her horse carries her to the edge of a steep drop, stops. Henry leans back, aligns her backbone with her mare's. Looks across the wide valley at Turtle Mountain, not yet fallen, will not fall for another seventeen years. Through the valley, Old Man River slicing a clean deep gash, west to the gap between Turtle and Goat Mountain. Through her shirt, her horse's heat.

No one around but bulls and magpies and gophers. She speaks to her horse's ears twitching back and forth. "Two years ago, that river pulled me beside it, and in the gap between Goat and Turtle, I smelled the devil, but my father said the devil doesn't live here."

Her back warm, the mare kicks at a fly on her belly. Henry shifts with her, her spine pressed into the mare's. "And when I got home, my mother held in her arms a baby who was the fish she had inside her. I told her I smelled the devil. She laughed and said the devil was white."

Her spine on her horse's, she rolls up, one vertebra at a time. Slides forward along her horse's back, rests both hands on her withers. "But a girl on horseback knows when she smells the devil."

Henry Reed picks up the hackamore reins crossed over her horse's neck, turns them away from the sun sliding into the gap. "A girl knows how to keep herself on the back of a horse." She squeezes with her knees.

Through the dusk, Henry will let her mare find her way home. The mare walks fast, rocks Henry gently back and forth, back and forth, warm on the insides of Henry's thighs. Down the wide valley, hills growing dark blue on their left, the river on their right murmuring out of earth, out of dusk.

Fast down the narrowing valley, hills and mountains closing them in. Her mare's hooves sure along the margin between earth and the space falling away to their right. From down there, the river sings loud over rocks and boulders.

Henry pats her mare's neck, laughs. "My mother knows horses. Who knows better than a woman how to get a horse. But look, the river has fire in it."

Henry leans out from her horse, over the black space that smells of cottonwood, poplar, willow, wet earth and water. Down in the bottom, in the blackness, flames dance and flicker, light up hills and mountains and arms and her horse's mane rising and falling.

The river laughs, the flames disappear.

Clouds and hills and mountains grow black, move closer. Faster, her mare carries them through scent of pine and poplar, wolf willow and grass.

Horses. She can smell them. A deep rumble in her mare's chest. Her sides tremble against Henry's inner thighs. Henry strokes her neck. "Easy now, easy."

Past a ridge, close and black. She can smell the earth, feel the cold solid beside them. Her mare's neck warm under her palm. Suddenly, the meadow opens before them, grey in the dusk. Henry blinks as her eyes adjust. Tents. Tunics draped over poplar bushes.

Henry whispers, her hand stroking her horse's neck. "They've left empty coats to guard their horses." Henry turns her horse back toward the river, squeezes her knees. They make a wide half-circle. Horses. Her groin aches.

Henry lets her mare pick her way through the trees, back toward the bays hobbled along the edge of the meadow. She pushes her stomach and chest flat into her horse's back, holds the reins loose against her neck.

The mare moves quickly, her hooves soft thudding between tree trunks. Her mane stings Henry's cheek. Branches hook Henry's shirt, her hair, her skin. Ahead, twelve bays rip and chew tender grass, stamp against flies. When he stamps, the stallion's prick smacks his legs.

The mare steps to the edge of the clearing. Henry pulls back on the hackamore. "Easy now, easy." She breathes fast, hot against her horse's back. Slides softly to the ground, pressed against her horse's side.

Sixteen horses. Twelve men asleep across the meadow.

Henry hooks an arm over her mare's neck. Leans into her shoulder, feels the sound rise from her chest, split the darkness. She grabs the reins under her mare's chin, pulls her head around. Her horse follows her into the trees, her breath hot on Henry's shoulder. Behind them, twigs snap.

Henry sets each step down lightly, slips past dark poplar trunks. Her mare breathes hot against her shoulder. When the snapping twigs sounds too far back, she stops to wait. "Breathe into a horse's nostrils so they always know who you are," her mother said, and she will tell Allyn Davis sixty years from now. Henry blows, inhales her mare's breath sweet and warm. When the forest thickens behind them, Henry drops her mare's reins, turns and walks back slowly through the trees.

She stops, stretches out a hand to the horse whose eyes she cannot see in the dark. "Easy, boy, easy." Takes a step, stops. "Easy, boy, easy." Stretches out her hand again. The horse is taller than her mare, taller than any horse she's ridden. "Easy, fella, easy." The black shape of horse, of muscle, flesh, sinew, bone. "Easy now, easy." Smells the horse's desire, quivering, front legs hobbled.

"Easy, boy, easy." Smells horse's breath blow across her face. She stands still before the stallion, stretches out her hand. "Smell who I am." Reaches for the curve of neck above her. Hot, quivering, under her fingers. Runs them forward, patting. "Ah, see how easy, see how easy." Forward to a cheek hard and round. "They won't know what I've taken. So easy, so easy." Down his nose to his mouth. She holds her hand open under the horse's nostrils. "Smell who I am." In the dark, Henry wraps her hand under the horse's chin, blows softly into his nostrils. "Smell who I am." Inhales the horse's hot breath. Finds the stallion's shoulder with her own. Runs her hand down the stallion's chest, leg, over his knee, down his tendons, around to his fetlock, down. Under her fingers, the leg trembles. Under her fingers, the leather hobble. Above her, shape of horse, quivering. "Ready now, ready."

Henry's fingers slide along the leather thong, find the knot. With both hands, unknots. She looks up at the shape of stallion. "Remember who I am."

Henry crouches, muscles tense, ready to jump out of the way. Blood rushes in her ears. Above her, the stallion trembles.

Henry's haunches tight from squatting, tight from waiting. Between her legs, steady throbbing. Her mare nickers.

The stallion snorts, flies over Henry's head.

In the dark, in the trees, Henry crouches. Horse rears on its hind legs, comes down on horse. Thud and squeal and groan and teeth and wet flesh.

In the dark, in the trees above her, all around. Henry arches forward, pushes cheek into knee. Wet flesh, her flesh, horse flesh. Rides. She rides. Her flesh, horse flesh. Shudders up her haunches. Leans against balsam poplar. Wet. Her hand. Her forehead. In the dark, in the trees, all around, panting.

Henry walks her mare through sleeping balsam poplar back to the meadow, now completely black. Behind them, the soft thump of hooves. In the clearing, Henry runs her hand down the stallion's chest, his knees, finds the joint between fetlock and hoof. Across the meadow, loud sighs on the west wind. The stallion sighs into Henry's hair. Henry ties the hobble, doesn't need to see. Pats the stallion's shoulder.

She crosses the hackamore reins over her mare's neck, slides onto her back, turns her downwind, downstream. Gives her her head.

Henry Reed has stolen her first horse.

SPRING
IN THE
WIND

ALL WINTER IN BELLEVUE, it snowed and snowed. Snow climbed the walls, ridged the bottom ledges of windows, climbed the windowpanes.

Before they went on shift, miners took their shovels, cleared door-ways, cleared spaces in front of windows so they could look out on snow-covered mountains. By the time they drank their coffee, collected their buckets from their wives, kissed their children good-bye, the snow was already filling in their footprints, the spaces in front of doors and windows.

To get to the mine, a half-mile away, or a mile or two or three, they shovelled and tunnelled through snow, replicated above the earth in white their black subterranean mazes. By the time they arrived at the mine entrance, where they had another half-mile, or mile or two or three, to walk underground before they climbed into their rooms and began work, sweat soaked their wool long johns and their tongues stuck to the roofs of their mouths.

Inside the school, lost and grey in snow, rows of connected desks gathered dust. Children stayed home with their mothers, spent the days burrowing just outside their doors, their mothers dropping their knitting, baking, mending, cooking long enough to pry open the door and check that snow hadn't caved in and suffocated their children.

Inside or out, shovelling snow that settled like concrete around their homes, it was women who recognized the danger. More than one mother, her heart beating in her ears, praying she wouldn't find her child's bloated body in the spring, dug out a child unable to move her hands or feet, breathed into the child's blue-rimmed mouth until the child sputtered, choked, opened her eyes and cried.

Through that winter the women learned their own techniques for digging labyrinths, their children lined up behind them, even the baby who couldn't quite walk yet, across town, through fields, to their neighbours' homes where they sat over tea or coffee reading in each others' eyes the fear of a fox caught in a leg trap, then back home to put on supper, knead bread, wash clothes in the galvanized tubs their husbands soaked in when they got home, hung shirts and pants and long johns, but not their own undergarments, which they washed after dark and took down before morning, from rope stretched across rooms until they could not turn around without bumping into sleeves, trapdoors and pantlegs.

Porcupines and deer stripped the bark from poplar and lodgepole pine. Horses dropped from thirst and exhaustion after digging for days, sunk belly deep.

Milk wagons and coal wagons paralyzed, people in the Pass that winter, Samaritans and thieves, followed their personal labyrinths to neighbours' homes, mine yards, friends' or enemies' barns, pulled from their pockets and the fronts of their shirts and dresses lumps of coal or bottles of milk, or just as easily stuffed into their pockets coal, milk, cheese. In the courthouse files in Blairmore, there are no recorded charges of theft.

Many a night, those who could tunnel their way to the Legion sat around small round arborite tables, argued for hours about the depth and weight of snow.

"What d' ya say there, Jack. Snow up to your second storey windows yet? Must be, what, twenty feet deep?"

"Nope. Ain't up to my windows, and them windows are only ten feet off the ground."

"You're both lying. You don't even have a second floor, Jack. I'm five-seven, my arms are two-and-a-half. If I stand flat-footed, reach straight up, my fingertips just reach the top of the snow. That makes her deep all right, eight-one to be exact."

"Well now, if you're standing flat on the ground and reaching straight up, how can the snow be deep? Has to be tall or high now, don't it?"

"High, deep, tall. None of that matters, does it, when you have to shovel the stuff. What matters is how much it weighs."

"Doesn't that depend on how long she's been sitting? Obviously snow that's settled in solid is going to weigh more than snow that's new."

"You all make me laugh. I watched the snow all day, tunnelled through it three times. I can swear on a stack of bibles, a pound of snow is a pound of snow."

"Yes, but is a foot of snow always a pound? That's the question we gotta ask ourselves."

"Christ, you're all drunker than a piss-eyed chute rider. What matters is how much snow can a cloud hold."

Too drunk to dig home, they spent the night in the back room, curled on the floor between cans of paint the Legion executive kept buying because they couldn't decide what colour they wanted the walls.

CURLED ON THE FLOOR in the Legion's windowless back room, Bran Davis stretched, swiped at grey dawn. Her elbow thunked a full can of paint. A pain jolted up her funny bone. She slid the can toward her, squinted at the printing on the side. The letters merged with the grey beery air. She brushed off an arm fallen across her stomach, hoisted onto her elbows, counted. Three, four, five of them and herself sleeping it off. The room stank of old beer, open-mouth snoring, dirty carpet.

She groped around her for her handbag, hauled it out from under

Jack, snoring face down on his belly. Muffling the clasp with one hand, she pried her purse open with the other and stroked the empty pill bottles inside. On her hands and knees, she crawled from one paint can to another, unable to see what colours, levered off their lids with a nail file, dipped her pill bottles, filled them to the top with paint, swiped drips with a tissue, snapped them shut.

Her purse loaded with colour, hanging from her shoulder, she crept among arborite tables for the lobby, took a shovel that may or may not have been hers from the forest of handles and blades lining the walls, and braced herself against the door as she loosened the bolt. The weight of that winter stronger than her own, she resisted the door shoving open, snow dumping into the lobby, pushing her back, her shoulder muscles straining, resisted until the door pressed her back against the wall. She stepped out from behind the door into snow.

Last night's tunnel had collapsed under a night of snowfall so Bran turned the blade of her shovel backward, raised her arms, sliced down at the wall of snow between her and the stores and homes of Bellevue, the wall between her and Stan Yurek asleep in their bed in Bogusch's field way at the end of town.

The backs of her arms ached as she raised her shovel over her head and sliced, raised and sliced. Snow collapsed around her knees. Sweat flowed between her breasts, down her back into the crack of her ass. Hot and shivery, Bran turned the blade of her shovel face up, heaved the snow settling around her legs over her shoulder. She could no longer see the door of the Legion. Nothing around her but snow. Pain pinching her shoulders, she bent, heaved snow behind her. All sound muffled except her own panting and the ssshhhooooo of her shovel.

Snow between her and Stan Yurek rolling over in their bed.

Bran bent, thrust, heaved down Main Street, past Cole's movie house and the Bellevue dairy and Green's Garage, all invisible through snow, around the curve of highway curving away from Main, past the Baptist and the Dutch Reform churches, whiter than the snow they were lost in, through Maple Leaf, Fidenato's and DeCilia's tall red grocery somewhere out there past all this weight of snow, across Bogusch's field at last to their shack.

Her blood pulsing red in the backs of her eyes, Bran heaved snow away from the door, fell inside. Muscles hot and liquid, she lined the pill bottles along the stump Stan Yurek put beside Allyn's bed.

"Play my muscles cool, play them blue," she whispered into Stan Yurek's sleeping ear, slid under the quilt, pressed her sweat into his skin.

ALLYN DAVIS DIPPED her brush into a pill bottle, brought it down dripping onto a sheet of paper. It slid across the page, alive in her hands. She dipped into another bottle, brought the tip down under the first thick shiny line. Fluid and alive.

Clouds. She dipped into a third bottle, filled the clouds with colour she couldn't see. Underneath, she painted tilted earth, Fidenato's and DeCilia's store as tall as the mountains, leaning into the street, its walls at crazy angles, then Green's Garage. Gas pumps with hoses around each other, cars with square wheels not touching the ground, the bakery, show hall, United Church. On the street, lumpy people without faces. People, houses, stores—Bellevue alive under her brush.

That's when her mother drifted in with the snow, whiskey on her breath, leaned over Allyn's shoulder.

"You've made the buildings red and purple, the clouds green and orange, the faces blue and lilac and turquoise."

That's when she painted her mother floating in the clouds on her side, naked, her hands behind her head, eyes closed, one knee drawn up, painted her in broad strokes, the brush alive, her mother's round arms and thighs alive, circles for her breasts and nipples.

IN MARCH, people in the Crowsnest Pass sniffed spring on the west wind. "Spring is just around the corner," they said, "just up the valley in B.C. there. Probably already having it in Fernie."

But the snow lay heavier than ever, caught in that torpor between falling and melting. Crystals slumped together, fused, lined peoples' tunnels with ice so that adults had to shuffle slowly, for if they fell, their fingers scraped ice while their bodies slid out of control however the ice sloped. Children loved it, chiseled the tunnels round, aimed their bodies high up one wall, swooped down, around, and up the other side, back and forth until they slid to a stop. They stole tallow from their mothers' pantries, greased their sleeves, pantlegs, backs, fronts, hurled themselves at curved ice. Patches of rusty blood dotted the insides of tunnels, blue black bruises spread under children's skin. Their mothers could not stop them. Their fathers did not know.

People complained of pulled muscles, chest pains, aching bones. Once they built a wide straight system of tunnels leading to their store, marked with signs, Fidenato and DeCilia did a booming business in horse lineament.

ALLYN DAVIS SAT at the table, painting figures on the backs of painted pages. Outside, the wind howled through dark pine, shook Turtle Mountain, howled through wall cracks and down the chimney.

She experimented with faces. How few lines to make a person look like a person? How many strokes to make a person look like herself? If she painted figures in groups in the background and made them lean toward each other, she saw faces even though she did not put them in. A glob of paint slithered under her brush, flowed into the shape of Tenor, only half a face, the eye a quick stroke. Another glob of paint, and the other half of Tenor's face shaped like Henry Reed's, Henry Reed's eye looking out of the paper from Tenor's face and her face. When the snow melted, Henry Reed would bring Tenor back to Bogusch's field. "A horse winters better with other horses," said Henry Reed.

Across the table, Allyn Davis' mother spooned ground meat and onions onto boiled cabbage leaves, rolled them into neat parcels, placed them in a roasting pan. Out of her throat rose and fell strange sounds that chased the wind around the room, like Stan Yurek's saxophone. In the bedroom, Stan Yurek slept before afternoon shift, the musky smell that moved in with him swirling around Allyn and her mother with her quick hands. Limp cabbage leaf, beef and her fingers square and sure.

Allyn dipped her brush, studied her mother's hands, let the paint glide. She shook her head, dipped, forced a slippery outline. She sighed. Dipped. Quick strokes. Her mother's fingers hooked around the cabbage, thumbs prodding the ground beef. Allyn held her brush over the paper.

"Keep your eyes in your head, you little bugger. You know what happens when you look too hard."

Her mother's hand around a tin of tomatoes. Juice flowed over the cabbage rolls, tomatoes plopped, split, seeds flecking, all in sepia like an old photo. But her hands.

Three sharp raps on the door.

Her mother's hands in beef and cabbage.

"Don't just sit there, answer it. They'll wake up Mr. Yurek."

Allyn Davis leaned her whole weight into the door. It swung open, hit the side of the shack.

"Good God, you're worse than whoever's knocking. Don't just stand there, ask them in."

Allyn Davis stared at the man standing feet apart, hands behind his back, waited for him to redissolve into the wind and sun-sculpted snow he'd emerged from. The man stood absolutely still in his khaki uniform.

His square face broke into a grin. He saluted, snapped his heels together. "Remember me, kid? I'll give you a clue. The best diver in the whole world."

"Owen." Allyn Davis' mother stood in shadow behind Allyn, her voice flat. "If it isn't the oldest son come home. Where's your father?" Her words flat.

"Hell if I know. I didn't see him after England." The man's face frowning.

Allyn Davis' mother's hand reaching, brushing the man's frown, pulling back, adjusting her own hair.

"You going to stand out there all day? Come in and I'll brew tea."

"ONE MINUTE I WAS IN ITALY, running past a stone wall, next minute I woke up in England in the hospital. Didn't know where I was, all these women floating around in white. Thought I'd gone to heaven, until I heard their English accents."

The man laughs in his chest, coughs. The cigarette in the corner of his mouth jerks up and down, shakes ashes into his tea. Allyn Davis cannot take her eyes off the man's square jaw, his skin without freckles. She could paint a boy's round face, round body, diving straight down into the Crowsnest River, his bum round. She could paint this man with the square face, square jacket, square boots. But she cannot paint Owen, this she knows. Owen went overseas. This man is here in Bellevue.

Ashes flecking his tea, the man wraps both hands around his cup, throws back his head, downs it. Wipes his mouth with the back of his hand.

"Don't think I didn't see women in Italy. I did, mostly in the dark, if you know what I mean. They had to sneak away from their Poppas, we had to sneak away from camp. We'd find them in the shadows of stone walls. They build everything out of stone over there. Huddled in a group, silent as church. Didn't know how old they were. First thing you'd touch is a metal cross hot from their skin."

The man laughs deep in his chest, wheezes, chokes, wipes his mouth. Allyn Davis' mother stares, eyes dark as coal, at the curtain across her bedroom.

"Yup. A metal cross."

He shakes his head, stares into his cup, then looks right at Allyn, one eye squinted behind coils of smoke.

"Shrapnel, that's what got me. Right under my helmet. Didn't know I'd been hit. One minute running, the next somewhere else flat on my back. Don't remember how I got there, nothing. Don't remember a damn thing. Come here, take a look."

The man drops his head forward, squints up at Allyn.

"Come on, take a look."

Allyn slides behind the man's chair.

"Move to the side there, kid, you're blocking the light."

Allyn steps sideways, weak yellow-brown light falls on the man's neck. At the base of his skull, a shaved patch and in the middle—"Do you see it, kid? Here, touch it."—a perfect cross. The man's square fingers stroke up and down, side to side. His raised wound pales, darkens.

"Shrapnel. Nestled right in there in my spine. Doctors left it there. Said they wouldn't dare touch it."

The man's fingers stroke.

"Come on, kid, you can touch your brother's scar. Shit, you used to follow me around like a pet mule."

Allyn Davis raises her hand to the stranger's neck, lightly strokes his crossed wound. Up, the wound pales, darkens when she lifts her finger. Across, pales, darkens. Allyn presses harder, the wound rigid under her finger, harder, if she keeps rubbing, keeps her finger pressed into the man's skin.

"Hold it, kid."

The man's fingers grab her wrist.

"You can't feel the shrapnel. It's buried too deep."

Allyn Davis' mother draws on her cigarette, looks from them to the hanging blanket.

ON HER BACK on her cot, Allyn Davis listens to the man snore from the cot against the far wall. She listens for the sax Stan Yurek puts at night in the box under Bran's bed.

In the evenings, the man eats with them, his elbows on either side of his plate. He fists food with his fork.

"What do you call these things?"

Allyn's mother keeps eating as if she hasn't heard. Stan Yurek chews his mouthful, swallows.

"Cabbage rolls."

"Oh."

The man with Owen's name nods, tines a cabbage leaf, lifts it dumping steaming beef into the air.

"Isn't this what they call bohunk food?"

He looks at Allyn.

"Must be what they feed boarders here in the Pass. We had polacks in our regiment. Not bad fighters for bohunks."

The man snores late into the morning, his mouth wide open. His legs twitch. Allyn paints his profile, daubs paint on a piece of brown paper, daubs on more and more. As the paint dries, fissures run through the man's profile, bits flake off. When the man wakes up, he lights a cigarette, dozes off again, the cigarette hanging from the corner of his mouth, ash falling onto his chest.

Allyn's mother sleeps in as long as the man, emerges from behind the curtain blanket in her housecoat, her hair matted around her shoulders. The man rummages around in his covers, finds his trousers, pulls them over his long johns, sits on the edge of his cot coughing, runs his fingers through his hair standing straight up. Allyn Davis' mother pours two cups of coffee from the pot Stan Yurek left on the stove. She bangs the pot, bangs the cups on the table. While the man steps outside, his fly open, his eyes crusty, she stirs three spoons of sugar into her cup, lights a cigarette, inhales. Her eyes look over the dirty cups, plates, pots on the table, over Allyn Davis' head, Turtle Mountain in her pupils. The man sits kitty-corner to her, pours coffee into his saucer, tips the saucer to his mouth. His eyes rise over the rim, squint at Allyn.

"What do you say, kid. I didn't hear the boarder make his bed this morning." He laughs, wheezes, leans across the table toward Allyn, fakes a whisper, his breath—coffee and the bottoms of ashtrays. "I stayed awake half the night listening, but didn't hear much of anything, except a few snores. Gets quieter all the time." He swipes his mouth with the back of his hand.

Her little finger in the air, Turtle Mountain in her pupils, Allyn Davis' mother sips her coffee, draws on her cigarette.

The man leans closer. "Course women over there weren't loose, just wacky religious, if you know what I mean." He winks. "And polacks knew their place." His square face squints at Allyn, closer and closer. He laughs. His breath and bristled chin closer.

Allyn dips her brush, flicks. The man stares at Allyn. Paint runs off one eyelid into his eye. Allyn dips, flicks. Paint dribbles down the man's forehead. Allyn dips as fast as her hands can, flicks as hard as she can. The man's mouth open, he lunges across the table, paint streaming his face.

"You little shit."

His chair flies back, smashes the wall.

"You goddamned little shit."

His square fist flying across the table and Allyn Davis' mother's voice low and flat. "Touch her, and you can go to Hell."

The man's fist smashes the people on Allyn's paper, paint splashes his chest, Allyn's cheek, her mother's throat. Her mother looks at them, eyes lit inside, raises her hand to her throat, wipes, examines her fingers. Lays back her head and laughs, the husky laugh like Stan's sax late at night before the man who stole Owen's name.

"Get your coat, you bastard. You owe me a drink."

ALLYN WATCHES their square dark backs disappear into snow. She stuffs her pockets with bottles of paint, pulls on Owen's old wool jacket, Stan's muffler that she sees as yellow-brown, remembers as blue.

Through the icy tunnels, she jogs uptown. In her pockets, the pill bottles click together. Where Main Street should be, the tunnel straightens out. Allyn guesses where the street ends, flicks the cap off one of the pill bottles, dips her brush. The paint glides across the ice, oily and smooth. Sticks just enough for thick glistening lines. Allyn paints from memory—the Bellevue Inn on the corner, where it should be, where it is, hidden behind ice and snow. She paints from the bottom up. The low cement wall bordering the Inn's lawn. The glassed porch, old men's faces peering out. In their eyes, the buildings from the other side of the street. The first floor windows. In the one on the corner, a young woman smokes a cigarette, waits for her new husband to maze through tunnels, pin her against the nubbly bedspread, the smell of the mine in his mouth. The second floor windows—gabled, empty. Allyn paints clouds and Turtle Mountain in each window frame. She steps back, smells the heavy oil of paint, surveys her hotel painted in colours she cannot see.

Where the tunnel wall curves away from her, the hotel curves away, warps the tops of the old men's narrow heads, encaves the young woman in her waiting. Where the sidewalk should be, Allyn paints a huddle of kids without faces. Their hands and feet stretch out of the curve of wall, make them appear to run, throw a ball. Over their heads she swirls gobs of paint that fly like birds.

She turns to the other wall, flicks open a new bottle of paint. Where she guesses the Legion should be, she paints into the tunnel's curve a tall narrow building. Outside the Legion door, she paints a drunk leaning against a telephone pole, puking into the darkness behind the painting. Allyn wipes her hand across her face, feels the paint smear her cheek, reaches into her picture, pats the drunk on the back. "Go home and sleep it off, you silly bugger."

All along the tunnel, she paints buildings where they should be, buildings flying in and out of the centre where the tunnel curves, buildings in motion. All afternoon, while the ice inside the tunnels turns darker sepia, Allyn paints people and mountains, curvy houses and flying horses, dogs and birds upside down, giant cakes with plums on top, Stan's daughters twirling, their hair whipping out of the curved wall, Stan's wife plump and square holding a bag of cheese to the children running out of the opposite wall, the brass bell of Stan's sax blowing colour Allyn cannot see.

She paints her way home. Paints Green's Garage on the other end of Main, cars lined up where the corner should turn off Main, their headlights shining into the tunnel, the Dutch Reform church, the Dutch choir on the steps outside, their mouths yawning out of the painting. Where the tunnels run along the edge of the cliff, she paints tipple and stacks and smoke and shacks with boxcar doors and women picking dandelions and herself skimming down the chute.

She paints after the sun goes down and shape and colour dissolve into blackness. At the edge of Bogusch's field, she paints the picture of her mother on her side, her hands behind her head. In the dark, Allyn's hands shape her mother's round thighs, her round breasts. Even though she can't see them, she knows her mother's eyes are open.

Allyn paints until her bottles are empty.

At the base of the ridge behind her shack, she wriggles each bottle into ice until the wall is full of round colours she cannot see, turns and runs for the shack where Stan Yurek boils potatoes and cabbage and sausage. The colours Allyn cannot see stare holes in her back.

WHILE SAUSAGES, POTATOES AND CABBAGE BOIL, Stan Yurek soaks in the galvanized tub next to the stove. In the hot water, the hairs on his skin loosen, flakes of coal float to the top. He sucks in his breath, slides his buttocks along the bottom, submerges his whole head, hears underwater the rhythmic squeak of his skin on metal. He slides back up, lathers soap in his hair, slides down. He stays under, listens to his throat hum, until he has to come up, his hum breaking the surface of the water, and there is Allyn standing by the stove watching him bathe, paint wild in her hair, on her clothes. Stan Yurek nods.

"I saw them, Allyn, she will see them, too. You paint music, I play colour. She knows. Now, you put the potatoes and cabbage and sausage on some plates, and I'll finish washing."

The skin under Allyn's eye twitches, but she does not move. Stan Yurek nods at the pots steaming on the stove.

"Go on. How does the saying go—I'm as hungry as a moose."

Allyn Davis stands still, her hands hanging at her sides. Stan Yurek looks into Allyn's eyes, old like his daughters', thin dark skin underneath.

"You must eat, Allyn. Soldiers I have seen before, boys dressed up as men. Owen will leave before I do, I know. Now we eat, and after I'll play for you every colour you can imagine."

Stan Yurek stands, reaches for his towel, the wind through the wall cracks blowing his skin cold, light as air. When the soldier leaves, he will play for Bran this cold lightness, and she will shiver and laugh, "You know me well, Stan Yurek. You did not try to make me see."

EARLY IN APRIL people in the Crowsnest Pass began to taste spring up the valley.

"Just taste that melting snow and warm mud and buds on the trees."

"You can taste spring coming. It's in the wind. We'll have spring any minute." They loosened their scarves, undid their top buttons.

By noon, the icy roofs of their tunnels had melted and been blown to a thin waving crust. Children walked with their heads back, watched through the thin ice clouds move beneath them, ran home shouting, "I walked on water. I walked on sky."

By afternoon, the ice melted through, rained on the heads of women and their children on their way to the nearest neighbours'. Women gazed at the sky naked above them, at the arc of clouds over the sky, at wafer-thin arabesques of ice flowing into different shapes along the tops of tunnel walls, placed their hands on the wet heads of their children. "We will live a little longer." They threw open doors, curtains, chased out shadows that had mouldered in their rooms all winter, hung sheets and trousers and shirts and dresses in the west wind. At their neighbours', they drank strong coffee without sugar, watched each other's eyes for the first sign of green.

Underground, the men tasted spring in their jam sandwiches. Above ground, they walked upright through white labyrinths alive with Allyn Davis' wild coloured figures, purple and green horses, violet and emerald and ocher buildings, green and red and orange birds in crazy flight. At the edge of Bogusch's field, a naked woman floated, violet, sapphire, chartreuse on her side, one knee up, hands behind her head. Her blue-black eyes watched them approach, watched them leave. None of them stopped to stare.

Near home, their children ran to meet them, swung on their arms. "Daddy, today I saw the sky. Today Mommy made a spring cake without eggs." Reached into their lunch buckets for bits of grey crust. "Daddy, you left some jam on." By evening, water sluiced knee-deep down tunnels, and the west wind whipped across sculpted ice, left people breathless and laughing.

In Bushtown, at the bottom of the cliff, Italian men dug trenches around their shacks, connected them to spillways running to the river. Before bed, they ate plums preserved in brandy, then drank the brandy.

Connected by one deep valley, one green river, bounded by limestone mountains, Ukrainians and Russians and Germans and Italians and Poles and Scots and English and Welsh gathered around wirelesses with cups of sugared tea, wine, beer. Surely spring meant the end of war.

Mothers wrote long letters to their sons overseas.

I remember when you were born. . . .

Do you remember the time you mixed black powder with Grampa's tobacco? . . .

I cannot wait to hold you. . . .

All my love . . .

Women who all winter fought to warm both sides of their beds wrote to their husbands.

Spring is here and my skin is thirsty. . . .

They said you were missing in action but the wind whispers you will come home. . . .

Don't stop to knock. . . .

Men, women and children went to bed with full stomachs and bladders, fell asleep while wind blustered and water sluiced through their dreams. They did not know what woke them in the middle of the night, aching bladders or wind. They staggered for the door, "Spring is here, why use the pot under the bed."

A shrieking Arctic wind blew up nighties, froze streams of urine in midair, whitened exposed flesh in seconds. They stood stunned, adrift in a lake of shattered stars. Ears and fingers and calves grew numb. On the clothesline, sheets and trousers and shirts and dresses stiffened, cracked. Sleeves, legs, skirts crashed to the frozen ground, tinkled into a million pieces. Still the people stood, their breath freezing into ice needles that blew in their faces, stung their eyes, slashed their cheeks. At last, they closed their doors, crept back to bed. Huddled shivering under blankets, they whispered all night to themselves fragments of wireless news.

"The Allies have stormed hills and ridges."

"The Enemy occupies high places."

"He has moved into the monastery at Cassino."

"Winter our Enemy."

"American troops frozen in position."

"Faith."

In the bowels of the mines, men moved closer to their partners, warmed blackness with their communal sweat. In the morning, women bundled in their husbands' long johns, trousers, shirts, over-coats, socks, boots, bundled their children five layers deep, stepped out into the Arctic wind, their children lined up behind them. The wind snatched their breaths, filled their mouths and lungs with icy needles. Their faces stung, went numb. Feet apart for balance on black ice, they wrenched pieces of frozen clothing from the line, slid them stiff between their children's outstretched mitts. Unable to move their arms, the children shuffled in solemn procession to their doors, sat their frozen charges on kitchen chairs, laid them out on tables. They shuffled back out into the stinging wind, bent with their mothers to the black ice, scooped with their numb mitts shards of frozen cloth. These, too, they laid out on tables close to the coal stove. All after-noon and late into the evening, they huddled around the stove, wait-ed for pants and shirts and dresses to thaw, slump over the backs of chairs and edges of tables. Fingers swollen from the cold, they stitched the shards of cloth together. They sewed while the mine whistle blew, sewed when the door flung open and their fathers laid frozen jam crusts in front of them. Late into the night, women and children sewed cross-stitches, running stitches, lock stitches. None of their clothing looked the same as the day before. Flowered bodices on checked skirts, pants different colours from the knees down, a brown shirt with one green sleeve.

A teacher watching his wife and children sew by lamplight wrote in his diary, "None of us are untouched by war." An Anglican minis-ter in Blairmore looked out at the stars reflected in ice, wrote the first line of his sermon—"I don't recall whether Milton or God first used the image of angels on the frozen lake of Hell, but surely that is an apt metaphor for our condition in these troubled times." A young woman alone in her shack wrote to her dead husband overseas, "Wind is wind, and snow is snow. There is no blame. Yet there grows under my breast a hollow dead thing. That would I kill."

ALLYN DAVIS WADES through the tunnels, water flowing over her boots. All around her her people and animals and houses liquefy, flow into each other, run down the walls melting behind them. Sepia, yellow, brown, flow into the brown water. She stamps her foot. Water splashes her groin. She lays back her head. Bulging brown clouds in yellow-brown sky. "Bullshit." She kicks a bird dripping upside-down down the wall.

"Colour." She shouts at the brown cloud. "I need colour." She slams her knee into a melting man's groin. "Do you hear me?" She raises her hands, screams over the pressure in her head. "Red. Green. Blue. Heliotrope. Cinnabar. Cerise."

All around her, endless yellow-brown. "Bullshit, bullshit." She pounds the water rising past her knees. Slush splashes her face, trickles off her chin. Yellow-brown.

She shakes her head, shields her eyes, surveys Bogusch's field covered in a brown sea rippled by the west wind. Across the field, windblown waves curl, roll for the edge of the cliff, drop off the horizon.

Bushtown. Water slaps Allyn's knees, fills her boots. She forces her legs to run. Every time she lifts her leg, mud sucks her gum boot off her foot. She flexes her toes, pushes her boots straight ahead. Her gum boots ripple against her shins. Bushtown. Il Bosc.

She stops at the edge of the cliff. Waves lap the backs of her knees, tumble in braided streams over limestone, into the raging brown torrent sweeping the valley below. Two rooftops swirl downstream, bobbing and circling each other. An iron bed, covers pulled back, pillows fluffed, a coal stove, belly up, TRIUMPH scrolled across its oven door, a barrel-bodied washer, SUPERIOR SOLID wringers spinning. Upstream, a knot of people run back and forth along the bank, point into the water, wade in up to their thighs, reach as far as they can into the swollen Crowsnest River.

A gramophone player floats by, disk spinning. A wooden washboard, a shirt stuck to it, an earthen crock, an empty cradle. Chairs around a table. On the wind, the wailing of women and children. Allyn finds footholds between braided streams, hops down the cliff. Her boots slosh, pop. A Singer sewing machine, treadle and needle whirring up and down. Allyn wades in to her ankles. The current sucks at her boots. She plants her feet, watches brown flood the valley. Close enough for her to smell the yeast, an immense mixing pan of rising dough. A book, *The Common Sense Medical Adviser*. Everything sepia like an old photo. A clucker floats by on her nest, *buckbuckbuckbuckbuck*. A pipe, a pair of gloves, a work boot. The water rises over Allyn's knees. A rocking chair, a hairbrush, an iron. Water rushes over her thighs. A pair of dice, a mug, a starched collar. Brown, drowning in brown. A set of false teeth, a bone corset. She leans into the swirling brown. A jar.

Plums.

Deep red. Purple.

Allyn blinks at the sealer jar bobbing toward her.

Deep, deep red.

She shakes her head.

Purple. Red purple. Purple red.

Allyn raises her eyes to Turtle Mountain. Grey and green. She lays back her head. Blue, blue and blue.

She staggers back in the water. Her boots. Black. Her hands. Red. Her trousers. Green. She cups her hands, scoops icy water over her head, icy water in her eyes.

"Colour. I see colour." She whispers, bites her bottom lip.

A burgundy wine bottle swirls past. An orange ball. A rusty can. Yellow. Magenta. Water dripping in her eyes, she squeezes them shut. Opens them slowly.

A flash of white. Bobbing under the water straight for her. Bump against her shins. Dizzy on colour, she crouches, peers into wide open blue eyes just under the surface of the water. On the west wind, the wailing of women and children. Against her shins, a baby in a white gown bumps, sways. Its eyes wide open under water. Allyn Davis cups one palm under its head the way she has seen women do it, her other hand under its back, straightens her knees. The baby's nose breaks the surface of the water. The baby's chin, cheeks, her body heavy on Allyn's wrists. The baby's gown trails in the river. Her head heavy on Allyn's palm, fine white hair dripping in her eyes. Allyn pulls the cold baby to her chest, cradles the baby's head in the crook of her elbow. River beaded on her lashes, the baby stares up at the sky. Softly Allyn blows on her face. Heavy in her arms, the baby stares at the sky. Allyn jiggles her the way she has seen women do it. The baby's lips are blue. Blue under her white, white skin. Allyn waves a hand over the baby's eyes. She stares straight up. Allyn touches her cheek, ice cold. She tips the baby face down over the water. River runs from her mouth. Cradling the baby in one arm, Allyn unbuttons her jacket, her shirt, folds the baby wet and stiff and cold to her chest, cups the baby's chin hard as stone to her own neck.

Behind her, the wailing of women and children. Allyn forces her boots into toeholds, climbs with both arms around the baby, the baby's knees sharp as stone in Allyn's stomach. Sweat trickles down Allyn's back, her face, the baby's cold body sucking heat. Across the road, past miners' shacks, onto Bogusch's field, their shack grey in the middle, stench of rotting leaves, mud, dogshit. From her shirt, cold river grass.

Fingers numb, Allyn shoves aside tea cups, plates, pots, lays the baby on the red-and-white checked oilcloth. The baby stares unblinking at the ceiling. Allyn cups a hand under the baby's head, lifts gently. Back and legs rigid, the baby's whole body lifts. Allyn peels the dripping gown over the baby's head, slides the quilt off her bed, slips it under the baby, lowers the baby gently, wraps the quilt around her head, her body. Only the baby's face stares out. With one finger, Allyn rubs her mother's whiskey over the baby's lips, inside her gums, on her tongue. Lays her gently in the roasting pan. The baby's round eyes stare blue at her from her quilt. Allyn opens the oven door, no fire since this morning, puts the roaster on the open door, the baby's head closest to oven warmth so she can look at the room. And Allyn can look at her.

Allyn digs her charcoal and sketch pad from under her cot. Dust balls skitter across the cover. All afternoon, she sketches the baby, black and white, shade and light, as the sun moves across the sky. All afternoon, the baby's round eyes stare unblinking from the quilt. The sketches Allyn spreads around on chairs, the table, her cot. In the blackness of the baby's eyes, a spot of light moves with the sun. When the sun dips behind Turtle, and the clouds blaze red and orange, Allyn Davis crosses the room, leans over the baby, pink in the light from clouds, strokes her cold head, closes her eyelids.

THE LAST CAR RUMBLES out of the mine. Careful for his fingers, he needs ten—once in Edmonton he heard a man play with nine, the notes he hit with his second joint falling out of the air—Stan Yurek throws the sprage between spokes. The car shudders, skids along the rails, sparks shooting ahead, stops. Behind him, the crunch of coal, and men with black faces emerge from the mine's concrete jaws.

"Hey, Yurek, where you play tonight?"

"Hillcrest Miners' Hall."

"Listen, play some blues, but no reds. Last time somebody talked socialism around here, the axe came down heavy."

"Tell you what. For you, I'll mix blues and reds."

"You could, too, you bugger. See you over there."

Outside their shack, Stan Yurek takes off his hat and coat, dances a jig. Spring, birds, sweet wind. In the spring, his wife dragged the couch outside, hung their down quilts in the trees. He cleaned out the tub under the grape arbor, filled it with warm water, lowered his daughters laughing and splashing, their bodies plump pink. "Play for us out here, Poppa." They stood dripping in the tub, danced to his music. Spring.

Colder inside than out, and dark. Stan Yurek stands inside the door, listens. Ragged breathing. He gropes for the lamp over the sink.

"Is that you, Allyn?"

"I tried. I tried, Dad, I tried."

The lantern cold in his hand, a hot wave washes over Stan Yurek. Allyn. Speaking. Allyn's voice. Dad. Poppa. Twenty-six years. He flicks a match against the wall, holds the flame over the lantern. The room jumps into three dimensions.

Allyn sits huddled on the edge of her cot, rocks back and forth, only her face lit, her body in darkness. She looks up at Stan, her eyes swollen.

"I tried, Dad, I tried." Her head falls forward.

Throat tight, Stan Yurek sets the lantern on the table. Light falls on Allyn's quilt across her knees. Dad. Poppa. Twenty-six years. Curled on their sides. Allyn slumped over her quilt. Like them, so young. Eyes so old.

Stan Yurek stands over Allyn. His shadow falls over her, over her cot, over the whole room. He lifts his arm, his shadow arm flickers across the wall, touches Allyn on the head.

"Trying cannot bring back colour, Allyn. Sometimes we spend our whole lives and never see anything."

Allyn's hair fine like his daughters', her head trembling. Such wars on this earth. His fingers pat Allyn's hair.

"Do you want me to play for you?"

Allyn shakes her head.

"We have time, lots of time, just you and me. I'll play in the dark, you tell me what colours you see."

Under his hand, Allyn's head like his daughters', their warm matted hair. She takes a deep breath. "I saw plum today, and green and blue and orange and rust. I saw white, but I couldn't bring her back." Allyn's voice, more words than Stan has heard her speak, muffled into her chest.

Stan strokes Allyn's hair. "Allyn, your mother always comes home at night. Right now she can't help it. Owen, too, is her child. You wait. He will go away, and she will come back."

Under his hand, Allyn's head trembles. "They went in the river looking for her. I found her, she doesn't look dead, I held her against my bare chest, I wanted them to have her alive. I prayed, but I didn't mean somebody else should lose something. I didn't mean all colour, all at once. I tried, I tried to bring her back, but it's too late. I see them all, all colours at once. I rubbed whiskey on her lips, I drew her. I tried. Her lips were blue. I didn't mean a trade, I didn't mean I wanted everything, I didn't mean a trade. Now I see them all, all colours at once. Now you will have to go. Henry Reed will go, Tenor will go. I prayed, but I didn't mean all at once. I didn't mean a trade. You will have to go."

Stan Yurek places both palms on Allyn's head, watches his shadow hands descend on the head of his wife, "I must die first Stan. Feed me to them, promise." The heads of his daughters curled on their sides in the field. And now Bran, her black hair in the river.

He slumps, turns to sit beside Allyn on her bed. Sees the dead baby, the drawings. "Oh, my God. I thought you meant Bran. I thought you meant she drowned. I thought—"

All night, he holds Allyn rocking the dead baby, holds tight, rocks back and forth. "I will stay here in Bellevue, Allyn, I will play colour, you paint. Me, you, your mother, we make a family."

ALLYN DAVIS RIDES Tenor across meadows so green she can taste them. Through poplar, tight leaves bursting green. Past pine, swishes their new soft tips.

She swings her legs, xylophones Tenor's ribs, each bone a note from winter. Clumps of red hair lift in the wind, red she can see, fly, catch on Allyn's pantlegs. Past the hoist, Tenor snorts, dances sideways. Allyn squeezes her knees, laughs. In the meadow beside the creek, Allyn slides to the spongy grass, rubs her cheek against Tenor's side as the horse rips and chews, green in the back of Allyn's throat. Tenor swishes through long grass to the creek, dips his nose. Allyn kneels beside him, dunks her lips, sucks in.

Down the mine road they trot, light staccato through trees, Tenor's back warm and solid under Allyn's legs. From the edge of Bogusch's field, Allyn watches between Tenor's ears twitching back and forth two figures emerge from their shack. One walks toward them.

Allyn looks down into the face of the man who stole Owen's name. The man has shaved, dressed in a clean white shirt, black pleated trousers. He salutes, holds out his hand. Tenor shies, the man rubs the side of Tenor's head. "Easy, boy, easy," holds his hand palm down to Allyn. Allyn extends her hand.

"Remember me, kid, the best soldier in the whole friggin' world."

He snaps his heels, marches past Allyn on her horse, his pack jouncing up and down.

Allyn fingers the gold cross on her palm, caresses the tiny man hanging rigid in the middle, his face carved in profile.

The man's square back disappears up the road.

"GONE TO CALGARY to find a job." Allyn Davis' mother runs crimson around her mouth, swoops her hair back and up, jabs in pins. "Won't go underground. Said he had enough dark." Traces her cheekbones with rouge. "What's the matter with you? These are my bones, my flesh. I like to dress them up." Her eyes flash at Allyn. "I'll be home late. I'm meeting Mr. Yurek at the Legion." Her hand brushes Allyn's cheek. "You look more like me than your father."

Allyn watches her mother's back merge in darkness with the hulk of Turtle Mountain. Across the field, her mother's voice rolls high and pure.

Chewing bread and jam, Allyn spreads her sketches of the baby across the table, across her cot, on chairs. Under kerosene light, she examines each one, leans close, leans back. With her charcoal, she prints on some, *Dead Baby, Bellevue Alberta, 1943*. On others, she prints, *Baby in White, Bellevue Alberta, 1943*. On the rest, she prints *Angelina Moretoli Sees Colour in Heaven, Bellevue Alberta, 1943*. She signs every one *A. Davis*.

RHYS DAVIS BOARDS the train in Calgary.

He sits with his cheek against the pane, looks into his own eye.

He holds his wounded leg out beneath the seat in front of him.

Stars flash by in the dark, behind his eye.

He knows when they are in the mountains, feels their peaks brooding in the dark, Turtle Mountain like the monastery at Cassino, a thousand eyes in a thousand windows occupying high dark places. Armed.

Rhys Davis lowers himself stiff-legged onto the platform by the river.

The train pulls away.

See you at Cassino see you at Cassino see you at Cassino.

In the dark behind him, rocks rumble like shells down the face of Turtle.

Fingertips like dead stone, he pulls his collar up around his neck.

He limps along the road beside the tracks, tastes creosote, river grass, limestone on the constant wind.

He limps across the bridge. Each step with his good leg cool as the river, each weighting on his bad leg hot as cordite before it explodes.

He ducks past the two houses at the bottom of the hill, aims for the Catholic church towering above, sentinel over the river valley.

Where the bluff folds, his feet find a path. His pack strains his shoulder muscles, increases the burn in his leg.

Sweat runs in his eyes. He shivers.

At the top, he slinks past the church, hides in the shadow of the Blessed Virgin to catch his breath.

He limps in the ditch grass alongside the church road, heads for Main Street. The yellow eyes of houses prick his flesh.

He flattens himself into shadow against the wall on the corner of Main.

Activity along the street, small explosions as doors close.

Rhys Davis rolls into the light swaying from poles on one side of the street.

His shadow crouches beside him.

His boots scrape the sidewalk. Each step he winces.

"Rheumatoid arthritis," the doctors said. "You won't last long if you go back underground."

Dark brooding windows on both sides of the street. Across the road, the Bellevue Inn watches him.

A gap between buildings, then the Bellevue Legion. Rhys Davis balances in the dank gap, tastes fox trot, smoke, beer, the brooding silence of soldiers who have been.

The door bursts open. Yellow light explodes into the street.

Rhys Davis melts into the dank gap. Smoke drifts past.

The door bangs shut.

Along Main, he dodges his eyes in windows.

Rhys Davis crouches on the edge of Bogusch's field, eyeballs the distance between here and the dark shack, scans the top of the ridge.

Runs, dodging side to side, flattens himself against the door, heart pounding.

Rhys Davis shoulders the door, falls into the dark.

"Hush, for God's sake. You'll wake the boarder."

Hisses near his left ear.

Rhys Davis covers his head.

IN THE FLARE OF THE KEROSENE LAMP, Allyn Davis opens her

eyes a slit, watches through her lashes the stranger at the table. The man sits with one leg straight under the table, slides his beret around and around in his hands.

Head down, the stranger looks up at the blanket curtain. Unable to stop herself, Allyn thinks the man's eyes are the colour of moss, his face the colour of milk left too long in the sun.

On the other side of the curtain, her mother's voice. "He's home. The man, my husband, came home." Before she can stop herself, Allyn thinks red, her mother's flushed cheeks.

Stan Yurek's voice, muffled, low. Blue, Allyn thinks, blue, knows she has gone too far when she hears the suitcase scrape the floor. She watches the stranger. The man, my husband. Allyn's heart pounds. I promise, she prays, I promise not to name every colour if Stan Yurek stays.

The blanket curtain flaps. Her mother enters the kitchen, an orange housecoat belted under her breast, a thin red line around her mouth. Allyn tries to unthink, unsee red. Her mother glares at the stranger who does not look up, glares at Stan Yurek swinging the suitcase through the curtain.

"Thank you, Mr. Yurek, you have been a most courteous boarder. You can settle your account with my husband."

Allyn sees the purple rise in Stan Yurek's throat, tries to unsee purple. The smell of rot seeps around the room.

Purple rises into Stan Yurek's face. He lifts his saxophone. Allyn squeezes her eyes shut. Hears Stan Yurek's feet cross the floor, feels Stan's lips brush her forehead. "You draw sound, Allyn. I play colour."

Allyn squeezes her eyes. If she can unsee one colour, it might not be too late.

The door of the shack swings open. A gust of cold wind blows in.

At first Allyn thinks it is the wind moaning, realizes it is Stan Yurek blowing his sax. Out the door, across the field, blowing louder and louder.

"I'm going to bed. Do what you like." Her mother's voice hard. Through the curtain, Allyn listens for the swish of her housecoat. All night, her mother's bedroom floor creaks.

All night, Stan Yurek's sax moans in the wind, rattles the windows, blows through cracks in the walls.

All night, the stranger sits at the table, his leg straight out.

All night, Allyn tries to unsee one colour.

AT THE KITCHEN TABLE, Allyn Davis watches the man wrapped in a grey blanket who calls himself Da-back-from-War. The man slurps soup with a big spoon, crams his mouth with bread.

On her sketch pad, Allyn draws Stan Yurek blowing his saxophone away from them across Bogusch's field.

At the stove, her mother glowers at the stranger, scrapes the cast-iron pan off the back, bears down on the man. "You bastard," smashes him over the side of the head.

The man's chair tips over, he crashes onto the floor, his hands at his sides. His eyes flutter, and the green stench of his wound leaks around the room.

Allyn Davis rips off and drops into the stove each page of her sketch pad. They curl, flame, whoosh up the chimney. From under her cot she slides drawings of Stan Yurek's daughters, horses' eyes, stone lambs, the main street of Bellevue in flames, a school of open-eyed babies swimming with the fish in the river, a naked woman in a truck at the bottom of Crowsnest Lake. Her hands hesitate over her paintings. Her mother on her side in the blue smoke over peoples' heads, Stan Yurek playing a lemon sky, his triangular eyes closed.

Allyn stacks them on top of her drawings. Every drawing, sketch, painting she ever did. She burns every one.

ALLYN DAVIS DOESN'T REMEMBER when the idea struck, to explode darkness. She did it once, accidentally, and lost colour. Now she means to fragment colour, choose the minimum she must give away to bring Stan Yurek back.

The stranger who spends more and more time on the couch, his face greeny yellow, brings home from the mine a can of black powder, stores it in the outhouse. Every day Allyn sifts a pinch into a bottle she snitched from her mother's handbag, until the bottle is full. Then she fills another.

Allyn rides Tenor down to the river bottom, circles the mine, watches the lights on nightshift disappear inside. The clamour of shunting cars drowns out Tenor's hoofbeats. In imperfect darkness outside, hazy from lights high on the tipple, Allyn checks the tobacco tin full of black powder, checks the fuse poking through a hole in the lid.

The last miner's light drowns in the perfect darkness inside the mine. The last empty car sits on the siding.

Allyn ties Tenor to a tree at the edge of the river, slips through hazy light past the tipple immense against the sky, across the tracks, between coal cars, up the slope to the mine's cement jaws. She flattens her back against one of the pillars, peers down a tunnel cold and gassy into perfect darkness. She slides her back over cement, onto coal, slides out of light into perfect dark.

She knows she must work quickly. The explosion must fragment darkness, not people.

She sets the tin of powder in the middle of the tunnel, strikes a match. Even in the flare of her match, she sees only darkness. The fuse sputters, burns toward the tobacco tin.

Allyn jumps the tracks, ducks past the tipple, holds Tenor's reins close under his chin. "Easy, boy, easy."

Allyn is unprepared for the flash of pure white light, the complete blackness it illuminates. The explosion thunders among the mountain tops long after the light explodes.

"HYAH."

Allyn drums Tenor's sides. Tenor jumps, stretches into a full gallop. Allyn stretches out flat on his back. Tenor's mane whips her face. Night and Bellevue fly past. Behind them, men whip their horses, slam their cars into gear, gun their engines. "Stop, you filthy little bitch. You'll pay for this."

Tenor's mane lashes her eyes. Tenor's neck rolls in her hands. The earth rolls past. Tenor's back undulates under her legs, her belly, her chest, tears sting her eyes, past the Catholic church, swoop over the edge of the bluff, sick joy of weightlessness in her gut. Tenor's hooves pummel earth, and they fly downhill in darkness. Behind them, other hoofbeats, voices.

"She's crazy, the kid's loony." Car lights swoop the long curve of road far to her left, men's voices.

"Cut her off. Block the bridge, block the bridge."

Falling with stars through darkness, Tenor's hooves and her heart beating.

The road just ahead, car lights bear down on their left. "Hyah." Allyn squeezes her knees, burst of muscle. Tenor's hooves leave earth, they arc over the road, thud of hooves on grass. Behind them car lights swoop right for the next curve. Tenor's sweat foams Allyn's hands. They gulp river air, the road again. Car lights bear down on them. "Hyah." They shoot across the road, the bridge ahead.

"Hyah." Before the bridge, Allyn squeezes her left knee. Tenor ducks right, crashes through low bushes beside the river. Indigo. "Hyah." Turtle Mountain on the other side of the river. "Hyah." Ahead, the trestle, smell of creosote, metal. Allyn tugs on the reins. "Easy, boy, easy," reaches for leather around Tenor's ear, flips the bridle off, slides to the ground, runs beside her horse in the dark, "Hyah. Get, get." Scrambles shale on her own two legs. Behind her, horses' hooves and car lights.

She steps onto the trestle blacker than black, jumps tie to tie, river damp between. Halfway across and the stars moaning like a tenor sax in an open field. Allyn Davis lays her head back, shouts "Red," shouts "Blue," shouts "Purple." Her feet skim cold metal, find black. Shouts "White." Falls.

Falls and falls through perfect blackness, falls past a miner singing, past a woman in a truck stripping, past a girl fishing with her father, falls through past, present, future

falls

falls

BENEATH THE TIPPLE. Shacks and coal cars and machinery and coal dust and smoke. And clanging all around you.

None of these things were here when you drove in. It was quiet then. Two clean wooden huts. A couple pick-up trucks. A sign—BELLEVUE MINE TOUR.

Pick your way through the metal on the ground. Crunch of coal under your feet. Duck past a full coal-car, step over the steel rails. Step through debris, around a cement pylon. Toward the highway, the highway you drove in on.

Looming out of the dark, a black mountain. Coal. Kick your toes in, climb up the slag-pile rising above you. Your book heavy in your sleeping bag slung over your shoulder. Climb the dark. Your heart racing.

Way up in the air. Darkness holds your feet. Across the valley, Turtle Mountain's grey face shivers in moonlight.

Way below you, the river. On the other side, the mine.

But the highway? Where is the highway?

Fluttering in the dark at your feet. Squat down. Paper. Bits of paper catching moonlight. Lift one to your face, tilt it away from you.

A picture of a building, flames shooting out the roof.

Pick up another one. A woman floating out the window of a truck.

A baby in a wicker buggy, eyes wide open.

Two girls curled on their sides beneath a tree, bones pressing out through their skin.

Swirl of people dancing.

Green writing.

There are voices we haven't heard yet. Voices we may never hear.

ON HER SIDE next to her father, Henry held her breath. Her legs twitched. Under her and around her and over her, silence.

"Girl or boy, girl or boy, girl or boy?"

In one ear, the sifting of bones.

"What if the baby in my mother's belly is a boy?"

In the other ear, the west wind.

Her heart pounded, her muscles cramped. She breathed out. "What if the men and women and children from the other ranches call me squaw?"

Bones and

Wind and

River

and

Cold seeped from the ground into Henry's ear. She listened for a baby's cry. For the cry of the fish in her mother's belly. "Girl or boy?"

"What if," she said to River, to Wind, to Earth, to Sky, "what if a girl changed the words? What if a girl had the earth under her and the sky over her and the river in her, and the earth and sky and river had the girl in them? What if?"

WHEN THE
WHISTLE
BLOWS

SUSAN MCRAE'S KNITTING NEEDLES probed shadows lurking behind the firelight. There by the window, the hump of Duncan asleep in bed swelled up the wall, bulged onto the ceiling. Her needles clicked, crossed, probed, knitted light around the bulging shadow, pulled it tight. Duncan, warm mound asleep under his patchwork quilt.

And there, gliding back and forth from one wall to the other, pulled in two as it glided through the corner, a shadow bigger than her husband could ever be. Her needles clacked, and firelight flickered from their tips. Grant beside her rocked in his chair, face flushed the red of his hair, hands asleep on his knees.

In front of the fire, Bonnie drew a comb through Evan Thomas' hair. Bonnie's hand dipped, curved, swooped like a white bird. Evan's hair black between her fingers, Bonnie sang to the top of his head. "Scuttle, scuttle, scuttle of coal, we need a scuttle, well bless my soul." Evan Thomas' back arching, his spine following his hair, her daughter's hand. On the wall behind her, their shadows lengthened, shivered up her backbone, the back of her neck, her scalp. Susan's needles clicked. Firelight in the tips of Thomas' hair. She pulled the wool tight into her finger.

Evan Thomas meeting her gaze, his blue-black gaze, his voice wrapping her in the double shadow of Turtle and Hillcrest Mountains. "Look behind you there, Susan. You've just knit a man with a woman's bones."

IT WASN'T THE SUN sending a watery shaft across the valley, washing the bumps on top of Turtle, nor the clock on the homemade chest of drawers metronoming her dreams that pulled Susan out of a sleep as black and smooth as Evan Thomas' voice.

Above her a piece of coal let loose, hurtled down on her from out of nowhere. Unable to move, she lay on her back. The coal slammed into her left temple. "No," she raised her hand to her forehead. "Not yet. Run," she whispered, "run." Thunder, and coal rolling, sliding, filling her mouth, waking her up to the sun on the tip of Turtle, her children, Grant asleep beside her. "Run, Evan Thomas, run."

"IS IT TIME, LASS?" Grant's burr under his arm. "Don't tell me it's morning already, I've only just shut my eyes."

"It's not time for you yet, though soon enough. If I don't hurry, Alex will wake the others."

In the dark kitchen, Susan's hands sought the wet baby in her cradle, Bonnie and Duncan asleep in the same bed behind the curtain. Her fingers traced Alex's warm legs, back, arms. "Look at you, as ruddy and hungry as the others. Just as well you came along. A wife and mother can't afford to get lost in another man's voice. But look, if you kick too much, you're not like to get fed." Her hands in the dark rolled her baby over, unhooked pins, slid the wet diaper out from Alex's bum, dropped it into the bucket of soaking nappies, slid a dry one under, pinned, wrapped Alex's nightie around her kicking legs.

Alex's head hot in the crook of her arm, Susan fondled her baby's toes curling and uncurling as she nursed. "Three are too many, but I'm glad you came along. I look at Evan Thomas's fine bones. His mouth is too soft for a man. I always thought I needed strong bones and lips like your father's, but I look at Thomas's lips and my breasts ache. Enough on that one, now try the other." She squeezed her nipple into her baby's mouth. "It's not just his lips, everybody has lips, it's the words and the voice that come out of those lips, and not knowing where the words come from. But you need me more, don't you?" She kissed her baby's downy head. "And for all his size and bluster, your father does, too, and the other two. Now down you go while I make his breakfast and his bucket."

Sunlight washed the brow of Turtle. Susan sliced bread, slathered jam, boiled water, brewed tea, fried bacon and bread and tomatoes.

"Six o'clock, love. Time to get up." In the cool puddle of dawn, Grant with his arm over his eyes. Susan rubbed his forearm. "Up, now, can't keep a good mine waiting."

"Don't you have to feed Alex?"

"She's eaten already. Now up you get."

"Don't you have to light the stove?"

"It's been crackling in there for almost an hour already. Surely, you can hear it."

"But is the water boiling yet?"

"Boiled and brewed, and your bucket packed. You've run out of excuses, Grant McRae."

Grant's arm, broad and familiar, sliding down his face, his eyes like robins' eggs looking into hers. She clenched her fists, took a deep breath. "I've laid your clothes out for you." Her voice gentle. She turned before he emerged from the covers. "There's hot water in the pitcher."

In the kitchen, she heaped bacon and tomatoes and fried bread on his plate, slid the plate into the oven, loud to cover water splashing, the razor scraping his chin.

Soft in his stockinged feet, Grant crept through the curtain. His shirt whispered as he leaned over, touched his lips to their children's foreheads, padded to her beside the stove, his lips hot on her neck. Her head bent, her body numb, she leaned away from him, slid his plate out of the oven. "You best eat while it's hot."

Big chunks of bread, slices of bacon. Grant chewed in silence, sipped his tea. Susan's hands dumped flour into the big bowl, cut in lard. Grant's knife sliced thin tomato skin, mashed it onto bread. He chewed in silence.

Dough curled around her fingers, Susan sat corner to him at the table. His eyes like robins' eggs. She fisted her fingers. Dough drying, sucking her skin.

"Are you ever afraid down under the earth?"

Red hair on his knuckles catching light from the lamp. "Afraid? Don't know what I'd be afraid of. Hillcrest is the safest mine in the whole Pass. A man does what a man has to do, and doesn't think overmuch about it."

"But don't you hear things down there, things in the dark?"

"Good Lord, lass, do you think I've gone deaf? That's a mining operation going on under Hillcrest Mountain. Of course I hear things. Picks, shovels, augers, horses breathing, men coughing, blasts."

Susan picked dough from her fingers, stretched it out like worms on the oilcloth. "Of course a man hears those things, but does he hear sounds men don't make? Does he hear sounds from the earth itself?"

"Some men hear moaning, some men hear singing, some hear the thunder of feet running overhead, but I hear rock. Rock settling, rock dust falling, rocks tumbling. One thing no man hears in a mine is a woman's voice. Women have no business in the mine. Bad luck. Is my bucket ready?"

Susan's fingers rolled the dough thinner and longer. "Aren't you afraid of getting lost in all that blackness? Aren't you afraid of finding yourself where you've never gone before?"

Grant's eggshell eyes on her face. Her nails digging crisscrosses into dough snakes. "Susan, my love, a man is born with a sense of direction. He knows he can only go where tunnels take him. He knows tunnels run two directions, forward and back. He knows that like he knows the cracks on his hands. Some men talk about mazes and labyrinths. Trouble is, a man can get lost in his own voice."

Susan's hands grinding the utensils into the washbasin. Dough floating on top. She dried her hands, twisted the dough from the table onto a baking pan.

Grant filled the doorway, his bucket over his shoulder. "I'm stopping off at the Hall after for a pint. Is there enough meat for one more for supper?"

"Who?"

His arm around her, his wool jacket wrapping her in dirt, coal dust and black powder. "Evan Thomas."

Grant walking away from her in a straight line for Hillcrest Mountain. Herding in with the others.

"Could be anyone," she whispered into the dawn humped around the valley. "Known him half my life, yet he falls off when I stop looking."

Men's breath rose above them in a fisted cloud. Behind her, the baby cooed, her children snuffled in sleep. She closed the door, ploughed her knuckles into rising dough.

AWAY FROM TOWN, away from the mine, through the liquid dawn. Evan Thomas runs.

His feet roll the earth behind him. Roll the village asleep at the foot of the mountain back into shade. Down the hill ahead of him, mist rises from the river.

Wind whistles in his ears, fingers his scalp, the roof of his mouth. Over the crest of the hill, he cannot see or hear the village behind him. Down, down, down, running into mist.

The heart of the earth beating under his feet, Evan Thomas unrolls time.

Grant chugging up the mine road beside him. "Thomas, a man must know the difference between past, present and future. A man can get lost in his own head if he's not careful."

The bridge rising out of the mist. Evan Thomas veers left, runs beside the river, mist in his face.

The earth beating under his feet, his arms beating his sides, past the three towers of the lime kilns, left, his body swooping. Evan Thomas runs. Molten heat from the centre of the earth flows in his veins, spews from his pores.

At the edge of the slide, he unzips his trousers, unbuttons his shirt, feet beating the heartbeat of rock, of earth, peels off the wet layer next to his skin. Steam rising from his naked limbs, Evan Thomas throws his clothes behind a boulder and runs.

Through labyrinths of stone, his naked limbs, wind, running, Turtle Mountain looming out of stone, out of green lake.

Running nude, his skin singing, ancient sea letters in stone singing. Running through time.

A century. Two. Five. Fifteen hundred nude Welshmen fighting for the slippery wooden cnapan bowl, fingers slipping over each other's sweaty shoulders, buttocks, over the wooden bowl, until one body breaks away, muscles dipping and bunching, breaks into his own territory, bowl under his arm.

In and out of dank boulder shadows, Evan Thomas runs into the past. In the washhouse, steam rising through the floor, men scrub the underground from cracks in their skin. He runs ahead of Grant into the washhouse, runs into a woman emerging from the steam, breasts and thighs and soft belly.

"Oh God, I thought your shift ended later. I wanted the feel of warm water falling. I wanted—" Susan's fingers around his wrist, laying his palm on her belly, "I want, Evan Thomas, but I'm not free." Dropping his hand.

Grant running up behind. "Good Christ, Lass, what could have possessed you to come close to a mine?"

IN HER DREAM, Susan squats on a flat plain, feet wide apart. She faces east. The sun blazes straight down. There are no shadows.

Her belly rests on her thighs. Her navel marks her belly's highest point of curvature. The line of hair from navel to matted triangle, her folded lips flushed slightly blue, have slipped off the horizon.

She holds her breath, too soon, too soon, too late, too late, hands light on her belly. Under layers of tissue, muscle, flesh, miners tunnel, blast, dig. In her bowels, a molten pressure.

Erupts. Her flesh heaves, buckles, folds. She pants, sharp pants. "Not yet, not yet, not yet." Rubs the surface of her belly, rubs flat her buckling skin, cannot rub out the buckling, squeezing inside. Rubs in small circles, not yet, too late, not yet, too late.

The explosion starts under her breastbone. Lifts her rib plates, heaves her belly, twists her organs. She rocks from the heels to the balls of her feet. Lays her face to the white sun.

"Run, Evan Thomas, run."

FRIDAY, JUNE 19, 1914, 7:30 A.M. Grant McRae struggles to the uncertain surface between waking and dreaming. Sweat tickles his balls, his armpits. On his back, he pants. He touches his tongue to his lips, dry and sticky, tastes for coal, mud, blood. Salt.

Around him, next to him in the grey, she moans, his wife, Susan, his mistress, the mine. Eyes closed, he waits in darkness for creak and groan and drip, drip, drip. Inside, his eyelids pulse red.

Calluses soft from sweaty sleeping, Grant strokes his wife's upper arm, runs his finger down the inside, impossibly white, impossibly soft. The crease of her elbow. Her wrist—sinews, veins, cords. But her skin, soft. He pries into her palm folded shut, pillowed, moist. Pushes his finger in, finds her fingers, tips ridged from jute strand, wool strand. "Not a far cry from winding, is it, lass?" Bonny and Duncan across the room, a sheet in between, Alex in the crib beside the stove. Not a far cry.

Back he drifts, down, down, down. His voice echoes after him. "Sleep my lass, sleep. No bucket this morning, no bucket. Afternoons, afternoons."

Down he drifts, down, down. Down the rock tunnel, grey around the mouth with stray daylight, into Slant 1, darker and darker. Down. On his back, feet first. Past rooms 5, 6, 10, 11. Down. Dark, but he knows they are there, no bigger, by Christ, than a coffin. A man can hardly turn over.

Feet first, on his back, Grant dreams past 26, 30, around a sharp bend into Level 1 South. No tapping, no dripping, no rasping in the damp, no cough or wheeze from deep-down lungs, horse or man.

He lies alone in her.

He lies. Yet he drifts on his back in the dark, feet first, so help me God.

Deep inside his dream, Grant whispers, "I do not dream, am not a

dreamer. Salt of the earth. Practical bugger. Love a pint, by Christ. Not
like you, Evan Thomas, you and your dreaming and singing, your
bones fine as Susan's and your eyes deep blue-black, but I never
dream. Never been afraid, never had a dream. Never, by all the saints
in hell."

Down, around, now up. Deeper into the seam running vertical.
Drifts into 32, horizontal, feet first. Up the ladder, floats into a room
so small, so black, by Christ, a man can hardly turn around.

Grant lies. Around him, she is lagged with brattice, walls and ceiling. Out she breathes. Up he floats, head back, presses his lips into
brattice. Breathes in breath of coal, moist and cold and sharp, before
the gas runs down the ceilings, down the walls, out into the tunnel
where no men dig or walk or cough or timber or swear.

"No. I never dream. You dream, Evan Thomas, you dream, and I
have looked at your fine body, hairless in the steamy washhouse, felt
your song steam on my skin.

> Hush my child and peace attend thee
> All through the night

I have looked into your eyes, blue-black, and have fallen, fallen
into your dream, your Goddamn singing, praying, poet-talking,
Welsh dream."

Grant opens and closes his lips, brattice rough under his mouth. She
breathes out cool and moist. He breathes in deeply. "But I never dream.
Never.

Your dream, I have fallen into your dream, Evan Thomas."

"What if I told you I were dead, Grant-the-Haggis, died ten or
twelve years ago when my limbs were supple, my eyes wide open?"

"By Christ, Thomas, you're daft even for a Welshman."

"No, consider this, Grant. What if I died in Wales twelve or fifteen
years before I walked the drover path beside my grandfather Dai
Samuels, he dead before I was born, and our hero, LLywelyn Olaf, his
wild red head in the crook of his elbow talking with his dead children for seven hundred years, up and down the valleys, the hills, bed-
ding down in longhouses with the sheep and cows or next door with
the family because they want to talk with Olaf's head before the fire

dies, all the way to Aberteifi wide open to the sea? And there had the choice, the Fine Fast-Sailing Triton leaving July 10, 1912, for Canada, or sail with Madog, off to the new world, 1170? Suppose before I am born, after I die, I clunk down a wooden gangplank, land here in Hillcrest, Alberta."

"Good Christ, Thomas, you offend my common sense."

"But this is common sense, Grant-the-Haggis, uncommonly common. Suppose I jumped onto the chute as a boy, should've gone to school, but no money and my da already underground, jumped onto the chute, coal jammed down to hell, bounced and she slid slowly, carried me down slowly, gently. And I thought she was jammed to hell, but the underworld can never be jammed full, so I bounced harder."

"I have to wake up now, Thomas."

"It's too early for a man on afternoons, a man with a wife and three children. The sun has hardly flushed the brow of Turtle. Limestone is slow to warm, quick to cool, not like coal."

"I never dream, Thomas, never."

"Listen, Grant. Out of the ground, out of caves flow springs and rivers and herds of pigs."

"I see only coal, Thomas. Only coal and men and ponies."

"Our chieftans coated their hair with lime so it would stand out wild. They rode horseback to the land of the dead."

"Pit ponies, Thomas, pit ponies. Blind in the dark, blind in the light."

"I will ride coal."

"Thomas, a man cannot afford to dream. A man's bones can be too fine, Thomas, underground."

"At Mynydd Newydd, we rode 774 black feet down, not like here in Hillcrest where we walk and, in the Six Foot Seam, solid coal, cut out a chapel. A chapel, Grant-the-Haggis, and whitewashed the floor, ceiling, walls. Who would think a body could paint coal white?"

"A man can be too much chapel, Thomas. Too much praying, believing and worrying death. A man with too much chapel goes mad when he drinks. A man with too much chapel goes mad thinking he's responsible."

"Seven hundred seventy-four feet down in a cage rattling through blackness. Six in the morning, from blackness to blackness. But this chapel, no blasting, hand cut, smoothed, white."

"A man sees too much in the light, Thomas, more than he should ever dream."

"And we stood together in our chapel. You should have seen us Grant-the-Haggis. We stood together, lanterns lit, and we saw the blackness around our eyes, in the blue-black slashes under our skin, and sang."

"A man needs to eat and sleep and provide for his family, Thomas. A man needs to stand a pint with his friends."

"But Grant-the-Haggis, the wild red head of Llywelyn Olaf sang with us, his murdered body deep in the earth beside the River Clywedog. And Owain Glyndwr, raging black hair and eyebrows, fierce and filthy from driving the English out of our Welsh mountains. And all the bodies not yet killed here in Hillcrest, singing."

"No man has been killed in Hillcrest mine, Thomas. Safest in the Crowsnest Pass."

"Listen, Grant-the-Haggis. Against the walls all white, we could see him, there over every head, Bran the crow. Ca-a-aw, Ca-a-aw, Ca-a-aw, he sang. You can walk a caw-caw-canary in front of you in a caw-caw-cage until the stupid bastard caw-caw-croaks, but you won't find me in the black, in the black. If a crow steals a man's purse, cast your eyes upon the crow and follow him unto the mountain, lest the earth fall in upon you and your brethren."

"A man should wake up, Thomas, when he's ready to get up."

"But you should have heard, Grant-the-Haggis, even the earth, our daear, sang with us. Look upon us, for we are black. Look upon us, for we are comely. Look upon us, for we have one foot in the pit we have dug for ourselves. A mighty song rising from our groins."

"A man needs a wife, Thomas."

"Listen, Grant-the-Haggis. In the hills around Y Bala, men and women knit long stockings out of wool dyed red and green and blue. Squatters stake their claims with yarn and knitting needles."

"A wife to lie with, Thomas."

"In Scotland, Grant, your wife wound jute. She told me when I met her on the train. Coming West she knit socks, prairie, sky, mountains. She knit me, Grant, she knit me. Yet she lies with you."

"Come up, Evan Thomas. When the whistle blows, come up. A man cannot live alone under the earth."

"When the whistle blows Grant-the-Haggis, when the whistle blows three times, step carefully in the pit we have dug. Shine your lantern on arms, hands, legs, faces, and when you have found the flesh of him you look for, cradle your left hand under his head, your right hand under his shoulder, and take him up unto you who have run your fingers over her skin, blue pulsing under white, down her back, neck, arms, feet, temple, thighs, fingers. Hold his cheek against yours, his chest against yours, and breathe into his nostrils that he may know who you are. Then take up his parts, one by one, his arms, legs, hands, out of coal, wash them in water, cool from the Crowsnest River, wrap his flesh smooth and clean in white linen."

"When the whistle blows, Evan Thomas, wash in the washhouse over the boilers. Come for dinner. She's roasting a rabbit fresh from the field."

"When the whistle blows and blows and blows, Grant-the-Haggis, hew a new tomb out of rock, lay my bones down gently alongside the bones of my brethren, while flesh is fresh on them. Look up at Crowsnest Mountain, lest you fall down with us. Cover us with soil and singing."

"No." Grant tries to say no, but his lips are pressed hard into brattice. He sucks in. The mine's breath catches in his throat. Up there, the whistle blows. He rises and rises and rises. Around him, she creaks and groans. Through layers of limestone, coal, limestone, dirt, he rises and rises. The whistle blows and blows. "No," he whispers, "no."

Grant sits up in bed, Turtle mountain white in the sun. The whistle blows and blows and blows.

AT THE FOOT of Turtle Mountain, Samuel and Henry pull pink flesh from fish roasted on green poplar over coals.

Samuel watches Henry drop the flesh into her mouth, chew as if she must think about each bite.

Son, he thinks, my son. Yet what if this new baby is a boy?

Until the day Henry slipped out bloody from between her legs, Coyote Woman rode her Paint, belly propped against its withers, miles east and west. Never a bit in his mouth, never flattened leather around his head. Just a round braided hackamore over his nose.

East through prairie grass swishing under her horse's hooves. At the confluence of the big Old Man from the north and the little Old Man from the west, she slid from her horse's back, squat beside the fire gone out, ran her fingers through the ashes. Slipped into the trees, gestured for him to follow.

He lay naked, the grass cool against his back, tree roots and hummocks pressing his nerves awake. She stood over him, her swollen belly and breasts eclipsing scattered sun rays filtered through leaves. Bent her knees, lowered herself, hands out in front, until she squat over him. Eyes focussed on his chest, white as the underside of a fish. Lowered herself, belly huge between her knees. Navel pushed inside out, her skin stretched. Slipped hot over his flesh, belly hot and heavy on his.

She rocked gently back and forth, knees pressed into his sides. Along his back, his arms, the backs of his legs, his stomach under her swollen belly. His nerves hummed. Back and forth, her flesh heating his groin, his stomach. She rocked hard, squeezed hard with her knees. Rocked back and forth, her finger tracing horses across her belly heavy on his. Dropped her finger to his flesh. He jumped, nerves singing.

Henry holds up the skeleton, fish's eyes white as milk. Picks up the skeleton on Samuel's plate. Flings the bones into the air, *phloop*, into a deep green pool.

VOICES
FROM
TOWN

WELL, JESUS, look at the picture. You can see how hard the bastards must've worked. No, no. Turn back a page first, the one where they're sitting on some kind of grandstand, fancylike in the sun. What the hell ridge is that behind them there? Here, hand me the book so's I can see up close. Don't see so good no more. Doctor changed my glasses just last winter, but hell, she don't know nothing. Don't know her ass from a hole in the ground.

Yeah, yeah, looks like the ridge up behind Bellevue there, above Hoist Hill. You must know the hoist, up by that what-do-you-call-it, that anti-cline there. No, syncline is where the rock folds down, like a soup ladle, forces the rocks together; anticline is where it arches up, you know, makes the rocks pull away from each other like this see. Christ, why do you want to get an old man to talk about this stuff, anyway, drag up an age that's dead and buried?

Nah, you find out this stuff working down there everyday. You should anyway. You just got to listen when the geologists come down, and the mine engineers, providing they know what the hell they're talking about. Lots don't, I can tell you that much. Out of the lab, don't know a rock from a pig's patoot, those guys. But the good ones, yeah, the good ones you listen to. Like Hutchinson. You ever heard of him? I'll bet you know more about Calgary. Could never stand the goddamned city myself. Felt more trapped with all them paved roads and high-rises than I ever felt underground.

Afraid? No, I was never afraid. One of the lucky ones. Some guys smelled like fear every day, from the minute they woke up to the minute they picked up their tags on the way out. A sour cold smell, fear, not like sweat from a good hard day's work. You could smell it worse at night. Don't know how we could tell it was night, but we could. The mine shifted and groaned more, don't know why. Maybe we just heard more, working quiet because it was night. You could tell the ones who were afraid. There were two types you could tell right away, before you could smell them. One type moved in slow motion. Didn't swing their picks, just pushed from the shoulder like this and waited between taps. Same with their augers. Turned them once, waited. Never spoke when they waited, hardly breathing, unless you spoke to them, and then they whispered. Like being in goddamned church, afraid to wake up the priest. You're not Catholic, are you? Too many Catholics around here in those days. If I want to confess, I sure the hell ain't going to confess to a man in a box. But it was spooky, I tell you, guys whispering, tiptoeing around, always looking up over their heads, looking up over your head. And when above us, right where they were looking, she did shift and groan, they didn't move a muscle. Stood there still as a lump of coal. But you could smell it, cold and wet and sour right through the poor buggers' clothes, and I'll tell you, we lugged around a hell of a lot of wool on our backs. I was relieved, see, that she finally moved, but they would just get quieter and quieter. We never said nothing either. Pretended we didn't know. One day, one of these guys hanged himself. Guido Molina, you must know the story. Picked up his tag, walked down the hill to the hoist house, Christ, almost in my backyard, strung himself up by a length of cable. Didn't wash, didn't say good-bye, nothing. The wife said she looked out the back window about five o'clock, thought something was strange. The hill was too quiet she said, none of that god-awful wind, and the rest of us hadn't come down yet, clinking our buckets, telling jokes. She wasn't nosy, either, not like a lot of women.

What? The other type? They were the hurricanes, always talking, always chipping away at rock and coal, clunking their pick and auger and bucket. You couldn't relieve yourself without them trying to drown out the sound of your pissing. Got so's you'd find a good hollow rock and aim straight on, just so you could hear something else under all that noise. But you knew it wasn't you they were trying to drown out. It was the mine, shifting and groaning. You could tell. When she moved, they'd move faster, talk louder, but you could smell fear, the same cold sour smell under their clothes. One morning in the Bellevue mine, must have been about an hour after shift change, took me an hour to get to the room I was working on, I heard some kind of loud bohunk talk off one of the tunnels. Every second person was a bohunk back then. Buggers worked hard, got to hand them that, but didn't know nothing about mining. Big shipment of them came over all at once. Got hired on all at once, too. Scabs and they didn't even know it. Firebosses had to post gas with an X. Most of them had never dug deeper than the potatoes in their gardens. Yeah, well on and on and on he talked in bohunk. Started off real loud, then run downhill quieter and quieter, faster and faster. Just when you thought he run out of steam, off he started again. Crazy bastard, I thought, so busy arguing and pleading with fear that he missed shift change. I couldn't hear his partner, probably got sick of trying to convince this bohunk orator to come up where the sun shines. There's no arguing with a bohunk, you know. Either he don't understand you, or he pretends he don't. The women are worse. I knew he was okay. I knew they'd send someone down for him soon enough. But all goddamn morning, every time I pulled my pick back, I could hear bohunk pleading and bohunk arguing right through the goddamned coal. We were loading a serial blast. You dug out from the bottom, see, so the coal would fall down, not out. Then you could stand on it while you loaded the next one up. Damn hard work cutting up like that in a steep pitch, but you had to cut at thirty degrees to keep the pitch optimum for getting the coal out. It's cheaper, you see, if you use gravity. Mining down is more expensive. But you don't want to hear this stuff, do you? Why the hell would you want to hear technical garbage?

So I was down on my side, see, digging out from the bottom, cramped in close to the face. And all this damned begging and fighting coming through the coal, and I couldn't understand a word. Jesus Christ, I thought, I hope one of you wins soon. But no, on and on, his voice rising and falling right under my damned pick. So I picked harder, pulled her back and let her have it. Damned if his voice didn't get louder. So I pulled her back and let her have it again. He must have saved the loud parts, because every time I pulled my pick back, his voice got bigger. So I just kept picking and picking and picking. I was in good shape in them days. I could smash that coal real good. As long as I smashed and smashed, I couldn't hear nothing else. But a man has to bring his arm back no matter how fast he works, and damned if his voice didn't grow between smashes. Pleading and arguing, arguing and pleading. I swung faster and faster, and soon I wasn't swinging at all, just hitting from the shoulder, as hard as my goddamned muscles would let me. And his voice through coal arguing and pleading. Maybe I wouldn't have minded one or the other, but all that up and down, and I couldn't understand a word. So I pounded and pounded, my own grunts answering his begging, fighting his voice. All morning, hammering, grunting, sweating, and that bohunk voice begging and arguing. My hands grew numb around my pick handle, my arms burned, my ears rang from striking coal over and over, but I could still hear the bugger. But she stopped me, by God, the mine herself took hold of my pick and pulled it right out of my hands. And you know, except for my own breathing and my partner's breathing, it was dead quiet.

No, I don't know what happened. What do you want to talk about these things for? They're gone, buried. Here, let me see that picture again. See the shape of that ridge there against the sky. Sleeping Indian we called it. Look at this part here, just like a long forehead, and see, that's his nose and chin.

They're sitting down in this picture all right, spit and polished, three rows, but Christ, mine rescue was hard work, harder than hammering away with a pick and shovel, I'll tell you. At least at the face— you know what a face is? Good, you learned something, though why the hell would you want to know about a coal face? What was I saying? Yeah, the face was predictable, you found rock or you found coal. But Christ, when the emergency whistle called you down, you never knew what you'd find. You know what happens when you burn coal? You release sunshine one hundred million years old.

See these packs on their chests. What does it say? Goddamned glasses. I gotta go to someone who knows what he's doing. PROTO. See, emergency packs. Heavy, and tubes hanging on you, racing through black-damp, hoping if you found one, his head—

See these tubes? Look like intestines don't they, stuck on the outside, up by the shoulder. Found a man in that condition once down the Mohawk. Must have loaded his own blast. Looked shocked as hell, poor bugger, eyes wide open, his hands—

They're for oxygen, that's the cannister there in the right breast pocket. The other one there in the middle, that's a filter. You can't see in this picture, yeah, turn the page, but those are goggles pushed back on their foreheads. Those round things in their hands? Gas meters, just like the canary in that cage there, on the ground in front of the fellow with the beard. If the little bugger fell off his perch, you high-tailed it for the surface. Wasn't smart to have a beard. Absorbed gas. You can't smell methane. Here, give me that pencil. Your gas meter looked like this, see, a circle with a line down the middle. One side was the reference section. It didn't change colour. This other side did. It was the indicator. Turned blue when you wandered into gas. *Reference. Indicator.* Written right beside so you'd know what the hell was going on, if you could read English. This whole thing is called the Permissible Mine-Rescue Breathing Apparatus, Type N Gas Mask, MSA Cannister, Type N. Am I getting too technical? The fireboss also used the Wolfe Lamp to check for methane. Ever heard of the Wolfe Safety Lamp? Jesus, where did you say you grew up? Had a glass globe like this, see, with two screens of 26-gauge Birmingham steel wire. Known as the bonneted safety lamp. We called it the bonneted whore. Walking around with one of those bitches was like sneaking around Bushtown after women or homemade hooch, never knowing when you might run into the wife. Fireboss went in first. If the blue tip on the flame stretched up to about here, he got the hell of out there, posted gas for that section.

That's how old Pete Jones there lost his arm. Got to be fireboss myself. Couldn't afford fear going down first, walking miles in the dark, around and around like a goddamned maze, your light too weak to make a shadow. You watched your flame pretty damn careful, case it fizzed up and danced. Just you and the dark and water dripping, ceiling creaking, and that wet smell you could taste. Had to watch you didn't get seduced into thinking she wouldn't hurt you or the bastards coming on shift. No, I didn't wear a mask. Fireboss was supposed to, but nobody did. Took her on her own terms, or you had no business being down there. Close calls? Yeah, but you expected them, see, what with you going down first. We had a superstition. If the fireboss came out safe, she was safe for everybody. If the fireboss got hurt, she was still safe for everybody because you knew where to keep your ass out of. No. Can't you see I got two eyes, all my fingers, and look here, no doubt about these legs being my own flesh and blood. No, she didn't hurt me. I got careless, but I got away with it, Christ knows why. Not like a fireboss in Frank, forget his name, held an open flame over a box of blasting caps. Boom, blew his goddamned hands off. Yeah, of course he knew better, you always know better. Another Frank miner, James Turnball, brought an open flame down, caused a gas explosion. Burned most of his body, laid up for four months, piddly compensation from the union, not like now when a man gets hurt. But, by God, when they asked him right there in his hospital bed if he still preferred open flames, he told them every time, at least you could damn well see. Then the Mine Branch took it in their high fallootin' heads to order locked safety lamps and restrict blasting. That's when the new guys hired on in Hillcrest. You know about Hillcrest? One hundred and eighty-nine killed. Went on strike to protest. Buried them all together, bits and pieces, in three big graves down by the foot of Turtle there. One guy they never found. Don't remember his name. You don't question, only those who never been down snoop around asking questions. You ever been down? No, I just fell asleep, no explosions or nothing spectacular. Was after nights went up, before mornings come down. I'd already inspected the main haulage and cross-cuts, turned down the new slope, north of the haulage. Didn't have a Permissible with me,

just a Wolfe Safety Lamp. Couldn't see worth a damn. She seemed darker there where we were opening her up. Didn't have nothing to do
with what kind of light you used. Couldn't tell pillars from rooms.
Kept walking into solid coal, bruised my goddamned knuckles. You
know the room and pillar method? There's the main entry, see, and the
counter entry, which runs parallel to the main entry. Main and counter
are pretty level. You drive your own room or tunnel up off the counter
entry, see, at a thirty degree pitch. Every sixty feet or so you dig a
cross-cut at a ninety degree angle to your room, so now you got tunnels between rooms, see. Now, common sense tells you you gotta leave
pillars of unmined coal in your room or you're gonna be like that fool
Samson. But to make it more complicated, once you mine out your
room, you retreat back the way you came, only now you're driving a
new tunnel parallel to your old one, so you got a square with a pillar
in the middle. When the managers get greedy, you blast the pillars
behind you and hope to hell the whole mountain don't fall on your
head. Turn the page there. Look at that blueprint of Hillcrest Mine.
Looks like a goddamned beehive. No point in looking at that thing. You
just gotta know where you are.

Why the hell you asking about buried mines? Christ, you can't
even get down them anymore to take a look. Bellevue's barred up,
though they're talking about opening it up for tourists. Hillcrest's
blasted shut, can't even tell where you entered. What's down there is
down there, and I can't open it up for you. And why the hell would
you want to know all this stuff?

Hutchinson? No, I don't want to talk about Hutchinson. A mine
engineer, that's all. Down the morning Hillcrest blew. How did I fall
asleep? Gas, methane. Just drifted off. No, don't remember what I was
thinking. Turn back to the mine rescue team. See that big open box?
See all those bags and tubes? Pulmotor apparatus. Forced oxygen into
your lungs. I woke up with a mask covering my goddamned mouth
and nose, looked up at the faces looking down at me, at the mountains and the blinding sun and the tipple and smoke. As I turned my
face to puke, all them looking down on me, I thought why not just
go on sleeping. That's what the hell I thought.

AFTERDAMP

O N THE PLATFORM the people from Bellevue and Hillcrest have built tonight, beside the river, each board lovingly carried under an arm, pressed to the heartbeat between ribs, down the steep hill from Bellevue, under black smoking stacks of the tipple, across the tracks, metal smell swollen with heat, across the bridge, the river's breath cool and green around their ankles. They kneel, hold the nail just so, raise the hammer, let the weight of its head swing, strike the nail straight, shiver as metal strikes metal, a silver echo piercing blackness between black mountains.

A million stars.

Beside the platform beside the river, men hammer a table out of boxcar doors, women lay down plates, roasters, bowls. Across the valley, the sun rides the tip of Turtle, reddens the secret steam rising from the table. Cabbage rolls, meat pies, fruit dumplings, prune colaca, pyrohy, verenoki, gnochi, butter, onions, lasagna, boiled potato, sour cream, mushrooms, trifle, drunk prunes in Grappa. The sun falls.

Aha. Look. Beer. *Prosit. Sante. Skol.* Mud in your eye. From the washhouse above, a piece of sky breaks off, hurtles rolling down the cliff, bounces, clears the tracks, rolls to their feet. They clap. "Send us another keg, such a night for beer." A piece of sky breaks away, hurtles down the cliff, bounces, smashes on the track. Foam sprays their faces and clothes. The men laugh, the women cheer. Beer gets the coal out of your throat you know. *Prosit. Skol.*

AROUND THE PLATFORM beside the river, stars and lights on the tipple and a full moon. The band plays a two step, and Evan Thomas's hand on the small of her back, and the smell of pastry and spice, boards humming under her feet. Susan holds his spine in the palm of her hand.

Around the platform beside the river, caught in the warm nudge of elbows and hips, piano and accordion and saxophone, and her skin inside her dress, and his spine under her fingertips through his soft wool shirt.

Around the platform in river damp, Grant in a huddle of men in the dark, his burr beyond the edge of the platform, lost in piano and accordion and saxophone and her body gliding. She laughs into Evan Thomas's eyes.

His hand on the small of her back. Her skin stretches inside her dance, rubs the thin skin of night, rubs the thin skin of her nipples. His hand, his mouth, his blue-black eyes between stars, his voice rising and falling. "A miner's parts are cheap underground. They send the ponies up first."

The music slowing, saxophone in the night, her body sliding through music, her unstayed breasts, hips. Her belly curves into his.

His breath against her ear. "I saw a drowned man, Susan, a man and his son. I was working alone when the water came down. Chipping away at the face. Heard it, like the river there. Ran for the sound but never got past the cross-cut. A wall of water caught me, drowned my light, slammed me into a pillar. In dark so thick I could taste it, wet and shivering, I prayed, prayed they would find me alive. Something bumped my shoulder. I reached out my hand. Water. A floating timber. A man's hand. Before I could grab it, a wave lifted me to the roof, scraped my neck along the lagging. Carried me kicking and panting up the cross-cut, dumped me on a ledge. Then the thump of someone else beside me. "Here," I shouted, "I'm here." He didn't answer, Susan. I groped in the dark for the front of his shirt, his face. He'd stopped breathing. I found his mouth with my hand, my mouth, breathed into him—"Don't die, dammit, there's air here." The first words he vomited were, "My family, who will look after them." He kept vomitting, his body jerking, and I knew he'd go if I didn't get him warm. I couldn't even see him, Susan, couldn't look into his eyes and say, "You'll be okay, you'll make it." So I felt in the dark for the buttons on his shirt, his belt buckle, peeled his clothes off, wrung them out, rubbed his arms, legs, chest, cold and rubbery, until I could feel blood pulsing. But he was still shivering, Susan, so I peeled off my own clothes, held the man close to me in the dark, his heart beating with mine, my legs around his, his head on my shoulder, both of us naked. Held him while I tapped to the rescue crew on the other side of darkness. Held him in continuous night until a faint light pricked the dark, and dry hands pulled him from me. That's when I saw them, Susan, on my way out. They were sitting against a timber. A man with one arm around his son, the other around the timber, both of them drowned. While I walked out into the blinding light and the white faces of the women clustered around the entrance."

Evan Thomas's breath in her ear, the saxophone, his spine under her fingers. "I headed straight for the pub, drank and drank but could not drown the white light, the fear in the women's faces. The next day when the sun burnt a hole in the sky, I went back down."

LOOK NOT UPON ME, for I am black.

In a cleft in the rocks, river at their backs, Evan Thomas slides Susan's dress up her thighs, over her hips, up her ribs, his fingers soft as river grass, touching, for two years he's imagined touching.

Look not upon me because I am black, because the earth hath looked upon me.

Between his fingers, the breath of his words on her flesh.

I am black but comely.

He slides her petticoat up the nape of her neck, the back of her scalp, his words on her forehead. He lays the dress and petticoat on a ledge above their heads. His fingers in her hair, his lips at her temple. His lips, his breath, the dark moist against her eyes.

"Grant loves you, Susan McRae."

"He loves you, too, Evan Thomas."

"In the steam of the washhouse, he scrubs my back."

"He will forgive you, Thomas."

His teeth close over the thin skin along her neck, roll it back and forth against itself. Down her neck, over her shoulder, trailing circles of evaporating skin. Down her stomach, her thighs.

Susan hooks her fingers under his shirt, slides it up over his head, slides her naked skin along his. Wraps her fingers through his hair, bends and licks the back of his neck. "I can taste you, Evan Thomas, but I can't save you."

Cleaved by rock. Laughter and piano and violin and saxophone and their naked shoulders.

Black in the shadow of rock, her hands she cannot see knitting the fine tendons in his feet, the sinews along his haunches, the cords in his throat.

Black in the shadow of rock.

My loins are filled with burning, and there is no sound part in my body.

"He will forgive you, Evan Thomas."

Cleaved

> in the shadow
>
> of
>
> God
>
> oh God oh God.

FRIDAY, JUNE 19, 1914. Two years I lived in the Union Hotel on the main street of Hillcrest, took my meals with whomever of the forty bachelors were not tunnelling under the mountain. I ate fish head soup, roast moose, spicy dumplings. I carried my bucket packed like a double boiler, sandwiches on the bottom. Childless, I crunched my sandwiches in the dark, all the jaws of all the men crunching in the dark, saved my crusts for the children of Grant and Susan McRae who met me on the corner, swung from my arms, "Come to our house, Evan Thomas, come to our house."

Friday, June 19, 1914. A hot morning after two days shutdown because of overproduction. Kiss ass was the word sifting through the tunnels when the market slumped and 1913 slipped off the calendar, kiss ass and stay on contract. For two years, I went to union meetings at the Miners' Hall under Turtle Mountain. For two years, paid for the powder to blow up coal so the Whiteshirts could make money off my back. For two years, scrubbed the sweat off the backs of men who had worked this mountain since 1905 when, under the measuring eye of Charles Plummer Hill, U.S. customs official, they pitted their muscles against rock and ripped the mountain open. Only two among us did not belong to the United Mine Workers of America, District 18, and they were new in town.

Friday, June 19, 1914. 6:45 a.m. and the road up to the mine black with two hundred and fifty of us, flecks of coal embedded in our clothing, soaking up the morning sun.

"Hey, Cullinen, what the hell you doing up this time of the morning? Aren't you on afternoons?"

"Switched with Knicky Knack Redmonson. His kid came by last night, said Knicky had a pain in his side, couldn't get out of bed."

"Don't we all get pains in our side on Friday?"

"Friday is a pain in the side."

"Not as bad as the pain in your head after payday."

"Notice the red in Unilowski's cheeks? His wife's coming in from the Old Country on the five o'clock. Belopotosky traded with him so Unilowski could meet her."

"Let's all go meet her. We'll all go to the station, then follow them home, not give them a minute alone."

"You're a cruel bastard, you are."

"Hey, Corkhill, you lucky bugger, isn't this your last shift?"

"Yup, heading out tomorrow. Gonna trade this can of shit for a plough."

"A farmer. You're gonna be a farmer?"

"Bet your ass I am. Sweet piece of land south of Lethbridge."

"C'mon, Corkhill. Miners don't make good farmers. You know that."

"Best of luck, Cork. Been a long time coming. Better to get out before the arthritis gets you."

"Don't listen to him, Cork. Once a miner, always a miner. You love her, you hate her, get's under your skin."

"I survived one blast. I'm getting out while my luck holds."

"Luck, shmuck. That was Kenmore. They don't got the same charm out there on the prairie. Mining belongs in the mountains so's you can use gravity. Ask Elick. Hey Elick, wasn't it the mine that saved you when Turtle fell? Took him and sixteen others thirteen hours to dig out, but they were alive."

"Wallis and his brother-in-law Neath are heading out Monday."

"What, they going farming, too?"

"They're going back to farming. Nova Scotia."

"See, farmers don't make miners neither."

"They'll never wash the black out. Don't matter how long they farm. Don't matter if they never go down again."

"You going to the Hall after shift? I'll stand you a pint."

"Am I going to the Hall Friday night? What did you do, leave your brains in the outhouse this morning?"

Friday, June 19, 1914. 6:45 a.m. The sun at our backs, coffee on our breaths, the mouth of the mountain out of sight at the top of the long hill, two hundred and fifty of us. For two years, I swung my bucket, my arms in time to arms and legs of thirty-five different nationalities, each man with his own day and night inside him, up the steep mine road, Hillcrest dropping out of sight behind us, into the same mountain. Two years, I ran naked among the stones of Frank Slide, silent as a churchyard, burrowed a labyrinth through the mountain's black veins. I found fossils in coal. Grasses, branches, leaves.

Friday, June 19, 1914. 6:45 a.m. We walk black under the sun. Two hundred and fifty of us. Charlie Ironmonger, nineteen, his muscles supple in the sun, motion of riding rope, jumping between loaded cars in the moving dark, hooking, unhooking, twisting, the cable from the hoist never stopping, imprinted in his bones. Sam Charlton, fireboss, battery for firing a blast in one pocket, key to activate it in the other. Alex Petrie, seventeen, sleep crusted on his lashes, his fingers itching from the brattice cloth he will lay in our rooms, responsible for directing gas away from the coal face, away from the faces of older men, gas that choked his father, out into the main tunnel. Tight under his arm, his bucket that his widowed mother or one of his two sisters made before they descended into the miners' café they run together, James and Robert asleep still before school. Two hundred and fifty of us.

"Hey, Thomas, you taff, aren't you supposed to be on afternoons?"

"I switched with Verigin. His wife's sick, and he can't leave until her sister comes in from B.C."

"We want to hear you singing today, Thomas, but no sad songs, by God."

Friday, June 19, 1914. 7:00 a.m. The sun at our backs. We climb past the slag pile towering black above us, climb over the lip of hill, into the noise of shunting cars, coal sliding down the tipple, screech of bearings, axles, cables. Past the washhouse, engine house, the mouth of the mine square, dark and small, into the lamp house. We pick up our lamps, hand over one brass I.D. check to Robert Hood, timekeeper.

"Here you go, Mr. Hood. Lucky I have another one in my pocket so I know who I am."

"Mornin', Hood. What's this I hear about you claiming you know how to stop time?"

Friday, June 19, 1914. 7:00 a.m. Past the hoist house, cable and wheel groaning and squeaking, the last gulp of outside air until the whistle calls us up. Oil, metal on metal, sulfur, smoke. We light our lamps, empty our lungs, enter Hillcrest Mine, No. 1. Breathe in the dark, the damp, hear the drip, drip of water, the sudden echo of our own breathing. Twisting black before us, the mine clinks, sighs, snorts. Mud grips our ankles, and we begin the long treacherous trek to our rooms under the mountain.

7:15 a.m. My boots slosh through water. I sidestep a loaded car looming out of the dark. My muscles feel loose and warm. My body sweats, a cold rivulet down my back. My eyes suck in darkness. The bones in my inner ear vibrate. Our lamps flicker over an X on a pillar. No working those rooms today, boys. Gas.

Two years, I have loved this mine from the inside. Two years, I have loved a woman through her husband.

7:45 a.m. I turn off haulage into Old Level 1 South, count the pillars of coal, the tunnels in between, not much different in the dark. . . . 31, 32, 33. My room. I lean back, hook my foot on the ladder, climb the flickering black. My room. Low, a pinched seam. I bend forward at the waist, make for the face I can smell. Men and horses breathing in the dark, loaded cars groaning the rails in haulage way behind and below, coal thundering the sheet metal in a chute in someone else's room. A horse coughs, a man's voice. "Get up there, you son of a bitch." I drop my shovel, auger, fork, lean into the face. Two years, I have chiselled, picked, blasted, shovelled, dug my way in. Two years, I have lived in the pale light of a woman's face asymmetrical as a quarter moon. In the black beyond the edge of my light, a pop, then rocks falling. I feel their sound through the soles of my feet, cold exhalation of gas on my cheek. Two years, I have loved another man's wife. My ears keen in the dark, pick out what my eyes cannot see, a boulder, rocks the size of fists, pebbles, crumble, slide, bounce. For two years, my flesh has ached. Susan's hands quick in the dark, stroke her children, wipe milk from their lips, smooth hair. Knit them together. Two years, I have craved her hands on my flesh. The last small rocks tinkle to the floor of my room. Dust billows through my lamplight. I cough, lift my pick, crouch, pull it back over my shoulder. In a cleft in the rocks, Grant, one riverbend away, Susan's hands in the dark stroking every aching inch of my skin, holding me, at last, holding me.

"There is no sound part in my body, Susan. I have sinned."

"He will forgive you."

Pop, from the ceiling. A rock thuds. Dust in my eyes, my mouth. I cough.

"My loins are filled with burning."

"He will forgive you."

"I have sinned."

"You must forgive."

Another rock, clear hollow thud. Another, one at a time. In the cleft of rock, our flesh cleaved.

"There is no sound part in my body, Susan. Grant loves you, Susan, he loves you."

"He loves you, too, Evan Thomas." Falling coal and rock loud in the bones of my ear. Gas fizzing, *dzzzzz dzzzzzz dzzzzzz*. I crane my neck, raise my face, my light to the sound.

Dust and falling rock and an arc of light.

The nerves in the back of my eyes. Along my hands, arms, feet, legs. Vibrating. Singing.

"That's how I think of death, Evan Thomas. A dark voice sets every nerve in your body vibrating until you can hardly stand it, and the only thing you can do is strain toward the singing."

My flesh flying into darkness. Susan, your hands. There is no sound part. I am filled with burning.

"I can taste you, Evan Thomas, but I can't save you."

BEHOLD MY HANDS *and my feet, that it is I myself, handle me and see; for a spirit hath not flesh and bone.*

Thomas Bardley's collar blows forty feet away. He stands on his own two feet, pick just off his shoulder.

"Tom," Evan Thomas whispers, "it's me, Evan Thomas. Tom." Thomas Bardley does not move, does not blink. No breath from his scorched lips.

Alex May falls to his knees twenty feet from the ventilation fan. Lays his forehead on coal. Brown smoke billows around him. He hugs his knees, coughs.

"Alex," Evan Thomas whispers in his ear, "Alex, it's me, Thomas." Alex looks wildly about, springs to his feet, disappears into brown smoke.

Charlie Ironmonger's supple body lifts from the car he is hooking onto the haulage cable.

"Charlie," Evan Thomas reaches for him, "Charlie." Ironmonger's supple body blows past Evan Thomas, sixty feet straight out the tunnel into light, along the cable still moving, slams into the hoist house. Concrete walls and roof and light crumple.

In Level 1 North, Charles Jones and Malcolm Link crawl along the tracks, press the outside of one leg to a rail. Brown smoke rolls along the ceiling. They plant one hand, one knee, lurch forward, panting.

"Malcolm," Evan Thomas reaches for the gash above Link's temple. Link shakes his head, coughs. "Strange draughts, Jones, something wrong, fans."

Jones pants into his chest. "Don't talk."

Jack Maddison and John Moorehouse slam to their knees, in the same movement, bounce to their feet, race for the entrance. They stumble over timbers, mangled cars, limbs of horses, dead men. Out of the brown smoke a shape runs toward them. "John Toth," he shouts, "I am John Toth. I'm alive." He sobs.

Evan Thomas runs after their backs in the dark. "Evan Thomas," he shouts, "I am Evan Thomas." He runs, leaps timbers and cars and dead horses, dead men. He pulls alongside them, "It's me, Evan Thomas." They run, eyes straight ahead, through brown smoke. Their backs disappear.

Behold my hands and my feet, that it is I myself. Handle me, and see; for a spirit hath not flesh and bones.

David Murray shakes off the constable's hands, runs into the mine. "I have three sons in there. Three sons, for Christ's sake." Disappears into smoke and dark. "Robert." He shouts as he runs. "Samuel. Answer me for Christ's sake. David."

Evan Thomas lunges for him. "They're dead, already. Turn back."

David Murray trips on a dead man's legs, coal digs into his knees. He slumps forward, drops his cheek on the dead man's buttocks. "My sons, my sons."

Evan Thomas leans over him, whispers into Murray's breathless mouth. "I told you. I told you. Why didn't you listen?"

Bill Guthrow's boot catches in a track switch, throws him face first. His ankle twists, his boot lodges into the switch. He whimpers, stretches out flat, scrabbles at the coal. The switch hangs onto his boot. Around him, choking, coughing, sobbing, shapes in the dark and smoke. "Help me, God help me." Guthrow wrenches his foot, hurls himself forward. The switch hangs on.

A shape swoops down beside him. "Guthrow? It's me, Moore-house. Afterdamp. Blackdamp. Got to get the hell outta here." Moore-house unlaces Guthrow's boot, pulls on his leg. Guthrow groans. "Christ, it's swollen. Can't get my boot off. Lord, help me."

Evan Thomas squats beside Moorehouse and Guthrow, shouts in Moorehouse's ear. "You go, I'll work it loose."

Moorehouse looks at the brown smoke swirling up Slant 1. "Son of a bitchin' wind patterns." He yanks on Guthrow's calf.

"Wait." Guthrow giggles, slides his hand into his back pocket. "My fucking knife." He stabs the point into the instep of his boot, slices up his ankle. His foot slides free. They disappear up Slant 2, Guthrow listing left.

Joseph Atkinson feels sound sucked out of the air. He drops his auger, doesn't hear it hit the ground. He heads up Slant 2, closer than Slant 1. He does not hear his boots ring against the rails, the groans of men and horses, the cursing, crying, praying. At the junction of Level 1 South and Slant 2, he stops, looks at smoke spewing out of Level 1. He keeps going straight up haulage, Slant 2. He does not hear the man on hands and knees crawling up the tunnel in front of him, does not hear his retching. Joseph Atkinson squats beside the man, lays his hand on the man's back. The man flops onto his side, his chest heaving.

Atkinson shines his light on the man's face. "Corkhill. Come on, man." Hoists Corkhill over his shoulder, drags him a few feet, staggers into the tunnel wall, falls back on top of him. "Can't. Carry. Too. Much." He leans Corkhill against the wall. "Walk. Man. Walk." Corkhill slides, rolls onto his back, vomits silently down his front. "Crawl. Dammit." Atkinson rolls Corkhill onto his stomach, hooks his hands under Corkhill's middle, props him onto his hands and knees. "Crawl. Dammit." Corkhill's head drops to the ground. "Shit. Farmer." Atkinson watches the brown smoke moil along the tunnel ceiling, toward the entrance. "Shit." He follows the smoke. Does not hear his own rasping breath.

Does not hear the men choking, dropping onto their stomachs, ripping their shirts, soaking them in the pool of water fifty or sixty feet from the entrance. Ahead, a watery square of light.

And a cloud of blackdamp. Evan Thomas tackles Atkinson with all his force. Atkinson shivers, keeps walking. "Blackdamp, you stupid bugger, look at it." Evan Thomas looks into Atkinson's face, mouths the words. Atkinson does not blink, walks into the black cloud, weaves on his feet.

Heaves himself backward, flattens against the ground, rolls back down the fifty or sixty feet, blackness spinning around him. Crashes into a mass of arms and legs. The smell of water. Water. He slithers between the men he cannot hear, dunks his face. He rips his shirt over his head, wets it, falls back onto something soft.

Evan Thomas leans his lips for Joseph Atkinson's mouth. "Hang on, man, hang on." No breath, anywhere, and Joseph Atkinson's eyes. Closed.

Between the mouth and Level 1 South, Evan Thomas drifts among the dead bodies. Dead bodies crouching, kneeling, walking. "You can't all go, just like that. What about your wives, your children?"

He drifts into Slant 1, hovers over the bodies huddled not fifty feet from the entrance. "Get up," he roars, "get up. Think of the grief of women and children."

Back into Level 1 South. Thirty men lie face down in water. Evan Thomas moans. "Please, you silly buggers, roll your mouths out of that water. Hang on, just a few more minutes. I hear a car coming down 2. I hear digging through rock in 1. God, you can't do this to them, I am the one who sinned. All of you, get up, get up, you can't die like this."

Evan Thomas plunges into tunnels 31, 32. Bodies, bits of bodies, flesh burned black, hair burned white. Evan Thomas skips 33, his own, drifts into 34, 35. An arm, a leg, a hand. A torso curled around a shovel. Burned, all burned.

Lights. Lights bob down the haulage in Slant 2. Evan Thomas runs toward them. Oxygen masks, oxygen pumps. "Thank God you're here. We don't have much time. There's a group off 1, if we get their faces out of water. There's a group up 2, you must have passed them. We have to move quickly. Thank God you're here. If we get them on the pulmotors right away."

Evan Thomas stares through smoke and thick lenses into Grant's blue eyes. "Thank God you're here."

Grant McRae shifts the mask on his face, bends, picks up a hand. "Pick up everything you find. Davis at the washhouse will clean them, match them up. Leave the worst until night. No sense adding to grief." He slides the hand into a sack.

"I said, thank God you're here, Grant McRae."

Grant bends, picks up a leg, tenderly brushes coal from singed hair. "Good Christ, you'd think you'd recognize the leg of your best friend, but I'm not sure, I'm not God-damn bloody sure." He cradles the leg, slides it next to the hand.

Behold my hands and feet, that it is I, myself. Handle me and see, for a spirit hath not flesh and bones.

Deep at the back of 33, pressed into coal, coal ground into spine, skull, liver, bladder, scrotum, the backs of his eyes, Evan Thomas breaks into low singing.

> *Sleep, my child and peace attend thee,*
> *All through the night.*

He sings. Sings as the rescue crew load coal cars with bodies, sings as their lights dust coal, sings as they joke, swear, fall silent.

> *Soft and drowsy hours are creeping,*
> *Hill and vale in slumber sleeping;*

Sings. The last car groans up haulage. Blackness. Sings.

> *I my loving vigil keeping,*
> *All through the night.*

Evan Thomas knows then that they will never. Find. His body. Sings.

> *I am grieved to hear through the press of the terrible disaster at Hillcrest coal mine by which it is feared hundreds have lost their lives. Please express my deepest sympathy with the sufferers and also with the families of those who have perished.*
> —His Majesty King George V

BEHIND THE TOWN a river of people rise up the black slope, flow around the mine buildings. Brown smoke pours out the mine's black mouth. The concrete walls, steel cables, wheels of the two hoist houses lay mangled in the mine's breath. A constable swings an axe at the swelling crowd. "Get back, there's nothing else we can do." Two miners, black-faced, strap masks over their heads, disappear into the brown smoke. A miner without a mask pushes past them. "I have three sons in there, three, for Christ's sake."

At the base of the black slope, Susan holds Alex to her chest, clutches Bonnie's hand. Duncan hangs onto her skirt.

"My da's on afternoons, isn't he?"

"He is, Duncan."

"This is still morning, isn't it."

"Yes, Duncan."

They join the bent backs and heads climbing the black slope.

"Evan Thomas said he was going down in the morning."

"When did he say that?"

"Last night when Bonnie combed his hair."

"You must have dreamed it, you were sleeping."

"I wasn't sleeping, I was listening."

All around them, the whisper of women's dresses. "Yours, missus?" "Yah yah." "Yours, missus?" "Two sons, my two sons." "Yours, missus?" "Can't think, can't think, don't know don't know."

Over the lip of the hill flow brown smoke and keening. Caught in a rising tide, Susan and her children clutch living flesh.

"When Evan Thomas comes up, I'm going to comb his hair."

"Are you, Bonnie?"

"Bloody rights."

Caught in a tide of sweat, whispering skirts, dear Gods, Susan and her children rise up the steep black slope.

Twisted concrete, smoke, wailing, stench of gas cold in her face, on the ground white linen bundles. She drags her feet, "Don't look Duncan, don't look." Elbows and faces and hands clutching rosaries, clutching living flesh, swell over the lip, onto the flat.

"When Evan Thomas comes up, I'm going to comb his chest."

Stench of smoke and gas catch in her throat. "Are you, Bonnie?"

"Yes, and the black hair on his hands." Her daughter pulls her hand from hers. "There's my da." Bonnie's red head dodges the swelling mass of hips and elbows.

Grant sits on a mangled dinky engine, cradles a white linen bundle. Susan shifts Alex to her other shoulder, touches her husband's red head. He looks up at her, his face the colour of curdled milk. "I thought this was his." He plucks at the linen. "I thought I would know his boot, his foot, his calf, but I don't know, I don't know."

His eyes almost white in the sun.

"I dreamed his dream, Lass. Last night. He shouldn't have been on days. He must have traded with someone. I dreamed his dream. His bones were too goddamned fine."

His shoulders shake. Bonnie lays her red head on Grant's black sleeve, strokes the linen bundle. "When Evan Thomas comes up, Da, you can comb his hair before me."

In the mine's cold brown breath, Susan jiggles Alex, lays her hand on Grant's head. Miners' lights disappear into the smoking earth, where Evan Thomas, Evan Thomas—

She presses her lips to her baby's damp hair. *His left hand should be under my head, and his right hand should embrace me. I charge you, O daughters of Jerusalem, that ye stir not up, nor awake my love.*

She squares her shoulders, breathes through her baby's hair, stares at the men and smoke and lights in the mine's mouth. Her lips move against her baby's head, *His left hand should be under my head, and his right hand should embrace me. I charge you, I charge you, that ye stir not up, nor awake my love.*

Nor awake my love, nor awake my love, nor awake—

Special Bulletin

A great tragedy has befallen the village of Hillcrest Mines. At 7:00 a.m. Friday morning 237 men entered the mine that was reputed to be the safest in the whole of the Crowsnest Pass. At 9:30 a.m. an explosion rocked the mine, blowing up the engine house 100 feet away. Of the 237 men who went on shift, 189 never walked out again.

Rescue teams from neighbouring villages spent day and night searching for survivors, of which there were very few. Long into the night they brought bodies, many unrecognizable, to the washhouse where volunteers searched them for I.D. checks, washed them, and in many cases sewed on severed limbs. The bodies were then wrapped in white linen for burial.

This morning, a long funeral procession wound down the hill to the tune of Saul's Death March, on their way to the mass grave prepared on the edge of town. As if the explosion weren't tragedy enough, a team pulling one of the drays shied and bolted for the ditch, spilling several coffins and their white bundles all over the ground.

Funeral services of various denominations will be held every day this week. A relief fund is being established to help ease the

burdens of all the mothers and children left without a provider.
Donations can be made at your local Miners' Hall.

THEY PRESS AROUND YOU—the women and children and rescue workers. Press you closer to the mouth of the mine, close to the men guarding it, shouting, "Move back. We're doing what we can. For God's sake, move."

Close your eyes, but you still see the fear and hope in their eyes. Smell their sweat. Smell the dank sulfur drifting from the mouth of the mine.

Bits of drawings in your fists, your book lost somewhere in this strange valley. Perhaps this moment in someone else's hands. Someone else reading. Someone else writing.

Voices around you—crying, praying, cursing. And your own voice, muttering. *Help, please help.*

Slip sideways through the press of bodies, voices. At the edge of the crowd, duck into the trees. Dropping the drawings behind you. These, too, someone else may pick up. Push through low branches and new green leaves to a cliff face veined with coal. Run your knuckles over limestone. Sharp and jagged against your skin.

Wedge your fingers into a crack between limestone and coal. Pull. A chunk of coal breaks loose in your hand. Rub the coal over limestone until you have a sharp edge. Run your fingertips lightly over rock until you find a smooth surface. Hold coal to rock.

Begin.

IN THE GAP between Goat and Turtle Mountains, before the bend in the river hugging the base of Turtle, Samuel and Henry Reed cast their lines.

When her float jigs in the water, Henry holds her rod straight up, reels in until the fish hangs thrashing in front of her face.

Samuel sniffs the air. "Smell that, Henry? Sulfur." He drops his rod, tromps through the tall grass, around the bend.

Henry raises her hand, grabs the thrashing fish, hangs on tight. With the thumb and forefinger of her other hand she slides the hook backward through the flesh of the fish's cheek.

"Come take a look, Henry." Samuel's voice wafts around to her. "A sulfur spring. Stronger than Banff. Cold, but we could heat it."

Henry kneels beside the river, slides the fish headfirst into the water, lets go.

"A healing place, Henry, we could build a lodge. Charge people to bathe."

The fish swims out into the current. Henry hoists her rod over her shoulder, walks through the long grass, around the bend in the river. The stench stops her. "Sulfur," the Sunday school story says, "the devil smells like sulfur."

Henry watches her father squatting beside a white spring gushing out of the side of the mountain, about to dip his tongue into the water cupped in his palms. She watches the thick white water run down over rocks, into the green river.

Without turning to see if he follows, she jumps the stream. White rocks and water and stench beneath her feet.

Without turning to see if he follows, she takes a deep breath, walks out of this book, this story. Makes her own way upstream. Has always made her own way. Will always make her own way.

IN THE COLD STILL MOMENT before the sun comes up you start to shiver. No matter how tight you wrap your sleeping bag, your teeth chatter, your muscles tremble.

Sit up, take a deep breath. Limestone, cottonwood, poplar. Just beyond your feet the river rushing, gurgling over rocks. A boulder cracking free from the top of Turtle. Ricochets down the face of the mountain.

Push your legs to standing. Your knees shake, your ears buzz. Two damp steps and you are at the edge of the river. Dunk one toe. Warmer than the air. Your whole foot. Both feet. Water wraps around your ankles. Your knees, thighs, waist.

Bend your knees, lay slowly back. The river tugs at your shoulders, your hair, pushes against the backs of your legs. Let the current lift your feet. In that luminescent moment before the sun comes up, the river fills your ears, and you are floating, bobbing, mountains and cottonwood and pine and boulders shimmering all around you.